Alone with Mr. Darcy

A
Pride & Prejudice
Variation

Abigail Reynolds

D0813450

WHITE SOUP PRESS

ALONE WITH MR. DARCY: A PRIDE & PREJUDICE
VARIATION

Copyright © 2015 by Abigail Reynolds
Cover by Jane Dixon-Smith
All rights reserved, including the right to reproduce this
book, or portions thereof, in any format whatsoever.
For information, address abigail@abigail-reynolds.com.

www.pemberleyvariations.com
www.austenvariations.com

To

Snowdrop

For fearlessly throwing herself into the story and displaying an amazing will to live beyond all odds.

Also by Abigail Reynolds

The Pemberley Variations

WHAT WOULD MR. DARCY DO?

TO CONQUER MR. DARCY

BY FORCE OF INSTINCT

MR. DARCY'S UNDOING

MR. FITZWILLIAM DARCY: THE LAST MAN IN THE WORLD

MR. DARCY'S OBSESSION

A PEMBERLEY MEDLEY

MR. DARCY'S LETTER

MR. DARCY'S REFUGE

MR. DARCY'S NOBLE CONNECTIONS

THE DARCYS OF DERBYSHIRE

The Woods Hole Quartet

THE MAN WHO LOVED PRIDE & PREJUDICE

MORNING LIGHT

Chapter 1

He remembered that old oak, the one with the split trunk. It had been in full leaf, a giant filling the sky, when he first rode to Meryton with Bingley. Now its bare branches reached out over the hedgerow as if to snare an unwary traveler. But Darcy was anything but unwary.

He knew the dangers of the road he followed. It led to Miss Elizabeth Bennet of the fine eyes, the woman who had almost made him forget who he was and what he needed to do. No longer. He had conquered that weakness and put it behind him. This journey to Meryton was for one purpose and one purpose only, and it did not involve seeing her.

Most of his acquaintances in Meryton had already faded in his mind. He could barely recall their faces, but that tiny wisp of hair which escaped Elizabeth's hairpins and danced over the nape of her neck – *that* he remembered in excruciating detail. He could practically smell her lavender scent and see the reflected candlelight on the engraved silver pendant she had worn to the Netherfield ball, drawing his eyes downwards and into temptation. And the music of her laugh, the flash in her fine eyes when she was amused, that pale blue dress she wore when Caroline Bingley invited her to take a turn around the room. The sunlight had shown through it when she passed in front of the window, and that image was seared on his soul. But now he was past all that. Should she happen to cross his path today, he would feel nothing. He was once more in control of himself, the master of Pemberley and of his fate.

The icy wind whistled past his ears and down his neck as a few lazy snowflakes danced in the air. With his free hand, he tightened his muffler and turned up the collar of his many-caped greatcoat. His thick leather gloves were fur-lined, but even so, his fingers were beginning to lose feeling as he held the reins. It would have been wiser to take a carriage in this weather, where he could have a warm brick at his feet and another for his hands, but he had wanted the freedom to come and go quickly when he reached Meryton. It was only a few miles now. His numb fingers did not matter. The sooner this was done, the happier he would be.

He squinted up at the grey sky. It had been clear when he left London, but now clouds covered every inch of it, not that he minded. The clouds matched his mood better than sunny skies. But now the snow was coming faster and the wind was picking up.

A serious snowstorm could trap him in Meryton overnight, and that was unacceptable. People would recognize him and ask questions. Perhaps he should turn back and find an inn on the turnpike. But he had not brought his valet or clothes for another day, and if he waited out the snow in an inn, he would have to go to Longbourn looking disheveled. Bad enough he could not hide the traces of his long, cold ride. Not that he had any need to impress anyone at Longbourn – far from it. He had no intention of giving anyone any expectations. None at all.

Most likely it was just a flurry and would improve soon.

A gust of wind sent snowflakes driving into his face. Mercury tossed his head and whinnied, most likely unhappy about the snow blowing in his eyes. He had probably never seen snow before. Darcy leaned forward and patted the side of his head, but the horse's ears remained flattened. Perhaps it had been a mistake to take the young stallion rather than one of his better trained horses.

But now the snow was coming down harder, making it difficult to see any distance down the road. Devil take it, he would have to go back. But when he pulled on Mercury's reins, instead of turning, the horse reared up wildly. Suddenly there was nothing but air beneath Darcy.

Elizabeth Bennet pushed her icy fingers deeper into her woolen gloves, wishing Lydia had not once again claimed the fur muff. Of course Lydia would just laugh and say it was her own fault for walking the long way home from the church. Lydia would never understand the need to get away from everyone, and today she would have run mad without some time to herself.

Why, oh why had she agreed to visit Charlotte in Kent? The last thing she wished to do was to travel all that distance for the supposed pleasure of sharing a house with Mr. Collins and all of his ridiculous platitudes and flatteries. How could Charlotte have agreed to marry that foolish man? What had happened to her good sense? Elizabeth would rather be a poor spinster than marry a man she could not respect.

It had been impossible to refuse the invitation, though. If only Charlotte had not asked her at the church door with everyone around them! She might have been able to find an excuse to avoid the visit then. But now she was committed, because everyone knew she was going to Kent in March. Oh, joy – she would no doubt have the *great* pleasure of meeting the famous Lady Catherine de Bourgh as well. It was not going to be a happy journey.

The snow was coming down in earnest now, swirling around her and painting the world in shades of white. How could she resist sticking out her tongue to catch a flake on it, even if she *was* half-frozen? She had always been the best of her sisters at this game, and chasing snowflakes was far more pleasant than thinking of the visit to Charlotte and her horrible husband. Her cold fingers were forgotten as she danced on the path, pausing here and there to examine the intricate shapes of the snowflakes as they landed on her gloves. Each was so different from the next! If only she had a way to preserve those fanciful forms. But they melted into nothing in a matter of seconds.

⚬⚬⚬

A burning knife was digging a hole in Darcy's skull. Why? All he wanted was to sleep. The cold had finally gone away. If only the knife would do the same!

"Mr. Darcy. Mr. Darcy!" A female voice called his name urgently.

He wanted to ignore it, but it stirred some memory. He forced his eyes open to discover the visage of Elizabeth Bennet only inches from his face. "You," he said distinctly, "are not supposed to be here."

"*I* am not supposed to be here?" Her voice rose sharply on the words. "You are the one who... oh, never mind. Are you well enough to walk?"

"Walk? Why would I want to walk?"

She closed her eyes as if hunting inside herself for patience. "Because it is snowing and you are injured."

"I am not injured. I am merely resting."

This time her lips twitched. "I see. You have chosen to rest by the side of the road in the middle of a snowstorm with a gash in your head. An interesting choice, Mr. Darcy. Personally, I would recommend a warm bed next time."

How tempting those lips were! "A warm bed sounds very good to me, although hardly for resting."

Elizabeth turned her face away, but he thought she was laughing. "Come, sir. I must take you to shelter. I fear you are confused from your injury."

He frowned. Had her normal intelligence deserted her? "I already told you I am not injured."

With a sigh, she pulled off her glove and touched her fingers to the burning knife, sending it ever deeper into his skull. He winced as she held up a bloody handkerchief in front of him. "Sir, you are bleeding. That is generally a characteristic of injuries."

Was she laughing at him? He tried to raise himself to a sitting position, since it was not polite to lie down in front of a lady, but the knife twisted painfully and he had to bite down on his lip to keep from crying out. So he *was* injured after all. That explained a great deal. "Ah, yes, I suppose it is."

An icy gust of wind blew past. Elizabeth grabbed her bonnet, holding it to her head. "Mr. Darcy, the storm is worsening. We cannot remain here."

"Where are we?"

"On the Hatfield Road. Were you travelling alone?"

"I believe..." He shook his head slightly, sending red-hot pain shot through his skull. He could not recollect how he had come to be there. He certainly was not about to admit *that* to Miss Elizabeth Bennet.

"Never mind. Do you think you can stand?"

The snow was coming down now at a slant, tiny ice crystals stinging his cheeks. Gritting his teeth against the inevitable discomfort, he lurched to his feet, his muscles stiff. He dusted off the covering of snow which had collected on his greatcoat. "I must have been unconscious for a few minutes."

"More than a few, I fear, from the amount of snow on you. You must be half-frozen. You might wish to press my handkerchief over your wound so it does not start bleeding again." She stood with her hand half extended as if prepared to catch him.

He did not need her help, even if the ground beneath him was moving noticeably. "I am well enough. Is there shelter nearby?"

"Meryton is almost three miles from here, though there is a tavern perhaps half that distance where you can warm yourself at the fire."

Two miles. He tried taking one step, then another. His vision blurred in and out of focus. Through the haze of pain he said, "I fear that may be beyond my strength. Might I request you to seek aid for me while I remain here?" Having to ask for assistance was always bitter. Having to beg it from Elizabeth Bennet was even worse.

Elizabeth glanced at the sky, though she could not have seen anything through the heavy snowfall, then to the spot where he had lain, already half filled in. "I dare not leave you alone for so long in this weather. There is a laborer's cottage nearby. I will take you there, then seek assistance." She bit her lip. "The accommodations will not be what you are accustomed to, but it will be warm and dry."

"I have been in poor cottages before. I can ask no more than warm and dry." Warm and dry sounded like heaven at the moment.

Had she passed by the cottage already? It could have been hidden by the driving snow, and she might not have seen anything even a mere thirty paces away. This was taking far longer than she remembered. It had seemed only a few minutes from the time she had passed the cottage on her ramble until she discovered Mr. Darcy lying by the side of the road, but now it seemed they had been trudging through the snow for far longer than that. Mr. Darcy claimed it was no trouble at all to keep walking, which would have been more credible if he did not sway whenever the wind gusted.

They must have missed it somehow. What should she do now? Should she suggest turning back? This direction would just lead them deeper into the countryside. Their chances of being found were better on the road... if they could *find* the road. They might end up walking in circles. If only she could stop shivering and think!

Her boot struck a hidden impediment, and pain shot through her foot. Apparently her toes were not as numb from cold as she had believed. Crouching down, she dusted off the spot her boot had hit. Her fingers found the shape before her eyes could. A paving stone - the cottage must be nearby! She laid her hand on Mr. Darcy's arm and peered around them carefully. Then she saw it, just off to their left, its shape a faint shadow in the snowy world. Had she not hit her foot, they would have walked straight past it.

"There it is!" She hurried toward the door and rapped loudly. No response. She knocked again. There was no light coming from the windows. Surely the owners could not be away in weather like this. What if it were uninhabited? She had no means to build a fire.

This was no time for niceties. She was freezing and Mr. Darcy was injured. Lifting the latch, she pushed the door open.

The room inside was dark apart from weak light filtering in through a small window, but it was blessedly free from the wind which had torn at her outside. At least it was free of the *force* of the wind; the *sound* of it rattled the walls. It boasted only a few pieces of rude furniture on a dirt floor strewn with straw. Elizabeth crossed straight to the hearth and used the small broom beside it to brush away the ashes banking the fire. Thank heaven – there were live coals underneath! The tenants must only be away for the day. She blew on the coals as she had seen the maids do, but was rewarded only with a rising cloud of soot and ash. She coughed, waving her hand in front of her to scatter the ash.

Mr. Darcy knelt beside her, his long-fingered hands setting one piece of kindling after another over the coals, then leaned forward and blew gently. This time small flames appeared, and with excruciating slowness the kindling took fire.

Elizabeth rocked back on her heels and watched as he set two pieces of wood across the kindling. Stripping off her gloves, she held her hands out toward the struggling fire. Even that slight heat felt like heaven. She would stay only long enough to warm her fingers fully. If she allowed herself to become too comfortable, she would not be able to force herself back out into the cold. She wanted to cry at the thought of putting her wet gloves back on.

Fortunately Mr. Darcy seemed improved, or at least less confused. As he scrutinized the growing flames as if his attention would cause them to burn higher, she attempted to catch a glimpse of his wound. Apparently it was no longer bleeding freely, and she could not make it out under his dark hair, slick from the melting snow. She suspected hers would look no better, but even if her bonnet had failed to keep it dry, at least it was covered. But it was hardly worth worrying about. Even Mr. Darcy, usually so careful of his appearance, looked disheveled.

Fatigue weighed down her limbs, but she would not give into it, nor show him her weakness. "I must go now, but I will send assistance to you as soon as may be."

He turned his face toward her, one side in shadow, the other catching the firelight. He looked exhausted. "Miss Elizabeth, I commend your bravery, but you cannot go out into the storm. How would you find your way to the road when you can only see a few feet away? No, we must stay here until the worst of the storm lets up."

"I cannot stay here! It will be dark soon." And if they were trapped there after dark, her reputation would never recover, even though everyone knew she was not handsome enough to tempt Mr. Darcy.

"It is unfortunate, but there is no other choice. I cannot have you risk your life in that storm."

He could not have it! Elizabeth tried to count slowly to ten before she replied. "It is *my* decision, sir, and I intend to go." Although heaven knew he was probably right, but heaven was more forgiving than Meryton society.

He shook his head. "I am weary, Miss Elizabeth. Pray do not force me to stand in the doorway and block your exit. I am no better pleased by the situation than you are, but I will not have your death on my conscience. If my current condition is not sufficient to guarantee your safety, I give you my word you will be safe with me." His mouth took on a bitter twist.

It was not the danger *he* posed that concerned her, but the danger of gossip.

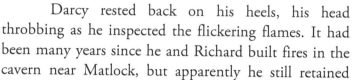

Darcy rested back on his heels, his head throbbing as he inspected the flickering flames. It had been many years since he and Richard built fires in the cavern near Matlock, but apparently he still retained some knowledge from their fumbling attempts. This tiny fire would do little to chase away the chill in the air, but the pile of coal and firewood beside the hearth would not last long if he built it any higher. The cold had sunk so deep into his bones he could hardly imagine ever being warm again.

He stripped off his sodden greatcoat and hung it over a stool near the fire. He doubted it would make much difference, but it would not help him if his clothes became wet as well. Wetter than they were, that is. His trousers were soaked through at the knees and caked with ice over his boots. As he knocked away what ice he could, he looked up to see Elizabeth wringing out the hem of her dress. She seemed to have fared somewhat better than he in that regard; but then again, she had not lain unconscious in the snow, just walked through it. Her pelisse seemed to have protected her well, though her stockings must be cold and wet. No. He should not think about Elizabeth's stockings or how they must cling to her shapely legs. Not that he had ever seen her legs except as a shadow through that pale blue dress, but he had imagined them often enough, usually wrapped around him. Devil take it! He needed to get control of himself.

He glared at the fire. This was not a good sign. Here he was, half frozen, stiff from bruises, his head pounding, and in an old cottage little better than a shepherd's hut. He ought to be immune to lust, not thinking about Elizabeth's legs – especially when those legs happened to be trapped in a small room with him. Perhaps the injury to his head had impaired his mental faculties more than he thought.

In a quest for distraction, he noticed two buckets sitting by the door. They would need water, and he might as well take care of that while he was still cold and wet. If only he were not so dizzy! Somehow he managed to put one foot in front of the other for the few steps needed to reach the door.

Elizabeth said sharply, "Where are you going? Did you not just say it was unsafe to travel in this weather?"

"I have no desire to travel, only to bring in some snow to melt. We will want water later."

"Oh." She sounded taken aback. "Thank you for thinking of that."

A deafening blast of icy wind burned his face and bit through his clothes as soon as he stepped over the threshold. This was worse than it had been just a few minutes earlier. He filled the buckets as quickly as he could and hurried back to the relative safety of the cottage.

It seemed oddly still inside again, even if he had only been out in the storm a short time. He set the buckets beside the hearth where Elizabeth stood warming her hands. "The wind has picked up. We were fortunate to find shelter when we did."

"I thought it seemed louder."

There was something odd about the fire. It seemed to be growing, fading in and out…

Elizabeth's hand clutching his elbow brought him back to his senses. "Mr. Darcy, I pray you, sit before you fall down. One head injury is enough for the day."

"I am perfectly well," he said automatically.

She huffed. "In that case, even though you are *perfectly well*, would you be so kind as to sit down purely to relieve *my* anxiety? You would not wish me to suffer for your stubbornness, I am sure."

How neatly she had trapped him. And how fortunate she had done so quickly, since the floor was showing a disturbing tendency to tilt under his feet. "Very well." Keeping a steadying hand on the wall, he lowered himself to sit on the hearth.

"Thank you." Elizabeth hesitated, then hurried away from the fireplace - not that there was far for her to go - and rummaged through a small wardrobe.

"May I assist you with anything?" It seemed polite to ask, though he doubted he could even stand up at the moment.

"No, thank you. I am simply looking for… oh, here they are. If you would not mind keeping your back turned for a moment, I would appreciate it."

"Of course." Darcy bit his lip so hard it hurt. Surely she was not changing her dress!

Fortunately for his sanity, she quickly rejoined him at the fire, still wearing the same dress. "Thank you. Now, if you do not object, I believe it would be wise for me to examine your injury while there is still light."

As if he did not feel enough like an invalid already, having been rescued by the woman he was trying to forget! "I think it is unnecessary. The bleeding appears to have stopped."

Her lips twitched. "I knew you to be a man of many talents, but your ability to see the back of your head is quite remarkable. Perhaps I misspoke when I said I should examine it if you do not object. If you *do* object, I still prefer to examine it."

Trust Elizabeth Bennet to make him laugh in the most unpropitious circumstances. "Since you insist, Miss Elizabeth, I will do my best to comply with good grace, but I *still* think it unnecessary."

"You may think whatever you like, so long as you allow me to check your wound. If you could turn away from the window so it is in the light – yes, just like that."

He could feel her fingers in his hair, carefully parting it around the wound. The movement stung, but all he could think of was her touch. How often he had wished for her fingers to run through his hair! This was not the way he had hoped for, but still, she was standing so close to him, he could practically feel the warmth radiating from her.

"I fear the eyes in the back of your head have deceived you, Mr. Darcy. It is indeed still oozing blood. Do you perchance have a handkerchief I could use to clean it?"

Darcy reached into his pocket and handed it to her without a word.

"Thank you. I am sorry to put your fine linen to such a messy task. I will try to avoid hurting you any more than necessary."

He was tempted to tell her it was too late for that. His inability to possess her had been a constant ache for over two months. In comparison, the gentle touch of her fingers in an open wound was nothing, and her concern was more soothing than he cared to admit.

It would be easy to allow himself to enjoy being cared for by Elizabeth more than he ought. He fixed his gaze on his drying greatcoat to distract himself. It had been joined by two long white stockings. Good God, she must have taken them off while he was gathering the snow! His imagination presented him with a tantalizing image of walking in while she was peeling those stockings off, one leg at a time. Wounded or not, he would have been delighted to offer his assistance, and then to…

"My apologies, that must have hurt. I will try to be gentler."

It was a good thing she could not guess the true reason he had stiffened. No more thinking of her legs, which must be bare and cold under her petticoats. It would only be kindness to warm them for her.

He was almost grateful for the blinding pain that suddenly stabbed through his head.

"There, I can see it now. Fortunately, the cut is not large, although you have an impressive goose egg around it. I would guess the bleeding will stop with a little pressure. I have folded your handkerchief, and perhaps you could press on it here." Her hand took his and guided it to the appropriate spot. "Very good. I will check it again in a few minutes."

What would she say if he told her the touch of her hand on his was the best healing he could have?

"How did this happen? Were you set upon by footpads?"

He winced. "No. I was...." Devil take it, what *had* happened? Why could he not remember? The road to Meryton was a safe one, and it would have been broad daylight. Surreptitiously he felt for his watch. It was still there, gold fob and all. Not footpads, then. They would not have left that behind. "I am not certain."

Her eyebrows shot up, but instead of saying anything, she crossed to the wardrobe and returned with a threadbare quilt. As she draped it around his shoulders, she said, "It is hardly fashionable, but it should warm you a little."

He should have declined, but the sensation of having Elizabeth worry over him was disquietingly pleasant.

Chapter 2

WHY HAD SHE not gone to the wedding breakfast at least long enough to fill her stomach? Apart from a roll and a cup of chocolate when she arose, Elizabeth had eaten nothing all day. "I had best see if there is anything we can eat here before the light fades."

"That would be most welcome."

At least he was being polite, even if he did keep staring at her. She began to rummage through the shelves and cupboards lining the wall. There was not much – a few items of simple clothing, a pair of shoes with holes worn through at the toes, a bag of rags. A shelf holding simples – dried leaves, flowers, bark – and a small knife. With a glance backwards to assure Mr. Darcy was preoccupied with the fire, she bit into a piece of bark, tasting the bitterness of willow. Excellent. She silently thanked the woman of the house. A cup and a wooden plate.

The last cupboard turned out to be the larder. Some onions, a cloth sack of oats and another of barley. None of that would help her. If only her mother had not been so proud that none of her daughters need learn to cook! At the moment, she would give a great deal for a few lessons from Cook. Half a loaf of bread so stale it would be given to the poor at Longbourn. Perhaps this one had come from another fine house. More onions. Could people live on onions alone? A few carrots, half a dozen wrinkled apples, and two turnips. She cast a glance at Mr. Darcy. The apples would do, but she imagined he would have to be very desperate indeed to gnaw on a turnip.

At the bottom, half hidden under another sack, she discovered a piece of frayed cloth rolled into a bundle. She lifted it out and unwrapped it. Dried meat! That was a welcome surprise. She would hardly have expected a poor laborer to afford so expensive an item.

"We are in luck." She showed Mr. Darcy her discovery.

"Indeed." He picked up a strip and frowned. "Venison. Apparently our host is a poacher, or has a friend in the business."

"You will not report him, will you?"

"I could hardly do so while taking advantage of the spoils, but it will go against the grain." He glared at the offending item.

Elizabeth hid a smile. "Well, we shall not starve, but it will be far from the fare you are accustomed to, unless you happen to make a habit of climbing apple trees in winter to pull down the last wizened fruit."

He gave her a sidelong glance. "It has been many years since I climbed an apple tree."

"I observe you do not deny ever tasting the forbidden fruit! Mr. Darcy, you have hidden depths. We shall not perish from thirst, either, unless you object to drinking from a wooden cup. There is a keg in the corner which I daresay holds small beer."

The corner of his mouth turned up. "A veritable feast! Dried meat, wizened apples, and small beer."

Who would have expected the stern Mr. Darcy to possess a playful side? She should be thankful for it. This situation was difficult enough without having to listen to complaints about it. Watching him feeding wood to the fire, she might almost think he was enjoying himself.

After filling the small kettle hanging over the fire with melting snow, she sliced the apples as well as she could with the small knife, collected the substance of their meager meal and brought it to the welcome warmth of the hearth. "As there is only one plate and one cup, I fear we will have to share." She watched him through her eyelashes, wondering how he would take this final bit of deprivation. If it troubled him, he showed no sign of it.

He offered her the cup so she might take the first sip. Why did he have to watch her as she set her mouth to the rough edge of the cup? She licked the last drop off her lip as she handed it back to him. "It is rather sour."

"Only to be expected." As he drank from the cup, his gaze remained fixed on her.

His look made her shiver. She had shared a cup with her sisters many times, but somehow this felt almost indecent, seeing him put his lips where hers had been, but there was nothing to be done for it. She looked away in embarrassment until the silence reminded her he could not begin to eat until she did, although it could hardly be called silence given the howling of the wind. She hoped the thatch of the roof would hold, or they would be in dire straits indeed.

Somehow he had managed to rearrange the apple slices so the best of the fruit was on her side of the wooden platter. Despite her hunger, she had to force herself to take one and bite into the soft flesh of it.

Once free to begin, Darcy attacked the remainder of the food with a healthy appetite, not hesitating in taking the most shriveled bits of apple.

"I am all amazement, Mr. Darcy. I would not have expected you to be so untroubled by our circumstances." Perhaps the blow to his head had sweetened his temper.

"When one is sufficiently hungry, even the poorest fare can be appreciated. This is not completely unfamiliar to me. There is a small hermitage at Pemberley, no larger than this cottage, which I have turned into my personal retreat. Naturally the furnishings, though simple, are better and there is always sufficient coal and firewood, but it is similar. We are fortunate our absent hosts take good care of their property. I have seen cottages like this which would be very uncomfortable to occupy even for a few hours. Not at Pemberley, of course. I would not permit such a thing."

"Of course not," murmured Elizabeth, shaking her head in amusement. "You have seen the homes of your tenants?"

"Naturally. I would be a poor landlord if I did not, or if I could not recognize the signs of good maintenance. This cottage is tidy, clean, and well cared for." He waved a strip of dried meat to indicate their surroundings, "There are no curtains at the window, but the walls have been well chinked to keep out cold air, and the chimney does not smoke. Apart from our host's unfortunate tendency to help himself to his master's game, he would appear to be a capable fellow."

"Or his wife may be the capable one."

"I will give her the credit for cleanliness, and her husband for chinking the walls. Of course, that may be of lesser importance here than it is in Derbyshire, where the winters can be bitter."

"This is quite bitter enough for me!"

"I speak only in generalities, Miss Elizabeth. A storm like this would be a notable event even in Derbyshire. And it has been twenty years since anyone at Pemberley lived in a cottage of wattle and daub like this. The few remaining mud houses there are used only for storage."

So Mr. Darcy was back on his high horse! She should be thankful they had managed a civil conversation for as long as they had. Once their simple repast was concluded, there would be no need for talking; they could each follow their own pursuits.

Their own pursuits... in a cottage lacking books, pen and paper, newspapers, or cards. No doubt there was mending to do somewhere, but not of a sort she was accustomed to, and certainly no embroidery. She had found only a small tallow candle, and that would shed little light. No, she and Mr. Darcy were trapped in a small room together with nothing to do but talk to one another for the entire night – and to attempt to avoid thinking about the ramifications of their plight.

A thought occurred to her. "Is Mr. Bingley returning to Netherfield?"

There was a pause. "I have no reason to believe he plans to do so."

Poor Jane! "I do apologize. I did not mean to be impertinent; I simply could think of no other reason for you to be on the road to Meryton, but no doubt you have many concerns of which I am unaware."

Darcy looked away before answering. "I wish I could tell you, but I cannot recall that either. I do not even know what day it is."

How odd! Clearly he remembered who she was, so the memory loss could not be profound. "The ninth of January, three days after Twelfth Night. Does your memory go back to that?"

He frowned as he thought. "I recall Christmas and the New Year, but not Twelfth Night."

"It has not been long, then. No doubt your memory will come back to you soon. It often does after an injury like yours." She was more concerned about the wound itself than the loss of a few days of memory.

"What of you? What brought you roaming so far from Longbourn on a cold winter's day?" It sounded somehow accusatory.

A good question. Had she any sense, she would have made for home after the wedding. "I did not start out from Longbourn, but from the church. Charlotte – Miss Lucas – was married there today. Afterwards, there was to be a large wedding breakfast at the inn, if you can call it a breakfast when it includes free ale for all the townsfolk. That is no doubt where our absent host can be found. I decided to take a walk because I did not wish to join the celebration, and I failed to notice how far I had roamed." No need to mention her desire to avoid seeing Mr. Wickham dance attendance on Mary King at the breakfast, especially with everyone in town watching to see how she responded to it. He might not have broken her heart, but his quick loss of interest in her still stung.

"I am surprised you wished to miss your friend's wedding breakfast."

Elizabeth shrugged. "She and her husband departed from the church door, so she would not be there. He lives... he lives far from here."

"It is unfortunate you will have fewer opportunities to see your friend."

If only that were the case! "Not really."

"Pardon me. I had been under the impression Miss Lucas was your particular friend."

She would not have expected him to notice such a detail. "She is, or she *was* until she decided to marry a foolish man, sacrificing every better feeling for worldly advantage. I had expected better of her." Why was she telling Mr. Darcy this? He disliked her, and could not possibly have any interest in her confidences. Perhaps *that* was why, and she had so longed to say those words aloud to someone.

"It is unfortunate, but that *is* the way of the world."

"It is not *my* way! I cannot imagine marrying a man whom I could not respect, no matter how much he had to offer. I knew Charlotte's opinions on marriage differed from my own, but that she should sink so low! I can never feel the same confidence in her as before." The words seemed to hang in the air.

"How long have you been friends?"

She had said so much already; she might as well tell him all of it. "Since I was fifteen. She is seven years older than I, and like all girls, I thought older girls were wonderful and sophisticated. I was flattered she wanted to be my friend. But she has no sisters near her own age, and she is a clever woman in a household where cleverness in women is not appreciated, so she sought companionship in me. And now she is married to a man who cannot even recognize her cleverness!"

"Have you other complaints about her that you no longer felt you could trust her?"

She dropped her eyes. "No, only that." But that was enough.

"I cannot imagine ending a long friendship because of my dislike for my friend's wife. Is it such a sin to be married to a foolish man?"

"No." It was true. If Charlotte had married Mr. Buscot, who could barely string two sensible sentences together, she could have forgiven her that. "Just this particular foolish man. I had mocked him often when I was with her, and…."

His silence was more of a question than words could be.

"And I had just refused an offer from him

because he was such a fool."

"That *is* embarrassing."

"Indeed it is, and now she wishes for me to *visit* them! Can you imagine how awkward that will be, with his incessant conversation and his anger at me for refusing him?"

"Highly awkward. Your friendship must mean a great deal to her if she still asked you to visit, putting your companionship ahead of her new husband's comfort."

"I suppose." Yet Charlotte had risked her friendship to marry Mr. Collins. Had she not considered how uncomfortable Elizabeth would be with her choice? But it was not as if Charlotte had other choices if she wished to marry. No man had ever offered for her, and she was close to becoming a spinster. If she ever wished to be independent of her family, this was likely the only opportunity she would have. Still, to marry *Mr. Collins*? But Elizabeth could have forgiven her even that, if it had not also embarrassed *her* so mightily.

How humiliating that Mr. Darcy, of all people, could recognize what she herself could not! It was one more thing he could criticize her for. Of course, she suspected he would run a hundred miles from something which embarrassed *him*. And still he kept watching her!

To disguise her discomfort, she checked the kettle. The willow bark tea was still weak, but it might be helpful. She poured it into the wooden cup and handed it to him. "This may ease your discomfort."

He sniffed it. "Willow bark tea?"

"Yes."

"At the moment I am happy to drink anything warm, even if it is willow bark tea." He took a sip and made a face at the bitter taste. "Thank you for making it."

"Tea is the only thing I know how to prepare. Cooking would be more useful to us now, but unfortunately it is not an accomplishment admired in young ladies. However, should you find yourself in urgent need of having a purse netted or a screen painted, I am at your service." She remembered his extraordinarily long list of skills necessary for an accomplished lady, most of which she lacked.

"The tea is adequate, thank you. We must do the best we can in these surroundings. " His eyes travelled down her body.

The weight of his critical gaze was more than she could bear. "Mr. Darcy, my hair is in complete disarray, my gown is ruined, my hands are red, and I am in the most unprepossessing surroundings possible. Surely it cannot take that much effort to find things to criticize about me."

His words, when they came, were as icy as the air outside. "Pardon me. I meant no criticism."

What did it matter? She would never see him again after tonight. She might as well speak her mind. "It was not what you said, but how you are always looking at me, trying to find fault in me. I have faults a-plenty, I assure you."

"I fear you are mistaken. I do not try to find

fault in you. I…" He stopped abruptly.

"Then why would you spend so much time watching me? Even Charlotte noticed it."

He looked away. "It was simply out of… interest. Your…expressions are so lively and changeable I enjoy trying to guess what will come next, what witticism you might make. You do not feign indifference to everything as so many ladies do. I apologize; I meant no offense by it, and certainly not to embarrass you. Had I found you displeasing, I would have looked away, not *at* you." To his credit, he did seem genuinely bemused by her accusation of looking at her only to criticize. Perhaps he even meant it.

"Oh. I had not realized…that." She hoped the light was dim enough to hide her blush. Of course he had not looked to criticize; in the presence of someone like her mother or Lydia, he always seemed to look out the window. What had happened to her common sense? Apparently she might not have been pretty enough to tempt him at the assembly, but her expressions were intriguing enough to draw his notice. But he *had* asked her to dance at the Netherfield Ball. What was she thinking? Men like Mr. Darcy did not show interest in country girls with nothing in particular to recommend them. She must not read too much into his words, especially not under the circumstances.

He rose and stirred the fire, then placed another log on it. At least he did not appear to sway this time. "I wish I could build it higher, but then there would not be enough wood to last through the night. I will spread the bedroll in front of the hearth for you."

"You are injured, and I will not have you attempting to take care of me! I am perfectly able to manage the bedroll, and *you* shall sleep on it. I will be quite comfortable sitting on the hearth. Besides, I would far rather freeze than have to face the responsibility of telling Miss Bingley I allowed you to perish from the cold." Not that she planned to sleep, but there was no point in telling Mr. Darcy that.

He gave a snort of laughter. "Even though that dire fate may lie before you, I cannot permit it. My injury is minor, and I am still a gentleman."

Men! Why must they always deny illness or injury, and take on tasks even a child could see they were unsuited for? Rather than argue, she took action, tugging at the bedroll to draw it nearer the fire. Who would have thought a simple bedroll could be so heavy? Was it filled with rocks?

Before she had managed to move it even a foot, Mr. Darcy appeared by her side. At least he did not tell her to stop, but instead pulled at it with her. Now it slid almost easily toward the fireplace.

Elizabeth watched as he wrestled with the ties preventing it from unrolling. He paused, muttered under his breath, then reapplied himself, without any apparent progress. Odd; it looked like a simple knot, and certainly the owner of the cottage would not want a major task untying it every night. Then she saw the tremor in his hands.

She leaned forward and placed her hand over his. He stilled instantly, then slowly turned to look at her. "Sir, I have great faith that under ordinary circumstances, you could tie and untie knots far beyond my ability, but these are not ordinary circumstances, and it pains me to watch your efforts. Pray permit me to make an attempt."

For a moment she thought he would refuse, but then he stepped back without a word. Before he could change his mind, she reached past and quickly untied the bedroll. Free of its restraints, it unfurled with unexpected rapidity, nearly bowling her over. She staggered back, but strong hands caught her from behind. Fully unrolled, the bedroll stopped at the toes of her boots, and Mr. Darcy was at her heels, his hands still gripping her arms. Apparently his strength was less affected by his injury than his dexterity.

With a breathless laugh, she said, "I had not bargained for that. Feather ticks are simpler to manage. This adventure is proving educational." Educational. She hoped that sounded cool enough to defuse the impropriety of her present position, able to feel a man's warmth behind her while a bed lay before her. Why had he not released her arms?

"I apologize I was unable to manage it." His voice sounded unusually hoarse. She hoped he was not sickening with a cold. That was all they needed.

She looked down pointedly at his hand on her arm, not that he would be able to see her gaze, and retreated into teasing. "I am sadly disillusioned. I thought you capable of any task set before you no matter how adverse the circumstances, and now I discover all it takes is nearly freezing to death and a blow on the head to render you occasionally in need of assistance. If it were not for the fact that building a fire is currently a more beneficial skill than untying knots, I might have to dismiss you as merely decorative and not useful."

He peeled his fingers from her arms. "I do not believe I have ever been described as decorative before."

"There is always a first time." She slipped to the side, careful not to look at him as she spread the worn quilt over the bedroll. "There. I suspect that is the best that can be done. I hope you will be at least somewhat comfortable."

"Miss Bennet, I cannot…"

She held her hand up to stop him. "Must we play at ladies and gentlemen even in these circumstances, when there is no room for either? You are injured; I am not, and neither of us is a fool. Pray, let us be practical. The pallet is for you." It had been such a long day, with too many surprises. She did not have the energy to spare for this argument.

He was silent, his lips tight. At last he said, "Very well, but if we are to be practical and not bound by the rules for ladies and gentlemen, the logical solution is that we share the pallet. If we each stay to the side, there is room enough for both of us."

"I cannot share a bed with you!"

"If I planned to take advantage of you, I could have done so at any point in these last few hours. If it will help, I give you my word you will be completely safe." His face was pallid in the flickering firelight.

If she was too tired for this argument, he must be at the end of his endurance. The simplest thing would be to agree with his plan, then once he was asleep, she could escape to the safety of the chair. Yes, that was the best solution. "Very well." She did not look him in the eye.

"Thank you." He dropped to sit on the edge of the hearth, his exhaustion obvious, and gestured toward the pallet. "Whenever you please."

The sooner he rested, the better, so Elizabeth began slowly unlacing her boots. It was a struggle to remove them, as they were tight over her bulky borrowed stockings, but finally her feet were free. Her hair was a more difficult problem. She could not lie down even for a few minutes while it was up, at least not unless she wished to have sharp hairpins jabbing her scalp. It would be a terrible mess by morning in any case. Resolutely she turned her back on Mr. Darcy, then removed the hairpins and plaited her hair in record time, without bothering to remove the ribbons braided through it. That was as much preparation for bed as she could manage without stripping down to her shift, and that was not going to happen.

She padded back to the pallet, pausing beside it to remove a piece of straw which poked through her stocking. "I promise I will never again take the smooth floors at Longbourn for granted!" she said, but when she looked up, her mouth grew dry.

Mr. Darcy sat on a corner of the pallet in his shirtsleeves, only his waistcoat covering the fine linen. Frowning, no doubt at her shocked expression, he said brusquely, "My apologies, Miss Elizabeth. The current fashion in tailcoats favors style over comfort, and to be practical, it will be more useful as an extra layer to go over the quilt."

Elizabeth swallowed hard. "Of course." It was not as if her appearance were proper, either; she no doubt looked quite disreputable without shoes and with her hair in a plait. At least she need not worry about attracting the wrong sort of interest from him in her current disheveled state! "Perhaps I should check your injury once more before you sleep."

To her surprise, he smiled. "I shall not waste my energy arguing, since you will no doubt insist in any case." He turned his face away so the wound faced her.

"I am glad to know you are educable," she said tartly, but she breathed easier without his dark eyes on her. Parting his hair with her fingers, she peered at the lesion by the dim firelight. "It appears to have crusted over, and no more blood is oozing out."

"I hope you are satisfied," he said dryly.

His hair was silky against her fingers as she released it. "I would hate to leave bloodstains on our absent host's bedding."

"Indeed." He gestured to the side of the pallet between him and the fire.

Of course he would insist on her taking the warmer spot. Unfortunately, his gentlemanly act made it difficult to hide her flaming cheeks as she lowered herself into that space. This was without question the most shocking thing she had ever done, and with him in his shirtsleeves! It made her painfully aware of how near her own low neckline was to him, and she hastily tugged the quilt over her and up to her chin.

The scent of musk mingled with smoke as he spread his topcoat over her. It was an almost indecent intimacy, lying beneath his clothing. Squeezing her eyes shut, Elizabeth muttered, "I thank you."

She felt his weight settling on the pallet beside her. How many inches lay between them? Despite his bold assertion that there was plenty of room for both of them, she knew it had been said only to ease her concerns. Like everything else in this hut, the pallet was no bigger than it needed to be. She tried to still her breathing, not wishing to expose her embarrassment. If only he would fall asleep, she could escape this position.

"Sleep well, Miss Elizabeth." His voice was unusually gentle.

"A quiet night to you as well," she muttered.

Darcy closed his eyes, knowing perfectly well that, despite his exhaustion, it would be insufficient to allow him to fall asleep only inches from Elizabeth Bennet. He did not even wish to sleep; that would mean missing this extraordinary experience. Naturally, he had done the only gentlemanly thing and turned to face away from her, but even his inability to see her did not lessen the impact of having her beside him. Despite his headache and his earlier confusion, the evening together had only served to draw him deeper into her thrall.

He had been Master of Pemberley for five years, ruling over tenants and servants, and dictating the use of the estate. But he had never felt as powerful as he had when Elizabeth confided her difficulties with her friend

Charlotte. Even if he could do nothing to help, the mere fact she had trusted him so far was an unexpected gift. And her sweet persistence in caring for him could easily become addictive. At Netherfield, she had tempted him, but it was nothing to this.

The sound of her even breathing was like music. She was still awake, of course; no doubt it would take her some time to overcome her discomfort with the situation enough to fall asleep. But she was there beside him – Elizabeth Bennet, whom he had never expected to see again.

How strange it was that she, of all the people in Meryton, had been the one to discover him by the side of the road! It must have been a sign.

But that raised the ticklish question of *why* he had been on that road in the first place. There was nothing to draw him to Meryton; Elizabeth was the only person there whose presence would have tempted him, but he had already forsworn her. Had something changed? He could not imagine anything which would have made him suddenly decide she would be a suitable bride after all. That could not be it.

Perhaps he had gone on Bingley's behalf, on some errand he could not even imagine. What could he do for Bingley at Netherfield? Nothing, and from what Elizabeth had said, he was not even on the correct road for Netherfield. It made no sense.

An involuntary smile curved his lips. Only one thing made sense, which was that Elizabeth was with him. That was just as it ought to be.

Chapter 3

ELIZABETH AWOKE WITH unusual stiffness and curled closer to Jane to share her warmth. But the body next to hers did not smell of Jane's rosewater, but of wood smoke, wet leather, and something essentially male. Her eyes flew open, revealing fine white linen over a distinctly masculine chest. Good Lord! She was entwined with Mr. Darcy! If her heart pounded any harder, it might burst her chest.

She could not allow him to discover her in this utterly compromising position. She would have to remove his arm that surrounded her, holding her to his warmth, without awakening him. With the utmost care, she slowly raised her chin until she could see his face. And his eyes. Watching her.

Her throat constricted. Why was he looking at her in that manner? So intent, so serious, so...she did not even have words for it, but it made her feel quite odd. And he had not released her. What must he be thinking of her?

Sitting up so quickly it made her dizzy, she scrambled backwards away from him. The shock of cold air once she was a few feet from the hearth shook away any last vestiges of sleep, leaving her insides quaking over what had just happened. If anyone had discovered them, she would have been ruined or forced to marry Mr. Darcy. Which would be worse? At least he would be as invested in keeping the incident a secret as she was. He would not wish to be tied to a simple country gentleman's daughter. But even if no one else ever found out, *she* would still know, and nothing would ever be the same.

With shaking hands she smoothed her skirts, though they were wrinkled beyond any hope of presentability. Even her plait had become partially undone, though her hair ribbons had miraculously stayed in place. Nell must have used glue to keep them from sliding out! She combed her hair with her fingers, then quickly twisted it into a simple knot, all the while refusing even to look in Mr. Darcy's direction. She could not hope to play the part of a gentlewoman in her current condition.

"Have you any idea how delighted Miss Bingley would be to find herself in your shoes this morning?" Mr. Darcy's deep voice from behind her made her jump.

She turned to discover he still lay on the pallet, though he was now propped up on one elbow. It was frighteningly intimate to see him so different from his usual formal self. Her cheeks grew hot. "I did not plan it. I was completely unaware of where I was."

"I know that." He sounded perfectly reasonable, as if this were a conversation about the weather over the breakfast table. "Although other women have tried, I cannot imagine *you* attempting to entrap me." He held out his hand to her. Could he possibly be trying to invite her back to bed?

Her fingernails bit into her palms. "I have no expectations of you, beyond that you will never breathe a word of this to anyone."

"You may depend upon my discretion, of course, but I know my responsibilities as well as you do."

"Then I release you from those responsibilities. As long as no one knows we were both here, no harm has been done."

He raised an eyebrow. "The fact you have been away overnight is damaging already."

It did not matter whether it was true or not. She had no intention of being trapped in a marriage with a husband who regretted his choice every day of his life. "My fondness for long walks is well known, and no one would be surprised if I sought shelter until the storm passed. Most likely many people were stranded in Meryton by the snow. Everyone will assume I was one of them." She turned away to signal the conversation was over.

Why was he so calm about the idea of marrying her? It made no sense. Either she must be dreaming or he was still suffering from the blow to his head. In his normal state, she had no doubt Mr. Darcy would be furious at being forced to marry an impertinent country nobody. He should consider himself fortunate to be with one of the few women who had no desire to take advantage of the situation. Good Lord, married to Mr. Darcy! Her shiver had nothing to do with the cold.

It was imperative they leave this place as soon as possible, preferably separately. Bracing herself for the chill, she approached the window. It was completely frosted over, allowing only a weak light through. She scratched at the frost, then blew on it to clear a peep hole. Her shoulders slumped at the sight of white clouds of snow still falling. Deep drifts of snow covered everything in the small area she could make out. There would be no escape from Mr. Darcy yet.

Puzzled, Darcy allowed his hand to drop. What was wrong with Elizabeth? Surely she understood what must be done. Why was she not pleased? After all, he was a finer match than she could have dreamed of making.

Ah, perhaps that was it. She understood only too well the gulf between their positions and how inappropriate it was for her to aspire to enter the sort of circles he frequented, and wished to spare him the embarrassment of making such a match. Dearest Elizabeth! What other woman would think of *his* position at a time like this?

He stretched like a satisfied cat, conscious of the empty space beside him which had once been Elizabeth's warm body. He should have taken advantage of the opportunity to kiss her before she ran off. His lips still ached with the desire to do so. But it was no longer a hopeless desire. Once she overcame her skittishness, he could kiss her as often as he pleased –

and it would please him to do so as often as possible. He smiled at the thought.

After all, fate was smiling on *him* today. Elizabeth Bennet was no longer out of his reach, and at the same time, no one could blame him for marrying so far beneath him. She had saved his life, and in doing so, hopelessly compromised herself. He was not degrading himself by proposing to her, but doing the only honorable thing. People would respect him for that, rather than laughing at his poor judgment in falling victim to the wiles of a girl far beneath him. They might still laugh at Elizabeth, but that would not matter. She would be his.

He pushed the tattered quilt away. Damn, but it was cold in this tiny place! His sleep-stiffened muscles protested as he moved to stir what little remained of the coals. Setting one of the last logs on top of it, he carefully nursed the flames to life. As he did so, a gust of wind rattled the small building. Apparently the storm had not yet spent all its fury.

"I take it the snow continues," he said.

Elizabeth jumped at his words. "Apparently so." Her voice was lifeless.

"No doubt it will die down soon," he said reassuringly, though he was in no hurry for such an event. This cottage might be uncomfortable, but once they left it, he would have to surrender Elizabeth to the demands of propriety until such a time as they were married. He intended to enjoy this opportunity to have her to himself.

Elizabeth took one last look at the snow outside the window. There was nothing to do but to make the best of it. Rubbing her arms, she checked her pelisse. Still wet through. She would have appreciated its warmth, not to mention the extra distance it would allow between her and Mr. Darcy.

Since Mr. Darcy continued to lounge by the fire, it was difficult to avoid looking at him as she refilled the open kettle with the last of the water in the bucket, then hung it once again over the fire. She was almost becoming accustomed to the shocking sight of him in his shirtsleeves. After all, how could she be troubled by the sight of him in his shirtsleeves when she had slept in those shirtsleeved arms only a short time ago? A shiver travelled down her spine.

"Will no one think to confirm your story?" His voice took her by surprise.

"My story?"

"That you were stranded somewhere, presumably alone."

"Most likely not, in all the chaos. Besides, even if someone learned you were here as well, you are the last man anyone would suspect of compromising me."

"Why is that?" He had the effrontery to sound puzzled.

She gritted her teeth. Was he truly going to force her to say this? "Everyone already knows you do not find me handsome enough to tempt you."

"Not handsome enough...Why on earth would they think *that*?"

His incredulity only annoyed her further.

"Because *you* said so. At the assembly in Meryton where we first met. Pray do not attempt to deny it. I was there and heard you say it. My vanity easily withstood the blow of not pleasing you, but as it is not my favorite topic of conversation in the world, let us say nothing more of it."

Mortified by her admission, she turned to the cabinet which served as the pantry and began to rummage through it, more to get away from him than out of hunger. It was bad enough to be forced to repeat what he had said, but she did not care to see the reality of it in his face. Truth be told, his slight still stung. There had been gentlemen who had shown no interest in her before, but none had ever spoken of her in such a manner to her face.

Searching through the cabinet was unlikely to reveal something new which had appeared miraculously since the previous night. Choosing two more apples and some of the stale bread, she dumped them unceremoniously on the plate in front of the hearth. If Mr. Darcy wished for something to drink, he could fetch it himself. She was not his serving maid.

Nor were her labors appreciated, apparently. He ignored both her offerings and herself, looking anywhere but at her. Had she actually managed to embarrass the proud and imperturbable Mr. Darcy?

"I did not mean it," he said flatly, apparently speaking to the fire.

"I beg your pardon?"

"I did not mean it!" he snapped.

"What did you not mean? The offer to restore

my honor? That is hardly a surprise."

"Not that! I *did* mean that." He raked his fingers through his hair. "What I said at the assembly. It was not true. I do not recall saying it, but if I did, I was most likely trying to get rid of someone who wanted to speak to me."

Was he actually trying to apologize? It was more likely she was still asleep and dreaming. "Truly, sir, it is a matter of indifference to me." She did her best to sound bored with the subject.

"Surely you know… After all, you were the only woman I asked to dance at the Netherfield ball."

"What do I know?" She had moved from exasperation to bewilderment.

"That I found you too handsome for my peace of mind!" His gaze was more adversarial than admiring.

"Oh, come now. This is ridiculous! I do not know what you are playing at, but I wish you would stop."

"You are not the only one to wish I would stop." He pulled his overcoat around him and fastened the buttons. "Miss Bingley knew it, and she did not like it at all." He stomped to the door and wrenched it open, letting a whirlwind of snow in.

"Where are you going? You cannot possibly reach town!"

"I am going to find a woodpile so we do not freeze to death today!" He slammed the door shut behind him.

Elizabeth shook her head in bewilderment. What a strange man! Did he think her so wounded by his words at the assembly that he needed to create such a story? It was ridiculous. Was he trying to mock her? She would have to ask Mr. Wickham the next time they met. He might understand what Mr. Darcy meant, and why her statement had made him so angry.

A shadow crossed beyond the window. She rubbed a spot clear again, enough to see Mr. Darcy, his arms wrapped around himself and his head bent down, slowly pacing the space near the cottage. Had she seen a woodpile when she had walked past the cottage the first time? She could not recall, and by the time they had reached its shelter yesterday, it would already have been blanketed in snow.

What if he found no wood? Her gaze flew to the hearth and the two small pieces of firewood remaining next to it. Those would not last long. It might be enough if the snow stopped soon, but if it continued, the cottage might become very cold indeed. She did not even dare think of the possibility the storm might persist until it was too late to depart. At this time of year, the sun went down early, and they could not leave without a good two hours of daylight left.

Darcy kicked yet another snowdrift as if his worst enemy lay behind it. Nothing under this drift, either. Devil take it, what kind of fellow would hide a woodpile? An idiot, that was it. Almost as much of an idiot as he was, to be stranded with Elizabeth Bennet in a storm. As he kicked away the snow again, he yelped in pain as his boot contacted something solid. Perhaps this was finally it! But when he bent to brush off the snow, he found only another of the paving stones that had tripped Elizabeth the previous day. Why had he ever returned to this miserable corner of Hertfordshire?

He trudged on, the ache in his toes reminding him not to take out his anger with his foot this time. How could Elizabeth possibly think he found her unattractive? He had thought himself so obvious, had worried about raising impossible expectations…and on the subject of impossibility, why in God's name did she not jump at the chance to be Mistress of Pemberley? Any other woman would have been thrilled at the opportunity. What was the matter with her?

Her warm body had felt so right in his arms when he had awakened, at peace with himself for the first time in months despite sleeping in his clothes on a flea-ridden pallet of old straw. It had been a damned good thing he was fully clothed, or he might not have been able to resist the temptation she presented. He knew perfectly well he should not marry Elizabeth Bennet. It would be a mistake on so many fronts he could hardly begin to count them. Yet he had been pleased to have the decision taken out of his hands. She had saved his life, and he had repaid her kindness by compromising her. Marrying her was his duty under those circumstances, and he need not reproach himself for giving in to his attraction to her.

And she had refused to take him seriously! Even if they were fortunate enough not to be discovered together, did she truly believe no one would notice her absence? Ridiculous! The simplest solution would be to go straight to Mr. Bennet with the facts of the matter.

But what was he thinking — he should be trying to avoid the marriage by any means at his disposal! Perhaps that blow to his head truly had addled his wits.

If only it had addled his eyes instead! Being so close to Elizabeth, he could not stop himself from admiring her. Her beauty shone through despite her dishevelment, and it drew him to her, the moth to the flame. And now he had as much as told her so. Would she try to use that power against him? Where *was* that damned woodpile?

Why was he even trying to find it? Without more wood, they would have to huddle together for warmth. He could feel his passion flare even as he stood in the raging snowstorm. But he could not do that to her. He would not take advantage of her vulnerability. And he would keep repeating that to himself until his gentlemanly impulses returned from wherever they were hiding. They were probably with that blasted non-existent woodpile.

He had made almost a full circuit of the cottage, but felt every bit as unsettled as when he had slammed out of the house before he did something foolish like show Elizabeth just how attractive he found her. The woodpile must be farther from the cottage than he dared go. In this driving snow, he could lose their way completely two dozen paces from his destination. That would not solve any of his problems.

The woodpile tripped him when he was only a few feet from the door. Blasted thing! He would have found it immediately, had he only started in the opposite direction. Even inanimate firewood was conspiring against his sanity today. He dusted the snow from his trousers and rubbed his aching knee, then began filling his arms with firewood. It was a good thing his servants could not see him now.

Chapter 4

ELIZABETH JUMPED UP from the hearth when Mr. Darcy entered in a blast of wind, his arms full of wood and his head covered with snow. He took great care in setting the logs in a neat stack, then returned outside. Just leaving the door open that long had lowered the temperature inside the cottage substantially. If he had to make several trips, perhaps she should open and close the door for him to preserve what little heat they had.

He thanked her coldly for her assistance. After adding a third armload of wood to the pile, he stumbled and had to catch his balance on the mantel. Elizabeth started to hold out her hand to stop him from taking another trip, but she drew it back, not daring to point out he should not undertaking such exercise.

But this time when he went out, he did not return immediately. Elizabeth waited by the door, peeking out to see if he was waiting for her to open it, but he was not, and the swirls of white covered everything beyond the doorstep.

Had he fallen in the slippery snow? Or lost consciousness? A sharp piece of ice seemed to pierce her deep inside. Oh, why had she allowed him to go outside again? He had clearly been in no condition for it!

Without giving herself a chance to reconsider, she opened the door and stepped out into the fierce wind. But how could she find him when she could not see even a few feet away? "Mr. Darcy!" she called.

"Yes?" His muffled voice came from her left.

Relief flowed through her as she made out slightly darker shape. "Is anything the matter?"

"No. Yes."

Her breath caught on something halfway between a laugh and a sob. "Which is it?"

"If you could assist me here…" Strain sounded in his voice.

If Mr. Darcy was actually asking for assistance, it must be something terrible. Perhaps he was trapped by a falling log. She pushed her way through the blinding snow till she found him on his knees, digging with both hands in a snowdrift, pieces of wood scattered around him. "What should I do?" she half-shouted over the wind.

"Could you remove the logs leaning on my arm?" he grunted.

"Of course." She hardly even noticed the snow stinging her fingertips as she hurried to move them aside. "Should I take more?"

"No, that should be…." He bent down into the hole he had made, tugging at something, then suddenly straightened with a lump of snow in his hands. "…enough. Thank you."

"Are you injured?"

"Inside."

Was he waiting for her to go first? Suddenly aware of the ridiculousness of trying to converse when every word had to be shouted, she trudged back to the door. Her shaking hands struggled with the latch for a moment before it lifted.

She had to lean on the door to close it behind Mr. Darcy. It was blessedly still inside despite the constant sound of wind whistling over the chimney. She could not have been out there for more than three minutes, but it had seemed like an eternity. She shook off snow from her dress and shivered.

Mr. Darcy knelt in front of the hearth, examining his odd discovery. "Would you be so kind as to place another log on the fire, Miss Elizabeth?"

His formality reminded her of how angry he had been when he first went in search of wood, so after doing as he asked, she retreated to the far side of the hearth. The fire burned higher with the new wood, revealing more of the lump of snow Mr. Darcy was busily rubbing. Elizabeth blinked. Was it *moving*?

Forgetting her attempt to keep her distance, she leaned toward him and peered at it. Yes, it was alive! "What is it?"

"A cat. She was hiding in the woodpile." He lifted the animal and held it against his chest, murmuring something inaudible to it.

Now she could make out the tail and the ears. "Trying to find a warm spot, I suppose. It is a miracle he made it through the night."

"It may be too late already, if he has frostbite on

his paws."

"I hope not. I would rather have a miracle." Elizabeth realized the animal was not so much covered with snow as mostly white. A few buff-colored patches dotted his head. "Actually, two miracles. Only you, Mr. Darcy, could find a white cat in a blizzard! I thought he was a snowball."

He raised his head. "Snowballs rarely meow and bite people."

Elizabeth could not stop herself from dissolving into laughter. "Did he really bite you?"

"Not badly. I was disturbing his hiding place, after all."

Another new side of Mr. Darcy! That he would go to the trouble of rescuing a stray cat in the storm was surprising enough for a gentleman, but to do so after he had been bitten, and then to warm it himself? "You are covered in snow. Should I hold him so you can remove it before it melts?"

He looked down at his arms in surprise. "I suppose so." He detached the cat, who apparently was clinging to his shirt with his claws, and gingerly held it out to her.

The cat made no effort to escape, curling immediately into Elizabeth's arms. "Why, you are barely half grown! I can feel your ribs." Scooting closer to the fire, she turned so as much heat as possible would reach the shivering animal. Would its fur be soft if it were not so wet and cold?

She fluffed up the fur to help it dry, then felt along the cat's body to see if it might be injured. No, it was only the cold, and most likely hunger. There could have been no hunting in this storm. "You poor thing," she crooned. "You will be warm soon." There was little they could do for the cat's hunger unless it had a taste for raw onions. The last of the venison had been eaten that morning.

Mr. Darcy crouched down beside her. "How is he?"

"She."

"Oh. How is *she*, then?" He reached out to stroke the cat's head.

It felt oddly intimate for him to be so close, both of them touching the cat. "Still alive."

The cat picked her head up and sniffed at Mr. Darcy's fingers, then stood up in Elizabeth's lap and stretched. Delicately picking her way across to his legs, she curled up against his body and began to purr.

Elizabeth smiled at his surprised expression, feeling warmer than she had in some time. "You seem to have made a friend. She knows who saved her."

Awkwardly he reached down to pet the cat. "Are you certain she is female?"

"I believe so. I take it you do not have much experience with cats?"

He suddenly seemed to withdraw inside himself. "Very little."

His taciturnity reminded her of his earlier comments. Her concern first for his well-being and that of the cat had distracted her, but it still made her nervous. She hardly knew which interpretation of them she preferred – that he was mocking her or that he truly admired her. Either one was excessively embarrassing, especially after waking in his arms. Her skin prickled at the memory of his body pressed against hers.

How could she be so drawn to him when she had such a dislike for him before? She dropped her eyes and discovered the sleeves of his coat were peppered with splinters. Without thinking, she tugged one of the larger ones free. "I hope your valet is not the disapproving sort. Your attire may never be the same."

He looked down and began picking at the splinters. "Showing disapproval would be beneath Crewe's dignity. He will not say a word, simply spirit it away and I will never see it again."

"Why am I not surprised you would have a silent and dignified valet?"

Darcy tossed a handful of splinters into the fire where they sizzled and popped. "Dignified, yes. But sometimes he is anything but silent."

"Oh?" Surely speaking of his valet was safer than talking about his past.

"The only time Crewe speaks more than a few words is when he thinks I am about to make a serious mistake. Then he quite carefully explains to me precisely what I am doing wrong and how I should correct it." He furrowed his brow. "Is something the matter?"

"No, I am simply astonished you would choose a servant who criticizes you."

"I know I am not perfect. Crewe is a special case, though. He served my father before me, and on his deathbed my father told me to keep Crewe with me and always listen to him. So he is permitted liberties other servants would be dismissed for."

"And *do* you always listen to him?"

His eyes looked hooded. "Yes," he said shortly. "I have little choice."

"To honor your father's wishes?"

"No. Because he is always right." His lower lip jutted in an expression which was almost a pout.

Elizabeth laughed. "What a very annoying trait! I should not like at all having someone who pointed out my mistakes and was always right."

"And it is always when I least expect it." Somehow his aggrieved look was oddly appealing.

"And now you will have to explain why you have white cat hair on your trousers as well."

"Do not remind me!"

As if on cue, the cat jumped off his lap and sat on the hearth, carefully washing herself. Darcy took advantage of his new freedom to poke at the fire, sending the flames higher. But when he placed a new log on top, it sizzled and sparked, damping down the flames until he fanned them with his hat.

How odd he knew so much about building fires! Would it not have been beneath him to learn the work of servants? Perhaps that could be a safe topic of conversation. "I am all amazement at your knowledge of fire building, sir."

He spared her the briefest of glances. "I learned it as a child. My cousin and I liked to play in a cave on his father's estate, and we built a fire pit to keep off the chill. The fire went out quite frequently until we worked out the knack of keeping it burning. It took us months to figure it out. It looked much easier when the servants did it."

"Months? You must have been a frequent visitor there, then."

"I lived with his family for over two years."

Had he been fostered out, then? Some noble families did that, to be sure, but she would not have guessed it of him. "You must have been glad to have a cousin near your age, then." Surely that was neutral enough.

"That was the pretext for my presence. My uncle claimed Richard needed a companion since he could not go off to school at that time, and he would benefit from having a fellow student to share his tutoring."

If that had been the pretext, what had the true reason been? And why had he said that? It would be rude to ask him directly about it. "That seems a good reason. I hope it was not ill health that kept your cousin from school."

"Richard?" Darcy snorted. "He was as hale as a horse. It was all an excuse. My uncle did not trust my stepmother to care for me adequately, and felt I would be safer with him. He wanted to make certain that the next owner of Pemberley would have Fitzwilliam blood. Of course, I did not learn that until much later."

"Surely there must have been servants at Pemberley to care for you, even if your stepmother had no interest in doing so."

"Of course there were. However, it would have

been very much in her best interest were one of her own children to inherit, and I stood in the way of that."

He sounded indifferent, but Elizabeth was horrified. "That sounds like something that would only happen in a fairy tale."

He turned to look at her then, his eyes opaque. "Even fairy tales must have some basis in fact and human nature. Of course, it might have been complete supposition on my uncle's part."

Something in his expression told Elizabeth he was not as unmoved on the subject as he sounded. What a horrible thing for a child -- to know his stepmother wished him dead! Some of his remote, proud behavior seemed more understandable now. "But what of your father? Surely he would not have tolerated any danger to you." It was a far more personal question than she would have dared ask in normal circumstances, but somehow it seemed natural now.

"He would not have, but he was away much of the time. That was my uncle's opinion, in any case, and he was not one to be gainsaid. He disapproved of the marriage from the start, saying she was too young and hardly respectable. But my father must have agreed eventually, for after my sister was born, he sent her back to her family."

She struggled for some appropriate response. "Your stepmother sounds hateful."

"Not at all. I liked her very much."

He *liked* her? This made no sense. It must be more confusion from his injury. He likely had no idea what he was saying. "You liked her?"

"She was my friend before my father ever noticed her. We were visiting her parents, and when I played with her brothers, she often joined us at our games, as she was not yet out."

"So she was quite young?"

He considered this. "I suppose so, though from the advanced age of seven, she seemed quite grown-up. She must have been sixteen when they married."

"Did you still like her after your father married her?"

He closed his eyes and rested his head against the hearth wall. "Yes. She was always pleasant to me, and she encouraged me to do things my mother would have forbidden, like riding a half-tamed stallion or climbing a rock cliff. I did not realize her ulterior motivation at the time, only that she seemed to have extraordinary faith in my abilities."

"Did you truly climb cliffs? I would not have pictured you as such an adventurous child."

A slight smile curved his lips as he opened his eyes to look at her. "I suppose I do not look the part now, but that was before I realized the responsibilities I had. At the time, like all children, I did not believe any serious harm could befall me. I imagine you were much the same."

"Do you mean to imply I was not a ladylike child?" she teased.

"I meant no discourtesy," he said stiffly.

"In any case, you would be perfectly correct in your assumption. I was quite a hoyden as a child. It would have taken very little for someone like your stepmother to persuade me to do unwise things. As you say, children see things differently."

"And then they grow up, and everything changes." An echo of melancholy shaded his voice.

This was becoming too intimate for comfort. In a brisk tone, she said, "You were fortunate your uncle took notice of what was happening."

"He did not notice. It was my tutor. I disliked him for his strictness and insistence I spend my days in study instead of adventuring. There was a time I fell ill with influenza, a very severe case. My stepmother apparently told the servants to stay away from me lest the contagion spread to them, and she would nurse me herself. Needless to say, she did nothing of the sort. I was left alone for several days without food or drink until my tutor discovered what was happening. He stayed by my bedside until the danger passed; then, as soon as I was well enough to ride, he took me to my uncle and laid the entire tale before him." His voice was flat.

Nausea gathered in Elizabeth's stomach at the thought of him as a child, ill, helpless and all alone. She gathered the shreds of her self-possession together and said, "That was brave of your tutor to risk your stepmother's displeasure. He must have been very fond of you."

"As to that I cannot say, but it was courageous. Had my uncle not listened to him, he would have been sent off without a character, which would have ruined his career and future prospects. Fortunately, he did listen, and offered him a position tutoring both Richard and me. Or, as Richard would say, a position making both of us as miserable as possible as often as possible."

"Your cousin was not of a scholarly disposition?"

"Not at all. He delighted in exploration and adventure." The flickers of firelight illuminated his high cheekbones. Even in his current dishevelment, there was no denying he was a handsome man.

Somehow she must find a way to lighten the atmosphere. "I suppose it turned out to *my* good fortune, in any case, since I would be very cold indeed had you never learned to light a fire."

One side of his mouth quirked up. "Yes, sometimes events that seem troubling at the time lead to a desirable outcome. I, for example, am grateful you choose to take a long walk on a cold day, even though it meant becoming lost in a snowstorm. I would most likely still be lying by the side of the road otherwise, without any need of a fire."

Her mouth felt suddenly dry. "I certainly would not wish for that."

"I am glad of that." His focused gaze was almost hypnotic in its power. Slowly he leaned toward her.

Her heart pounded in her chest. She knew what was coming. Why was she not jumping up and running away? If she told him to stop, he would do so; her instincts told her as much. But her words were frozen in her throat as he drew nearer. Then her eyelids slid down as his lips moved gently against hers, a spot of warmth in an icy world.

Her insides fluttered at the sensation. What was

wrong with her?

Cold air replaced the warmth of his lips, and she opened her eyes to see him pulling away with a slight smile. "You see – it would not be so bad to be married to me."

His words chased away all the sensation of his kiss, and she covered her face with her hands. After a minute, she managed to choke out a few words. "Mr. Darcy, that subject is closed."

"Why?" His voice was quiet, persuasive. "Unlike your last suitor, no one has ever accused me of being a fool or talking too much."

"No, of those two sins I can acquit you."

"There is no need to be frightened."

"I am not frightened, and I am *not* Miss Bingley!"

He chuckled. "I know that. If you were, I likely would have chosen to remain at the side of the road."

She could not keep a muffled giggle from escaping. "Surely you would not go to that extreme."

"You might be surprised."

"You have surprised me quite enough for one day, sir!"

After a long moment of silence, he said, "Then I will endeavor to be more predictable."

"Why are you trying so hard to be agreeable? It is not like you."

He seemed to withdraw into himself. "I do not make an effort to be disagreeable – at least not usually."

"I did not mean... oh, never mind. This is a ridiculous conversation."

After a brief hesitation, he said, "I suppose it is. But I must add one thing, even if it is ridiculous."

"Oh, very well."

"Kissing you was very agreeable indeed."

She drew in a sharp breath between her teeth. "Be that as it may, it will not be repeated." Oh, it was so unfair, this game he was insisting on playing. Why had she allowed him to kiss her? Surely she could pity the boy he once had been without permitting him liberties now. If only she could walk away from him! But there was nowhere to go. She could stand a few paces away on the other side of the room, at the price of subjecting herself to the cold air, but it would make no difference. She would still be in his presence, so she might as well remain by the hearth. She leaned her head back against the rough bricks and closed her eyes. Hopefully he would take the hint and leave her alone.

"If that is what you wish. It will matter little in the long run, for I cannot share your opinion that a marriage between us is unnecessary."

Why must he insist upon pressing her on this? "Unnecessary or not, I appreciate that you are trying to do the honorable thing, assuming you do mean it."

"Assuming I mean it?" His voice was tight again.

"Mr. Darcy, surely it is not news to you that there are gentlemen who promise a lady marriage with the sole intention of enjoying her favors, and then deny saying anything of the sort. I do not *think* you are doing that, but I would be a fool not to consider that possibility – if I were contemplating accepting your offer, which I am not. That was all I meant."

"But you doubt my word. Have I ever behaved in such a manner to make you think I am not a man of my word?"

"To me? No."

"To whom, then?"

Why did they have to keep discussing this? Could he not let the subject rest? "It does not matter, truly. As I said, any young lady would be wise to consider such risks, rather than taking every gentleman at his word."

"Indeed it *does* matter, madam, if you are questioning my honor. Our circumstances are not ordinary."

"I cannot argue that point! But I pray you to forget I said anything. I am tired and cold, and I allowed an unconsidered thought to pass my lips. It meant nothing."

He made no reply, instead getting to his feet and pacing across the room. Not that there was much room to pace; a mere four strides took him to the far wall. Four steps there, four steps back, again and again. Were he not so obviously angry, it would have been humorous.

Suddenly he froze, his expression grim. "Permit me to guess. What is George Wickham accusing me of this time?"

For some reason, his sardonic tone seemed to cut into her. "It makes no difference what anyone has said."

"It matters to me, especially if it has made you

think ill of me."

She gathered the quilt more tightly around her. "Obviously I must think terribly ill of you to have allowed you to kiss me!"

"There is no point in trying to distract me. Whatever he has said, I deserve the right to defend myself and my good name."

"Perhaps I should express myself more slowly and clearly so you will understand me this time! I do not think ill of you." Oddly enough, it was true. He had become a real person to her in this last day, with all the complexities that went with it.

He leaned over her until his face was just a short distance from hers, his hands against the wall on either side of her. "Tell me, Elizabeth. I demand it of your justice."

She huffed and looked away from his intent dark eyes. "Very well, since you leave me no choice. He said your father had promised him a living, and you refused to give it to him. There – are you happy now?"

To her great relief, he stood again. "How very like him – to tell only those parts of the truth which paint the picture he chooses. My father did promise him a living, and I indeed refused to give it to him, but I suppose he did not mention that three years earlier he had requested payment in lieu of the preferment, and I gave him a sum of three thousand pounds. When he then returned on the death of the incumbent, requesting the living, I refused."

Elizabeth hardly knew what to believe. She had no reason to doubt Mr. Wickham, yet Mr. Darcy had produced his version without hesitation. It did not seem like something he could have made up so quickly.

Darcy returned to his pacing. "He should not be a clergyman. He is a scoundrel, a cheat and a seducer."

"A scoundrel? Come now. That is rather extreme."

"Is it? How should I refer to the man who contrived to meet my sister alone, convince her she was in love with him and to agree to an elopement – all when she was but fifteen years old? It was nothing but good fortune that I arrived unexpectedly and discovered his plans before it was too late. That was last summer. His inducement was her dowry of thirty thousand pounds."

His angry words felt almost like blows. She covered her face with her hands, hiding from his probing eyes. It could not be true, could it? Mr. Wickham would not have done such an evil thing... or would he? He had certainly been quick to abandon her and develop an interest in Mary King once he discovered she had ten thousand pounds. Charlotte would call it practicality on his part, but the speed of his change of allegiance had been shocking. She still could not believe he would attempt to elope with Mr. Darcy's sister, but at the same time, why would Mr. Darcy make such a claim if it were not true? It would devastate his sister's future if it became public knowledge. He had no reason to lie about it.

She had to respond somehow. "I am sorry. I hardly know what to say, what to think."

"You are far from the first to be taken in by his pleasing manners. He has a long history of plying his charm on one lady after...." He stopped abruptly.

Lowering her hands to see why he had stopped, she discovered him staring into space, his eyes alit. "Is something the matter?"

"*That* was why I was travelling to Meryton yesterday. I heard rumors to the effect that you were Wickham's particular favorite. I did not wish to see you become another of his victims, so I determined to go to Longbourn to tell your father what I knew of him."

So it was possible to feel even worse about her mistakes. That Mr. Darcy would undertake the mortification of seeking out her father for her protection was more than she could bear. In a small voice she said, "See, it is as I said. Your memory has returned. But I must beg you to excuse me; I do not wish to converse any further at present." In case he could possibly misunderstood that, she drew her knees up to her chest and buried her face in her arms. She could not even bring herself to care that he would see her weakness.

To her relief, he said nothing. But after a minute a weight settled over her, and her eyes shot open to discover he had placed his topcoat over her and tucked it in at her sides, like an embrace.

Chapter 5

IF THERE WAS a worse fate in store for him than having to watch Elizabeth's shoulders shake with silent sobs and being unable to offer her comfort, Darcy did not wish to know what it was. This was excruciating. He hated having caused her pain. Even worse, the fact that she was finding the revelation of Wickham's ill deeds so painful seemed to suggest she had come to care for that blackguard, and *that* idea made Darcy want to pound his head against the wall.

Why in heaven's name had he decided to depart from Hertfordshire when it meant leaving Elizabeth at Wickham's mercy? He must have been out of his mind. He should have warned her more thoroughly, not just a cryptic comment during their one and only dance. Or he should have forgotten all those ridiculous scruples about why he ought not make her an offer then and there. If he had done that, she would be his wife now, and she would be snug in his arms at Pemberley instead of freezing in a peasant's hut.

Finally, after what seemed to be an eternity, Elizabeth's breathing became even. A breath in, a breath out, and a tiny sigh, barely audible over the noise of the wind whipping past the cottage – the same sounds he had heard this morning when he awoke. She must have fallen asleep where she sat, no doubt exhausted after a night trying to sleep on the hard pallet in the cold cottage. Thank heaven! Darcy's shoulders sagged as tension suddenly left him.

The fire was growing low. Even sitting on the hearth, Darcy shivered. Elizabeth was wrapped in both the quilt and his topcoat, leaving him in his shirtsleeves. Stirring the fire might wake Elizabeth, so instead Darcy added another log to it. It was slow to catch, apparently still damp with melted snow, but once it finally caught fire, it burned merrily, hissing and snapping.

His greatcoat was almost dry at last. That could make the rest of their stay a little more comfortable, something which grew more important as the day passed and the storm continued. The chances of escaping the cottage were growing slenderer by the moment. Not that it troubled him personally; it would mean more time with Elizabeth, but he suspected she would not take it well. He spread the greatcoat out across the hearth to dry it more quickly. After its soaking in the snow, the bloodstained collar, and the cat hair sticking to it, a little soot would not make any significant difference. Crewe would not be pleased, but that was the least of his worries. The greatest of them was dozing on the other side of the hearth.

⚬⚬⚬

Elizabeth eyed Darcy as he handed her the cup filled with hot water. Had he truly filled the kettle and put it over the fire himself? The warmth was most welcome, in any case, especially as she had no idea what to make of the change in Darcy's behavior.

Since she had awoken, her eyes still swollen from crying, he had been acting as if they were at a public gathering, asking her about events in Meryton and her family's health, telling her about his sister's preferences in music and how winter in Derbyshire differed from that in London. It was starting to make her nervous. What was he thinking that would make him be so, well, distant? After the intimacy of some of their discussions, not to mention their disagreements, it felt wrong to be playing at ladies and gentlemen again. But it was a relief not to be quarreling. It was hard enough being trapped with him.

The wind whistled over the cottage, sending a gust down the chimney that caused the flames to jump. How long had she slept? "What time is it?"

Darcy checked his pocket watch, then closed it with a snap and shook his head. "Half three. Even if the storm abated this minute, there would not be daylight enough to get us back to Meryton." His voice seemed oddly muted.

Elizabeth said nothing. What was there to say, after all? She had never liked being indoors for long periods of time, and after being trapped so long in the tiny space without even a view of the outdoors, the walls of the cottage seemed to be closing in on her. They had broken their fast on the last of the venison and apples, and her stomach gurgled with hunger. The wind had picked up again, and she could barely hear herself think over the constant refrain of its howling. It felt as if the smell of smoke and wet wool would cling to her forever. And then there was Mr. Darcy, always only a few feet away. If only she could burrow down under a feather comforter and hide there until the storm went away! But all they had was the thin quilt, and there was no place to hide.

Reluctantly she rose to her feet. If they were not to be reduced to eating raw onions and turnips tonight, she would have to think of something to do with them. How hard could it be to make soup? She rummaged through the larder and brought out the onions, carrots and turnips.

It was simple enough to figure out how to cut up the carrots and turnips with the small knife she had found, though her pieces were distinctly uneven and she almost cut herself more than once. The onions were more mysterious. The brown, papery globes looked nothing like cooked onions. Finally she cut them into quarters, then poured all the chunks into the kettle. Rubbing her arm over her stinging eyes, she filled it with water and added a handful of barley, then placed it in the fire. If they were fortunate, it just might be edible eventually – or perhaps not. With a heavy sigh, she sank down on the hearth again.

Darcy sat down by her side, his arm only inches from hers. "I know it is not what you wish to hear, yet since we have no choice but to pass another night here, it seems impossible your reputation will be untouched. I do not understand why the idea of marriage to me is so repugnant to you. Most women would be delighted to make such a match."

Not this again! Apparently her reprieve was over. "I am not most women!"

"No, that you are not. Is there another man, then, who you wish to marry?"

She jumped to her feet, needing some distance from him. "Is that the only reason you can imagine I might not want to marry you?"

He took his time in answering. "I am attempting to understand your reluctance."

Running out and losing herself in the storm was starting to seem like an appealing alternative. "*You* do not wish to marry *me*, and the only reason you are even considering it is because you feel you have no other choice. You yourself have said your temper is resentful, and I do not wish to be resented by my husband. That should be reason enough."

"It is true I would not have made the offer were it not for our circumstances, but if you think I dislike the idea, I most assuredly do not."

"Even if I were to believe you are not personally averse to the match, can you tell me with honesty that you would never be embarrassed by my family? That there would not be moments when you would regret tying yourself to a woman of such low connections? You need not give me an answer to these questions, for I know it already."

He hesitated, his brows drawn together. "I cannot deny it, but I would not blame *you* for any of it."

"So you say now, and no doubt you even mean it, since you seem to feel you owe me your life. But years from now, when my charms have worn thin and my imperfections become more manifest, it will be different. Then my lack of a proper education will become an irritant, and you will realize that had I not found you at the side of the road, someone else likely would have done so soon enough."

He frowned. "You think me so fickle and unfair?"

"I think you are human. I have seen what happens in an unequal marriage, when a man loses his respect for the wife he once wished desperately to marry. I will *never* agree to be in that position, to be treated with scorn, not for all the riches of Pemberley."

He shook his head. "That would not be my way."

"Not deliberately, perhaps, but I have seen your scorn for those you feel to be your inferiors. Sooner or later, you would feel that way about me." To her horror, her voice cracked on her final words. She turned her face away from him in the vain hope of hiding the hot tears burning her eyes.

Mr. Darcy might be at a loss for how to respond to her refusal, but he had no hesitation when it came to answering her distress. His arms closed around her, holding her to his chest. She should have pushed him away, but the comfort he offered was too tempting and she felt warmer in his embrace than she had all day. She swallowed a sob.

"Shh, Elizabeth. All is well. I truly do not mean to distress you," he said softly.

"I know that," she whispered into his chest,

rising and falling with each breath. "It is just too much, the storm going on and on, and the cold, the lack of food, nowhere to go and nothing to do."

"I can do nothing about the storm or being trapped here, but perhaps I can at least help you be warm for a time. Come." Taking her hand, he led her back to the hearth, where he added two more logs to the fire, poking it to make it burn hotter.

"Will there be enough wood left for the night?" Elizabeth crouched down on the pallet and held her cold fingers out to the blaze. At least one side of her would be warm.

"I can always bring in more, since now I know where to find the woodpile." Darcy sat beside her, and a heavy weight came around her shoulders. It was his many-caped greatcoat, and he had wrapped it around both of them. His arm encircled her shoulders as well, and he urged her closer to him until her side pressed against his. She still felt the cold deep in her bones, but there was no doubt this was the warmest she had been.

She should not permit this intimacy, though. Reluctantly she said, "But if someone discovers us…"

"If someone discovers us now, it does not matter whether you are across the room or in my arms. Either way you would be hopelessly compromised. The question is whether you would rather be warm or cold when you are compromised."

She giggled. "Warm. Definitely warm. I adore your greatcoat. Why do they never make pelisses out of such lovely heavy wool? I suppose it would look too unfashionable." She snuggled deeper into the coat and

Mr. Darcy's arm.

"In summer, I envy the ladies in their light muslins and short sleeves, while we gentlemen must suffer with shirt, waistcoat and topcoat, no matter how hot it may be. But in winter, I am thankful for all the layers men must wear, and wonder how ladies keep from freezing."

"It is difficult for me even to imagine the warmth of a summer day right now." And a few minutes earlier, she could never have imagined that being encircled by Mr. Darcy's arm could be so comforting – or pleasurable. "Or even to imagine the snow stopping. I think I will hear the wind howling in my dreams for weeks!"

His chest vibrated with a rumble of laughter. "It has been rather constant."

Something poked at the greatcoat, and a furry face appeared inside it. How could she have forgotten the cat? "Hello, Snowball," she said as the cat stretched out across both Darcy's leg and hers.

"Snowball?"

"It seems appropriate, does it not?"

He scratched the cat's head. "Indeed."

Snowball began to purr. Elizabeth was tempted to share the sentiment. This position was altogether too pleasant, but what must Darcy think of her? "I hope you know I do not usually behave in this manner."

"I could hardly miss that fact, since it took you this long to realize the best way to stay warm," he teased. "I know it is unlike you, and unlike me as well. But this is a time out of time, and the usual rules do not apply."

"Most of those rules would have been impossible to follow." Somehow that gave her permission to rest her head against his shoulder. What would she think in a few days when she looked back on this moment? Would she be horrified with herself, or wonder why she had not enjoyed it more while she could?

"Under normal circumstances, we do not have to worry about freezing to death or starving. The reason we can have so many rules about propriety is because our servants take care of those critical problems for us, so well that perhaps we forget how important they are. More important than rules, in any case."

"Definitely more important," agreed Elizabeth.

They sat together in companionable silence for some time until the smell of onions began to permeate the air.

"Do you suppose your delightful concoction is ready yet?" Darcy asked.

She wrinkled her nose at him. "I have no idea, as you know perfectly well. We shall have to be adventurous and discover the answer the hard way. Or rather, *I* shall be adventurous."

"I insist the privilege is mine." He urged Snowball onto her lap, then wrapped his greatcoat around her before using a stick to move the kettle away from the fire. "As soon as it cools a bit, that is."

His smile truly was quite devastatingly attractive. It made her breath catch in her chest. "You are a very brave man, then."

"Either brave or very hungry. The aroma is good, in any case."

"It smells like stewed onions, carrots and turnips, which is hardly surprising, as that is what it is."

"It smells like hot food, which is something I barely remember at this point." He rejoined her under the greatcoat and took her hand back in his, squeezing it gently. "Not that I am complaining, mind you. The company has been excellent."

"You mean that the company, like the food, is excellently warm," she teased.

"The excellent company keeping me warm is far superior to the warmest of foods. Now, where is that spoon?"

"The one which is right in front of you?"

"Ah, yes, that one. I must be blinded by the beauty of the excellent company."

"Or the smell of hot food has gone to your head!" Who would have guessed Mr. Darcy had the capacity for banter and light flirtation?

He stirred the pot, then drew out a spoonful and blew on it. Raising it in her direction, he said solemnly, "To blizzards – may they always bring such companions."

Elizabeth choked back a laugh as he sipped from the spoon. "Your face is a study! You might as well say straight out it is terrible."

He eyed the spoon, then took another sip. "I would not describe it as terrible. It tastes of onions, carrots and turnips – but mostly of onions."

"I cannot see why. I put in as many carrots as I

did onions. Besides, have you never heard of onion soup?"

"The mysteries of cooking are far beyond me, Miss Elizabeth." He dipped the spoon in the soup again, then held it in front of her mouth. "Come, it is your turn to give an opinion."

With an arch look at him through her eyelashes, she obediently sipped from the spoon he held, then pursed her lips as if in thought. "There is a trace of onion flavor, it is true; but I would have to judge it as passable for my first try. Why, in another day or two, I shall be as knowledgeable as a French chef!"

"A *trace* of onion flavor?" said Darcy in mock indignation. "A mere *trace*?"

"Admittedly, it is perhaps a rather *large* trace. But I only put in four onions, although there were a great many more I could have added. I was successful in my other culinary goal, though."

"And what was that?"

"It is hot, just as I wished it to be – though I will have to give some credit to your fire for that."

"I am striving to improve my skills at keeping things – and people – warm," he said.

"Constant practice is the key to success, so pray, do continue to keep me warm. And if you object to my fine onion soup, why, there will be all the more for me." She attempted to tug the spoon from his hand.

He pulled it away from her. "Oh, no, Miss Elizabeth! I must have my share of your very warm cooking. I will give you another spoonful, then one for me."

"Mr. Darcy, I have not been fed by another person since I was out of leading strings!"

"Then it shall be another new experience for you. We have only one spoon, and it seems I cannot trust you with it."

She nearly choked on the next spoonful as his mock-stern expression made her laugh. "And I was accustomed to thinking you too serious!"

"I am very serious indeed, especially when it comes to hot food." His actions followed suit.

Poking him in the ribs with her elbow, she said more out of playfulness than necessity, "My turn."

He held up the spoon for her once more. "Your wish is my command."

She tried to take a sip. "This is harder than it looks! I have no idea how infants manage it." Finally she swallowed it down, then licked a few spilled drops from her lower lip.

Darcy's hand stopped in mid-air as he stared at her mouth. Had she missed some soup and allowed it to dribble down her chin? How embarrassing that would be. Once again she ran her tongue over her lips.

"You may have the spoon." Darcy's voice sounded hoarse as he dropped the spoon on the hearth.

Elizabeth's shoulders sagged. Once again she had managed to offend him without even knowing what she had done. And just when she had been enjoying his company! Was it too much effort for him to hand her the spoon? "Very well," she said equably. Unwilling to go hungry because of Mr. Darcy's moods, she proceeded to eat a few mouthfuls of the soup, then replaced the spoon precisely where he had left it.

Even the soup was less satisfying now, not that it had been flavorful to start out with. Perhaps she should have cut up the onions more or removed the papery skin which now floated in the soup. It might be hot, but her stomach still felt hollow. There must be something else she could do. Were not men generally in better spirits when they were not hungry?

On inspiration, she braved the cold and left Darcy's side in search of the stale bread she had seen the previous day. It was as hard as a rock, but she brought it back to the hearth anyway. Unfortunately, breaking off a chunk of it was more difficult than she had anticipated. She was overly conscious of Darcy observing her vain efforts.

Finally he took the bread from her without a word. He raised it over his head, and then smashed it down on the edge of the hearth. The loaf broke into several pieces, or perhaps it would be more accurate to say it shattered. Could bread shatter?

"Thank you." She did not look at him as she dunked a chunk of bread into the soup. She let it soak briefly, then removed it and held the dripping end over the kettle.

There was no way to eat such a thing gracefully, but what did she care for Mr. Darcy's good opinion? She clearly could not keep it long. Cautiously she leaned forward and bit into the soggy bread. Sitting back, she chewed it slowly, then swallowed.

"I cannot say I recommend the dish highly, but it is preferable to going hungry," she said.

"A clever idea." He followed suit with another piece of bread.

At least he no longer sounded upset. She would keep her peace in hope it would last.

The bread and soup disappeared quickly, leaving nothing for them to do but to sit huddled together for warmth. Initially Elizabeth resolved to say nothing, but the discordance between their physical closeness and emotional distance finally won out over her reluctance.

"You look very serious. Is something that matter – apart from the usual issues like being stranded here in the cold with an impertinent miss instead of a cook?"

"Not at all. I cannot imagine sharing my coat with my cook, so it is just as well she is not here. I am merely attempting to keep my thoughts of that impertinent miss to those of a brotherly nature."

That was not what she had expected to hear. "From what I can see, you seem to be succeeding in that."

"Do I?" His voice had an odd inflection.

She tilted her head to look up at him. "I do not understand."

He let out a long breath through his teeth. "In fact, I am failing abysmally at it, and have been ever since I gave you that spoonful of soup."

"Oh." Was that why he had withdrawn so suddenly? How was she to respond? Her lips began to tingle.

"I do not like it, but I must ask a favor of you."

Her pulses grew rapid. Was he going to ask for a

kiss? She had been thinking of the last one all day, and despite her brave words earlier, she did not know if she would refuse another. "What is it?"

"Do not permit me any liberties tonight."

Stung, she said, "I was not planning to!"

He sighed. "I know, but sometimes these things do not turn out as we plan. There are good reasons why young ladies are never allowed to be alone with men. So I am telling you now that, no matter how many rules we break, it would be very unwise to let me kiss you. And if I am fortunate, the mere act of saying so will be enough to prevent me from making a fool of myself by attempting to do so."

She straightened, shifting so that no part of her side came in contact with his. "You need have no worries on my part."

He laid his head in his hand. "Elizabeth, I beg your indulgence. I truly do not mean to quarrel with you or to imply you are lacking in any way. You are not. I, however, am sadly lacking in self control, and I said you would be safe with me. Above all else, I do not wish to betray your trust. But I am only human."

Again she had misjudged him, thinking him angry when he was struggling with himself – over his attraction to her. And he had not complained about it until she had asked him directly what troubled him. She hunted for the proper words to make her amends. "I am sorry the situation is so difficult. Despite my ruffled feathers a few minutes ago, if there is any way I can ease the burden, I hope you will tell me. Would it be better if we did not sit together?"

He shook his head vigorously. "No, if anything..."

"Yes?"

His voice was muffled. "If anything, it would be easier if I could hold you closer."

"I should not let you kiss me, but I *should* let you hold me? Tell me, do men always make this little sense when it comes to these matters?"

To her relief, he chuckled. "Yes. We make no sense at all when it comes to women."

"Well, that relieves my mind," she said with mock tartness. "I would hate to think you would make sense." She hesitated, then added softly, "I do not mind if you wish to hold me."

How he looked at her again. "You do not mind?" He sounded uncertain.

Her pulses raced. "It would be... comforting." It was not the correct description, but how could she tell him she longed to be closer to him, to resolve all their quarrels and find happiness together?

He made a sound of assent; then, before Elizabeth knew what was happening, he scooped her up and deposited her in his lap. He wrapped his greatcoat around her so it covered them both except for the area directly in front of her. Elizabeth reached out and completed the circle by pulling up the quilt to cover the remaining area, enveloping them in warmth as Darcy cocooned her in his arms. With a sigh, she rested her head on his shoulder, breathing in the scent of spice, musk and wood smoke. Oh, this was far too pleasant! Safe, comforted, yet feeling oddly alive, as if every inch of her were experiencing sensation for the very first time. And warm – oh, so warm! She curled and uncurled her toes in her stocking just because she had to do *something*. "Better?" she asked.

He rested his cheek on the top of her head. "Yes."

How could he think this was easier? Now she was the one struggling with thoughts quite inappropriate for a young lady to have towards a gentleman in whom she had no serious intentions. Unfortunately, she was no longer certain she did want to part from him after the storm ended. Oh, how unfair it was for him to make her want things she could not have! All her reasons for refusing him were still valid – except that she wanted quite desperately to kiss him, to make him laugh, to have him gaze at her with passion. Why did *this* have to be her weakness? Could she not have settled for flirting with the officers as Lydia and Kitty did? But no, she had to want Mr. Darcy, of all men.

If only there were something separating them, something to stop her from giving in to the temptation to press her lips to his. With a sudden movement, she pulled the quilt over her head.

Darcy's body stiffened. He lifted a corner of the quilt and peered under it at her. "Are you attempting to stay warm, or is something the matter?"

She ducked her head. It was remarkably difficult to lie when seated in someone's lap. "I am hiding," she informed him with great dignity.

"From me?"

"From everything."

"There is no one here apart from me to see you."

"You, and the fire, and the walls, and the roof, and the cupboards, and the snow." She stopped herself before adding the town of Meryton and the entirety of England and the West Indies as well. Everything that represented society, expectations and limitations.

"Perhaps I should join you, then." She could hear his smile more than see it as he ducked under the quilt with her."

It had felt too intimate before, and now it was double so. The warmth of his breath wafted over her cheeks. "That would defeat the entire purpose."

"How so? You are still safe from the fire, the walls, the roof, and the snow." He sounded amused and at ease.

Resignedly she tipped her head back to look at him, or at least at the vague shape she could see by the hint of firelight finding its way through the think quilt. Why did he have to attract her so? Even at the Meryton assembly she had been aware of him.

"What is it, Elizabeth?" His voice was tinged with concern now.

"Do you think..." She lost her courage for a minute, and touched her tongue to her dry lips. "Do you think you are the only one who finds this situation difficult?"

At first he did not seem to understand, and then he closed his eyes for several long moments that felt like an eternity. His voice was low when he finally spoke.

"You likely would have been wiser not to say that — but I am remarkably glad you did."

Afterwards, she was uncertain which of them had moved first, or perhaps they had both shifted so their mouths could meet. This was not the chaste pressure of his earlier kiss; this time she could sense the uncontrolled passion behind it as his tongue teased her lips apart. The sensation lit a fire within her, simultaneously shocking, intoxicating, and disturbingly exciting as she instinctively met his invasion with a response purely her own. How had her arms ended up wound around his neck?

He broke away, his breathing ragged. "I hope this means you have changed your mind about marriage, because very soon it is going to be too late."

He could not have brought her back to reality more painfully had he thrown her out into the storm. What had she done? She clapped her hands over her ears and squeezed her eyes shut. "I beg you, stop asking me that. I cannot do it. You do not know what you are asking."

She felt his chest move with each heavy breath he took, his body now rigid. "Very well, madam, if that is what you wish," he said coldly. He pushed himself away, leaving his greatcoat covering Elizabeth. "I will leave you alone."

She opened her eyes. "Where are you going?"

"To get more firewood." His voice sounded harsh even to his own ears.

"Then you will need your greatcoat." She began to remove it.

"No. I do not need it." What he needed was to be half-frozen to death. It was his best hope of quenching the hunger for Elizabeth Bennet that was devouring him.

He pulled at the latch on the door and strode out into the frozen world. The cold slammed into him like a runaway carriage, the fine linen of his shirtsleeves no protection from the icy wind. He stood on the doorstep, letting the cold seep into him until his teeth chattered. Still not enough; all he wanted was to make love to Elizabeth.

She did not realize what a dangerous position they were in. Alone together, having discarded the rules that kept them a safe distance apart, a long night ahead and attraction flaring between them. She probably imagined they could share a few kisses and then stop, but he knew better. It had always been obvious to him she was passionate by nature, and now he had discovered how much pleasure she derived from physical affection. One little spark and it would all be over.

Or perhaps it would be for the best that way. If he made her his, there would be none of this nonsense about not wanting to marry him. Even if she remained skittish, he would have to insist. Devil take it, why had he allowed these thoughts into his mind? Desire surged through him again, icy wind notwithstanding.

Why was she so frightened by the idea of marriage, anyway? She was far from timid by nature, but this question brought out a side of her he had never seen. Had some man hurt her or frightened her? He would not have thought so from the way she kissed him. Groaning at the recollection of her tongue against his, he clapped the heels of his hands to his temples. Why did she have to be so tempting?

Well, if she did not want to hear about marriage, he would keep his thoughts on it to himself henceforth. But how was he to control his own attraction to her?

A gust of wind whipped against him, icy pellets stinging his face. If only it could blow away his desire so he could act the part of the gentleman again!

Or perhaps that was part of the problem. Elizabeth knew he wanted her; there was no point now in wasting his energy in a vain attempt to keep up the appearance of indifference. Perhaps it was time to stop the pretense. If he allowed himself to behave naturally, showing his admiration and not trying to restrict every word that came out of his mouth, then he might be able to focus on the critical matter of convincing his hands to stay away from her clothing.

That was the answer. He would stop guarding his expression and his words, and would say and do as he pleased — as long as he did not touch her clothing. Unless, of course, she came to her senses and agreed to marry him, in which case none of it mattered anyway.

His teeth began to chatter uncontrollably. A little more of this and he would develop frostbite. Perhaps that would take his mind off Elizabeth! But he could not stand out here forever. He had told her he was fetching firewood, so he had best return with some. His legs were stiff with cold, but he forced them to take the few steps to the woodpile.

Chapter 6

As soon as the door closed behind him, Elizabeth shook off his greatcoat and retreated to her earlier seat on the hearth, her legs pulled up to her chest and the quilt covering her knees. Huddling together had been warmer, but it would be better to freeze than to have a repeat of what had just occurred. What had come over her? Simply being close to a handsome gentleman was no excuse for kissing him. It was not as if they were even getting along particularly well. For every conversation which went well or joke they shared, there had been a misunderstanding or quarrel.

Her opinion of him was better than it had been before the storm, but he was so difficult to understand. Admittedly, their situation was an unusual one and they had spoken with remarkable frankness, but she had never met a man of as many moods as Mr. Darcy, and only rarely did those moods make sense to her. Nor did her own reactions. What had happened to her vaunted ability to laugh at foolishness? She could not laugh at his sulks; instead, they made *her* unhappy. And none of it, *none* of it, was any excuse to kiss him!

How could she blame him for making the

assumption she would marry him when she behaved so improperly? The storm must have affected her wits somehow, for her usual common sense to have deserted her so badly. She would have to make certain to keep her distance from him, since apparently she could not trust herself.

She lowered her head onto her knees. It was only a snowstorm. He was only a man. The storm would certainly end soon, and they would be able to leave this tiny room tomorrow. There was no reason to panic – except that she had never had such powerful feelings about a man before, and she did not understand him at all.

The door opened, bringing with it a blast of icy air, but Elizabeth did not raise her head. She could not ignore him forever, but it was so much easier not to look at him, not to see his expression, not to attempt to guess his mood as he slammed the door shut again. His feet shuffled against the straw on the floor, then the sound was replaced by the clatter of wood being dropped and restacked. The poker scraped along the hearth, followed by the soft crash of a log breaking and an increase in the crackling and popping of the fire. What good did it do not to look at him when she followed his every movement by the sounds he made?

Raising her head just an inch, she peered over her knees at him. He was squatted in front of the hearth, closer to the flames than could possibly be comfortable. Even in the ruddy firelight she could see his face was pale, and his hand, where he held the poker, was almost blue. Had he gone out without his gloves? He must have. He had removed them when they ate the soup.

He must be half frozen, but he had not touched his greatcoat where it lay over the stool. Instead he remained as unmoving as a statue, his gaze fixed on the fire. Perhaps he was avoiding looking at her just as she had done with him.

The situation was embarrassing – mortifying, if truth be told – but there was no reason for him to suffer. On impulse, she took the quilt from over her legs and draped it over his shoulders, then pulled back into the position she had just left. Her legs felt the chill more now, but her heart was more at peace.

"I thank you." He drew the quilt around him more tightly.

Apparently he did not intend to say anything about what had passed between them. That would make it much easier. "Has the snow eased at all yet?"

"A little, perhaps. It is mixed with sleet now."

"How deep is it?"

He tilted his head to one side as if considering the matter, but he kept watching the fire. "That is hard to say. There are some drifts which look quite deep. Outside the door, it reaches my knees. It will be hard work to break a path tomorrow."

At least he seemed to think they would be able to leave by then. Surely they would be able to depart in the morning. She had never heard of a storm lasting as long as this one already had. "Once we had snow too deep for me to walk through, but as I was perhaps five years of age then, that did not necessarily mean it was very deep. I remember it melted after only two days, and I was heartbroken because I thought it was so beautiful."

"I imagine it will take longer than that for this to disappear, unless the weather is unusually warm. That would disappoint the people of London; it has been cold enough they are hoping for a Frost Fair. The Thames has not frozen over in almost twenty years, but they think it might this year."

She managed a smile. "I have seen pictures of Frost Fairs, and always hoped I could go to one someday, but I cannot say the idea of spending a day on a frozen river has any appeal at the moment."

"Perhaps another year, then, when this is but a distant memory."

"Perhaps." She could not imagine a time these days would fade into the past.

He said nothing more, but at least the atmosphere seemed peaceful, which was a great improvement. Perhaps a lack of trouble was the best they could hope for at this point. Obviously, they could not return to where they had been, no matter how pleasant it had been to sit pressed up against him under his greatcoat and to laugh with him. She rested her cheek on her knees, avoiding looking directly at him, but she could still see him out of the corner of her eyes. There was something comforting about keeping him in sight.

After a time, he roused himself to ask if she would prefer to have the quilt back or would rather wear his greatcoat, his question making clear he was not offering to share them.

"The quilt works well." It would be too hard to face the intimacy of being enveloped in his coat. She did not want to bring back the memory of his kiss, not now when everything was calm.

But there was one problem looming before her. When she began to yawn, Elizabeth could no longer ignore the question of where they would sleep. "About tonight…"

"Our sleeping arrangements?" His response was so quick he must have been considering the same thing. "Last night seemed to work well."

Her stomach fluttered at the memory of waking in his arms. "If you do not mind the impropriety of it."

His voice deepened. "As it happened, I did *not* mind the impropriety of it – far from it."

"You are not helping, sir!"

He sat up and touched her cheek with the back of his fingers. "No, I suppose I am not. But you must know by now that I do not intend to take advantage of you. At least not undue advantage. We might as well both be as comfortable as possible, since we will need our strength in the morning."

"I suppose so." She tried to sound dubious, but it was difficult when the proposition was so tempting. It was wrong to want to lie in his arms again, but she could not help herself, especially when she would have to say her final farewell to him in the morning.

To distract herself from that painful thought, she began yanking out her hair pins, ruthlessly pulling her hair out of the simple knot she had made that morning. Last night that had been enough, but now her hair was too tangled even for a simple plait. Yesterday morning, an eternity ago, Nell had braided fine lilac ribbons into Elizabeth's hair in honor of Charlotte's wedding. Last night Elizabeth had simply left the tiny ribbon braids in place when she plaited it, then put it back up in the morning. Now the ribbons were snarled in her curls. If she slept with the ribbons in again tonight, she might have to cut them out.

Earlier she had seen a rude wooden comb on the shelf. She took it to the hearth and began the slow process of untangling. It was like sorting through a rat's nest. Each braid needed to be teased apart from the rest of her hair, then carefully unbraided. Oh, why had Nell put in so many? She winced each time the comb encountered a tangle. Her brush at Longbourn would have made it much easier, but it might as well be on the moon for all the good that did her.

And she had an audience. Last night Mr. Darcy had turned away when she let down her hair, but tonight he made no pretense of looking away. He sat on the palette, resting back with his hands behind him, the look in his eyes as hot as the fire. The power of that look made her long for something more.

That was a bad idea. She wrenched her eyes away, concentrating all her attention on the large snarl near her scalp. Finally it came free, and she turned slightly as she began work on the other side. It was a good thing she had no other tasks to manage, since this was going to take quite a while. Mr. Darcy seemed prepared to admire each moment of her struggles.

"Gentlemen are fortunate they do not have to deal with these problems," she said. "No one ever wants to glue feathers in *your* hair."

"I am glad to say the question has never arisen. Do you really use glue?"

"Not I, since I refuse to wear feathers in my hair for that very reason. Most ladies do. Their maids spend hours washing it out later. Sometimes they must cut it out." She tugged hard on a particularly recalcitrant tangle.

"I am grateful you do not wear feathers, then. It would be a crime to cut even a strand of your hair." His voice seemed to reverberate in the small space.

She masked her discomfort by focusing on undoing another braid. The ribbon, when it finally came free, was already fraying. No wonder it had knotted so badly! She dropped it on top of its fellows beside her.

The back of her head was harder. Her hairstyle had never been designed for her to undo the braids herself, and she had to explore with her fingers even to discover where the ribbons were. The first came free easily enough, though unbraiding it when she could not see it was challenging, especially with Mr. Darcy observing her clumsy attempts.

The last braid was hopelessly snarled. She gave up on the comb and tried to separate her hair a few strands at a time, but it was impossible to tell if she was making progress or making things worse. Frustrated, she pulled hard at one lock, only to wince when her scalp protested. She blew out her breath in annoyance.

If only she could see what she was doing!

Mr. Darcy spoke from the shadows. "It seems the eyes in the back of your head operate no better than mine did in assessing my injury. Might I offer my assistance?"

To sit close to her and touch her hair? Her throat grew tight. She should refuse, but she doubted she would be able to untangle it herself. "I am certain it will not matter if it waits until my maid can deal with it tomorrow."

"I am not *that* untrustworthy," he said with a low laugh.

The question was whether *she* could be trusted, but if she refused now, he would see it as doubting his word. "Very well."

As he joined her on the hearth, she turned to face away to allow the faint light from the fire to illuminate the back of her head. She could feel his closeness, but he did not touch her hair. "Is it that hopeless?" she asked archly.

"I am examining the problem and planning my strategy and line of attack."

"So you view my hair as a battle?"

"You have no idea." He said it so softly she was not certain she had even heard him correctly.

Now she could feel the pressure as he did something, no doubt to separate the braid. Her scalp tingled at the sensation, almost as if he were caressing her. It was *not* a caress, she told herself firmly. She never thought of Nell as caressing her hair. Perhaps she should try to imagine Mr. Darcy was her maid. A giggle bubbled up.

"Is something the matter?" he asked.

"Not at all. I was merely considering whether you had a future as a lady's maid."

He chuckled. "Only if the lady in question has dark, curly hair which feels like silk between my fingers."

Oh, dear. The fire simmering inside her was putting the one in the hearth to shame. It did not help when she felt his hands slide through the hair she had already untangled. There had been no need for him to do that. He must simply have wished to do it.

Fortunately for what little peace of mind she had left, he returned to untangling. Each tug sent a spiral of odd sensation down into her body. How could she feel it so clearly when he only touched her hair? She dug her fingernails into her palms to distract herself from the strangely pleasurable feelings.

"Almost there." His voice was hoarse.

She bit her lip. "Good." She both wanted him to stop and to continue forever.

"I will need the comb."

Silently she handed it to him, bracing herself for pain, since combing through her tangles was not easy. The tugging sensation changed, but remained surprisingly gentle. "You do that well, for one with no experience."

"My sister used to like me to comb her hair when she was little. She pretended she was a princess and I was her knight. Her hair is straight, though."

"Whenever my hair tangles, I wish it were

straight."

The comb stopped moving for a moment. "Do not ever wish that."

She swallowed hard, her mouth dry. What could she possibly say in response? It was a good thing he could not see her face. It might be all too obvious how he was affecting her.

"There, it is all free now, apart from the braid. If you can be patient another minute, I will have the ribbon out."

Another minute might be too much. She might go up in flames by then.

His arm reached around her and dropped a ribbon in her lap. Before she could say anything, he resumed combing her hair. Or was it combing? She felt her hair being raised. He was running his fingers slowly through it from below.

Shivers ran down her spine, or perhaps it was a line of sparks. "What are you doing?" she asked, her mouth dry.

"Making certain all the tangles are out," he said huskily.

He was definitely taking more time than was necessary. She knew she ought to object, ought to tell him to stop, but somehow the words were stuck in her throat. As if it had taken on a life of its own, her scalp tingled with each movement of her hair. Then she felt something soft and warm caressing the back of her neck, and an exquisite sensation cascaded through her from that point. Her eyes drifted closed involuntarily. At least her face was in shadow; he would not be able to see her expression.

Then she gave a cry of pain as sharp, stinging pain intruded on the swell of sweet sensation. She clapped her hand down on her injured thigh, capturing a furry paw.

Darcy dropped her hair instantly. "My deepest apologies. I had no intention of causing you pain."

The cat batted at the ribbon hanging down from Elizabeth's lap, managing once again to snag her claws through her skirt. "*You* did not hurt me. That honor goes to your protégée, Miss Snowball. She seems to think my hair ribbon is a toy and my lap is a pincushion." She ought to be grateful. Who knows what might have happened had the cat not interrupted them? Could she have mustered the strength to tell Mr. Darcy to stop?

She took a deep breath and turned toward Darcy, but the words died in her mouth as she saw him staring intently into her eyes with obvious longing. She had to swallow hard before she could say, "Her claws are remarkably sharp, no doubt from hunting mice in the woodpile. I... I thank you for your assistance."

"It was my pleasure – totally my pleasure. You do not know how I have longed to touch your hair."

Forcing herself to break eye contact, she said lightly, "Likely you did not anticipate dealing with snarls, though!" She picked up the ribbon and drew it slowly across her lap, hoping Snowball would claw her again and bring her back to her senses.

Instead, the cat caught the ribbon in her teeth and tugged it away, then leaped onto Darcy's lap and began to purr. Elizabeth would have to find her own courage to resist his charm – but she wished it was her instead of Snowball he was caressing.

Elizabeth entertained herself for the next half hour or so by trying to recall as many of Mary's favorite quotes from Fordyce's Sermons as she could. Not that it helped her stop wishing for things she could not have, but at least it kept her mind occupied and provided a reminder of society's expectations. Who would have thought she, Elizabeth Bennet, would ever require such a reminder? Till being stranded with Mr. Darcy, she had never truly known her own weaknesses.

Finally she could delay going to bed no longer. She felt inordinately clumsy as she settled herself on the straw pallet, careful to lie as close to the edge as she could to leave as much room as possible and facing away from the remainder of the pallet.

Darcy put a fresh log on the fire, then stepped past her. The straw pallet rustled as he took the place beside her. Although she could not see him, she was acutely aware of his presence and his lingering of spice and musk.

It took a tap on her shoulder to make her look at him. He lay propped up on one elbow, the firelight playing in red shadows across his strong features. His expression was serious. "Warm or cold?"

She bit her lip. Time out of time. "Warm."

A smile lifted the corner of his lips as he lay back and extended his arm. She snuggled in beside him, resting her head on his shoulder, in the spot which seemed to be made just for that. When she reached up to brush a lock of hair out of her eyes, her hand touched his, sending a shock all the way down to her toes.

Darcy wrapped her hand in his, then rested them both on his chest. It felt natural, and far too pleasing. Somehow she kept her voice from trembling as she bade him goodnight.

His lips pressed lightly against her forehead. "Sleep well, sweet Lizzy."

Although she stayed still, in a feigned sleep, it was at least half an hour before sleep claimed her as she listened to the steady beat of his heart, still feeling the spot his lips had pressed. But it was much longer before Darcy joined her in that state.

Chapter 7

THE FIRST THING to cross Darcy's consciousness was an awareness of the presence of sunlight. Even with his eyes still closed, he could see it and feel the strangeness of it. He always awoke before the sun was up. The warmth in his arms was the next thing to register. He did not need to open his eyes to recognize Elizabeth Bennet. Her arm was across his chest, and during the night he had apparently captured her leg between his. Now that was a sensation he intended to enjoy! This was an excellent way to wake up to a new day.

Except for one thing. If the sun was shining, then the storm must have ended; and if the storm had ended, he would have to let Elizabeth go. That was not acceptable. As his arms tightened around her, he realized from the sound of her breathing she was not asleep.

So she had awakened first, but stayed in his arms? That shocking thought was enough to make him open his eyes. The room was more brightly lit than he had ever seen it, and it was silent. No roaring of the wind, no crackling of the fire. Just Elizabeth in his arms.

She shifted her head as it lay on his shoulder. "The quiet seems almost eerie, does it not?"

"Who would have thought you would miss the sound of the wind?" he teased.

"Mmm. Well, I do. It is too quiet." And she still made no effort to leave his arms.

No. He was not going to attempt to make sense of her behavior, and he was most certainly not going to suggest marriage again. That was how he had landed in trouble yesterday. He should just take the moment as the gift it was, and not think about the separation which was bound to follow.

He raised his head enough to see her face. Her expression was unreadable, but the relaxation of her body against his spoke of contentment, or perhaps it was something more. His own body was certainly thinking of things beyond contentment, and was becoming more demanding about it by the minute, but he did not want to endanger this precious time.

Except for one thing. If he had to say goodbye forever to Elizabeth Bennet in a very short time, he wanted to kiss her again first, a kiss which did not end with the image he could not forget of her pressing her hands over her ears and squeezing her eyes shut to block him out. No, he wanted a kiss he could remember without pain, that he could replay in his mind during long, empty nights without her.

He shifted his arm until he could reach her chin and tip it up with his forefinger. She did not fight him, and her dark eyes looked steadily into his, her lips slightly parted. There could be no doubt; she was expecting him to kiss her, neither inviting it nor avoiding it, just waiting.

That was good enough for him. He tipped his head towards hers slowly, savoring the anticipation as well as giving her the chance to pull away, but she did not move until his lips finally touched hers. Then her hand tightened on his shirt as she met his passion, straining against him as if she, too, had been longing for this moment.

It did not matter that he was trying to hold back, trying to limit the intensity of this kiss to avoid the explosion of passion of the previous night. He could keep the kiss slow, but the power of tasting her essence made him burn. How easy it would be to drown in her kisses? He nibbled her lip, exulting in how it made her shiver.

But he had to stop while he still could. Regretfully he drew back. "We should be going," he said gruffly. "There is no telling when someone might come this way."

She stiffened, then looked away. "Of course." She sat up, flipping her plait over her shoulder. "At least all of our clothes will be dry to start out with."

"That will help." He took one last deep breath of the air they had shared, then rose to his feet. If he looked at her now, he would not be able to stop himself from trying to kiss her again, so instead he started to prepare to depart. First his topcoat, then his heavy greatcoat. Today he fastened all the buttons on it, as he had not the previous day when he had shared it with Elizabeth. Next came his top hat and gloves.

How could it take so little to be ready to leave behind all the hours they had spent together? They were still wearing the clothing they had arrived in. He chanced a glance at Elizabeth who was folding the quilt, already in her pelisse and bonnet. It took him a moment to realize what was wrong. She had not put her hair up, but instead left it loose and stuffed it inside the collar of her pelisse.

She must have seen his surprised look. "It is quite improper, I know, but I have no scarf, and it will help to keep my neck warm."

"Very sensible," he said gravely. It would *not* be sensible to go to her and pull her hair free, run his fingers through the silky length, and kiss her until she was senseless.

He dug in his pocket and pulled out a handful of silver coins, then piled them neatly on the table. The food and firewood they had used would likely have lasted the frugal tenants for a week or more, and they should have fair recompense. He took one last look around the room, trying to commit it to memory. Something small protruded from the bedroll. Stooping, he discovered it was a violet hair ribbon. He glanced up. Elizabeth was facing the other direction and pulling on her gloves. Quickly he gathered up the ribbon and stuffed it in his pocket.

"I hope you stay warm, Snowball." Elizabeth reached down to scratch the cat's head, then straightened and said crisply, "Are you ready?"

"Yes." As ready as he would ever be.

When he lifted the latch, the door moved

inward of its own accord, fluffy snow spilling over the lintel. It must have piled up by the door during the night. He kicked it out of the way and stepped outside into a blindingly white world. Beyond the open fields, trees were piled high with snow, and he could see ridges which might be buried fences.

A flash of white fur moved past him and leapt off into the snow. "Snowball!" he called. Was she to die of cold after all?"

"She will be well enough. Cats are good at finding places to stay warm, like woodpiles. And she clearly did not care to remain inside." Still, Elizabeth looked after her wistfully.

"At least she does not seem to have difficulty managing in the snow." He stomped down a small area on the doorstep and stepped aside to allow Elizabeth to pass.

She peered around him and gasped. "This is what I imagine the sea would look like, only blue, and in motion."

"It is indeed a veritable sea of snow." He pushed his way through the drift of snow. Even beyond it the snow rose to the top of his boots.

"I have always wished to see the ocean, but since I have never been fortunate enough to visit the seaside, this will have to suffice for me." Elizabeth lifted her skirts and followed him, picking her way gingerly in his footprints.

Now what were they to do? It had been snowing fiercely when they arrived, and any landmarks had been long since buried. "Which way is the road?"

"It is..." Elizabeth pointed to the right, but then lowered her hand, her head turning from side to side. "I think...if those trees are the copse I came through, and that rise is Oakham Mount – no, that cannot be correct." She turned in a slow circle. "Of course! There is the tip of the church steeple, so Meryton is that way, and the road must be over there." She shaded her eyes with her hand. "Yes, I believe I can see a line which might be the hedgerow."

It all looked the same to him, buried under the blanket of snow. "We will try it, then. This may be slow going. Tell me if you see anything you recognize."

The snow was too deep to step over, so he had to kick it out of the way to move forward. He could have gone a little faster by himself, but he had to clear enough space for Elizabeth, who had the double disadvantage of skirts and shorter legs. The snow must be well over her knees.

Kick and step, kick and step. Who would have thought snow could be so heavy? He hoped Elizabeth's sense of direction was good.

Fortunately, she was proved correct when they finally reached the road. Darcy was beyond relieved to see tracks in the snow where someone had come through on horseback.

When Elizabeth caught up with him, her skirts kilted high, she said, "I think it may be some time before I feel the urge to take a long walk on a winter's day!"

Darcy pointed to the road. "It will be easier from here, since we can walk in the path the horse has broken."

Her breath made a frosty cloud. "I assume it would be best if we proceeded separately from here."

The words seemed to stab him. "If you wish. I would feel better were you to go first, so if you run into any difficulty, you need only wait for me. Would a quarter of an hour be enough time?"

She cast her eyes down at his legs. "If you do not walk too quickly."

"I do not believe anyone can walk quickly through this snow."

"Very well, then." She hesitated. "I appreciate all you have done these last two days, and your willingness to protect me, even if it is unnecessary."

"You will contact me if there are any repercussions to your reputation from your absence? I can be reached at Darcy House on Brook Street in London."

"If it seems necessary." Still she waited, as if somehow unwilling to leave him. "I wish you Godspeed."

He conjured up the image of awakening with her in his arms, then briefly stroked her cheek with his gloved finger. "Godspeed, Miss Elizabeth." The knot in his throat would permit no more.

She met his gaze for a long moment, then turned and trudged down the road. Away from him, away from this interlude, towards a future in which he played no part. After so long in her constant company, the emptiness she left behind was palpable. But it was no use. All the arguments he had used in London against making her an offer still applied. He had been able to set them aside when it seemed to be his duty, but she had refused him. He could not justify any further effort. Pemberley and Georgiana needed to come before his lust for Elizabeth Bennet. Besides, she had made her views quite clear.

The silent, snow-covered landscape seemed to reflect the bleakness in his heart. He checked his watch three times before the promised quarter hour actually passed. If nothing else, he would do her this last service of protecting her reputation. She had said there was a tavern before the town; he would stay there for an hour or two until his appearance in Meryton could not be connected with hers.

His feet began the weary walk. His boots pinched painfully where they had been soaked and then dried again. When he returned to London, he would remove these boots and never wear them again. As for his clothes, his valet would most likely think them beyond salvage. There would be no reminders – none except a thin violet hair ribbon.

Even with the snow tramped down, the path was treacherous in spots, requiring his attention to the placement of his feet. But a flash of a familiar red in an otherwise white world caught his eye. Elizabeth! Had he caught up to her despite his efforts to keep his distance? He knew he should stop to give her more time, but he wanted to be with her so badly his pace quickened. Then he realized she was moving towards him, not away.

Had she injured herself? He hurried toward her

as fear flashed through him. He should never have let her walk alone in this snow, regardless of what she said. As he drew near, he could make out the anguished expression on her face, and his heart threatened to stop altogether. "Good God! What is the matter? Are you hurt?"

She stumbled toward him and launched herself against him, her fingers biting into his shoulders as she pressed her face against his chest. As his arms closed around her – how could he have stopped himself? – her body shook, and it was not solely from the cold. "Elizabeth, what is it? For the love of God, tell me what has happened!"

Her breathing was ragged. "I am unharmed, but... at the tavern, when I reached it..." She drew in a sharp breath. "I opened the door to go in, and I saw...there were men, officers, and... and a girl. They did not see me, and I ran back. I do not...want to walk alone."

At first he could not make sense of it. It was a tavern. Of course there were officers and a girl, and even if Elizabeth had walked in on a scene unsuitable for a maiden's eyes, he could not imagine her reacting to it with terror. She was too level-headed for that. Then he understood. "The girl – she was not willing?"

"I *know* her." As if that said it all.

If the girl were an acquaintance of Elizabeth, she must be gently born. He swore under his breath. "Come. I will put a stop to it."

"No! You cannot! There are too many of them."

He tightened his arms around her. "Even so,

they will listen to me."

She shook her head without looking up. "One of them is Mr. Wickham," she said miserably.

Wickham! Of course, it would have to be him. Under normal circumstances, Darcy's rank would be all the protection he required, but if Wickham were involved, and particularly if he were drunk, Darcy could not depend on that. Wickham might take advantage of the situation and leave him helpless. Whatever else might happen, Darcy's first responsibility was to keep Elizabeth safe. He should have been there to protect her from seeing what she had seen, and instead he had let her go alone. "Then there is nothing I can do immediately. Who is she?"

This time Elizabeth's head shook more vigorously. "I cannot tell you that! It will go badly enough for her."

"Elizabeth, listen to me. I have cleaned up George Wickham's messes more times than I can count, but I can do nothing for the girl if I do not know who she is. You may trust me on this; I will say nothing to harm her."

She said nothing for a long minute. "Her name is Maria Lucas." Her voice was low and hopeless.

"Related to your friend Charlotte?"

"Her sister. You would not have met her; she was not out until Charlotte became engaged."

The poor thing. Wickham and his cronies would not even care they were ruining a young girl's life. And if Elizabeth had not been halted on her walk by discovering him lying by the roadside, she might have ended up at the tavern that day. He shook his head to free it of the painful image. "I will do my best to find a way to protect Miss Lucas."

Elizabeth's eyes were downturned. "You are very kind."

"I should have warned everyone here what sort of man Wickham was. It was my responsibility."

"Do not blame yourself. You did nothing wrong, and you cannot protect the entire world."

"I wish you would allow me to protect *you*. I know you do not wish to hear it, but it is true."

She raised her eyes to his face. "I promise to contact you if there is any difficulty, and I would be more than happy to accept your protection should those circumstances arise. Is that enough?"

No, it was not enough, but he could not say that. "Thank you."

"Now, we cannot stay here forever. We still have a long walk ahead."

They started forward again. More than once he reached to steady Elizabeth as she floundered in the snow. Her half-boots were ill-suited for the slippery conditions. As they approached the tavern, he could see her growing tense. He moved to walk at her side, even though it meant struggling through the deep snow.

Fortunately, the only person outside the tavern was a boy clearing a path to the stables. Telling Elizabeth to wait out of sight, Darcy approached him and gave him a coin. The boy ran inside, then returned with two thick slabs of bread. He found Elizabeth just beyond the curve in the road.

Her eyes widened at the sight of the food. She took the slice he offered and bit into it with alacrity, then closed her eyes as she chewed. "It is even still warm! And slathered with butter. I think I must be in heaven."

"I thought you might be hungry, after all this exercise on an empty stomach. I wish I could have brought you a real breakfast, not just a slice of bread." He took a bite of the other slice. She was right; it was heavenly. He had never before appreciated how good freshly baked bread and butter could taste.

"This is perfect. It could not be more delicious. Believe me, slaying a dragon would be worth far less to me than bringing me this."

He was oddly heartened to see her spirits somewhat restored, and to know he had played a part in it. "To tell the truth, I could not agree more."

Elizabeth was just finishing the bread when she gasped and looked down at a white cat clawing at her skirt. "Snowball! I cannot believe you followed us all the way here. You must be frozen!" She scooped her up and cuddled her close.

"She must have followed our path." He felt a little lighter just knowing the small cat was not lost in the snow.

"Oh, your little paws are like ice! Well, if you are determined to follow us, I suppose you might as well come to Longbourn where there is a nice, warm stable you can stay in."

He held out his hands. "I can carry her."

"She will no doubt be happy to keep her paws

out of the snow!" Elizabeth eased the cat into his arms.

He was even more grateful they had been able to slake their appetites when they discovered the rider who had traveled ahead of them had apparently stopped at the tavern, leaving them to face a long stretch of unbroken road. It would take them an hour to go a mile at this rate.

The pace was hard, and he was already weary when Elizabeth stopped him with a gentle hand on his arm. He was breathing rapidly as he turned to look at her.

"Although you would not know it now, there is a lane going off to the right here which leads to Longbourn. I think I prefer to try that, since it would allow me to avoid going into Meryton where we might be seen. It is not far; I am certain I can manage it on my own."

Allow her to walk alone through the snow, especially after what had happened at the tavern? Not likely! "An excellent idea, but I would prefer to accompany you, at least until we are close to Longbourn."

"That is very kind of you, but it would take you out of your way."

"It is no matter. I would much rather that than to worry about your well-being."

Her face lightened. "If you put it that way, I suppose I can only agree. At least it should provide you amusement to watch me gracelessly flounder through the snow."

He chuckled. "As you know, I enjoy watching

you regardless of what you are doing."

"If I were not entirely sick of snow and the cold, I would see if you enjoyed watching me throw a snowball at you, sir!"

"That would never do!" Although not for the reason she would think. Playing in the snow with Elizabeth would be far too dangerous. It would be bound to end in kisses. "Besides, I have the Snowball with claws."

Fortunately, Elizabeth was correct about the short distance. Despite his rapidly numbing fingers, Darcy slowed his pace as he noticed she was lagging behind him more. When they finally reached the intersection with the road to Longbourn, he turned to discover she was shivering. He cursed himself for his inattentiveness. He should have made her wear his greatcoat, even if she fought against it. The lines of fatigue in her face felt like a brand of his failure. "I think I had best accompany you to Longbourn," he said.

She shook her head stubbornly. "You can see it is very close. I will be fine, and it would be very difficult to explain your presence."

He wanted to argue, to somehow keep her with him, but more than that, he did not want her to suffer any longer. "I will bid you farewell here, then."

She reached out her hands, and for a brief happy moment he thought she meant to embrace him, but then he realized it was merely for the cat. He had to extract Snowball's claws from the wool of his greatcoat before placing her in Elizabeth's hands. He stretched out his arms, stiff from carrying the cat, but feeling strangely empty without her. Seeing her in Elizabeth's arms brought home that he would likely never see either of them again, and his gut clenched.

"Thank you for accompanying me this far. I appreciate it more than I can say. Perhaps we shall meet again someday, Mr. Darcy." Her smile was wan.

"I hope that will be the case. Now go warm yourself at Longbourn."

She nodded, her teeth chattering, and began to tramp through the snow. He watched her struggling to make her way, clenching his fists as if somehow that would give her his strength. God, but he hated to see her in such discomfort! His punishment was to stay there until she reached the door of Longbourn, on the chance she might fall and require his assistance. But she did not. He told himself he was not disappointed.

At the last moment, she looked back and froze for a moment when she saw him waiting there. Then she waved and went inside.

As he turned to leave, he took one last look at Longbourn. He had an odd foreboding he was making a terrible mistake.

Chapter 8

TEARS PRICKED ELIZABETH'S eyes as she hurried into Longbourn. It was not just saying goodbye to Mr. Darcy, or discovering he had watched after her to be sure she was safe. After her long, cold trek, all she wanted was to curl up by the fire underneath every shawl and wrap in the house. She stopped short at the entrance to the empty drawing room. The hearth was cold. Her footsteps echoed as she checked the dining room and the library. No fires there, either. Was the house as deserted as the little cottage? Had she not seen smoke rising from the chimney, or had it been a dream?

If there were a fire anywhere, it would be in the kitchen. After hobbling to the back of the house with all the speed her numb feet would provide, she threw open the door to the kitchen, and almost burst into tears of relief at the rush of warm air and the sight of Cook, asleep in her high-backed chair, snores issuing from her open mouth. The hearth was full of red, glowing coals. Elizabeth crouched as close to it as she dared, releasing Snowball. The welcome heat was almost painful against her cold skin.

Chair legs scraped against the flagstone floor behind her. "Is the family finally back then, Miss Lizzy?" said Cook with a yawn.

"I am the only one so far, it seems. Where is everyone?"

Cook heaved herself to her feet. "All gone off before the storm for the free ale and food, and none returned. There are a few of us here – Nell did not wish to go, and one of the scullery maids had taken a chill. Two of the stable boys had to stay here to watch the horses while the grooms went off."

Elizabeth peeled off her wet gloves and held out her hands to the fire. "No one has returned from Meryton yet?" It was odd, since it was a shorter distance than she had traversed, but presumably others were not in the same hurry to avoid being discovered and would prefer to wait until the roads were clearer.

"Why, did you not come from Meryton? And where did that cat come from?"

So much for her ability to disguise her whereabouts! Though if everyone in the area was stranded in Meryton, they would all know she was not there. "I found her freezing by the side of the road. I was out walking before the blizzard and took refuge in a cottage. Can you imagine – I have been wearing this dress day and night since I left for Charlotte's wedding two days ago! I daresay it will continue to stand up by itself after I remove it." Perhaps that would distract Cook.

Cook made a tsk-ing sound with her tongue. "Best you should change to something fresh before your mother returns!"

"May I leave the cat here? She needs to warm up." Snowball was already sniffing the kitchen floor, seeming perfectly at home in these new surroundings.

"Well, your mother will not be pleased to find a cat in the house, but perhaps she can catch a few of those pesky mice before the mistress notices. Nell can help you dress. I had best put myself to cooking dinner if the rest of the family will be here today. I tell you, Miss Lizzy, the five of us had quite a feast when no one returned from Meryton to eat all the good food I had made."

"And I am certain you deserved every bit of it!" The last thing she wished to do was to leave the hearth, but restoring her normal appearance would have another advantage. It might make her parents believe she had been at Longbourn all this time.

Darcy's feet ached as he finally trudged into Meryton, but not as much as his heart did. It had been a battle every step of the way not to turn back toward Longbourn and Elizabeth. It made no sense. He had always been perfectly satisfied with his own company. He should be eager for some time to himself after so much time trapped in a small room with another person, but instead the lack of her felt as if part of him had been amputated. He wanted to be able to turn to her and share his thoughts.

But he did *not* wish to speak to any of the townsfolk sweeping away snow from their doorsteps. It was only Elizabeth he wanted. Besides, his appearance must be unkempt at best, and he needed to avoid any questions. If he could only reach the livery stable without anyone stopping him, all might yet be well.

But not a dozen paces from the livery, a familiar figure crossed his path, almost as if Darcy had created him from his imagination. Mr. Bennet was wrapped in an overcoat thick enough to disguise his figure, but his face was plain to see.

Somehow Darcy managed a correct bow.

Mr. Bennet stopped short. "Good heavens, if it is not Mr. Darcy! I had not known you were in the area."

"Simply passing through," Darcy said with all the firmness he could muster.

"You have picked poor weather for it, I fear." Mr. Bennet gestured at the snow surrounding them.

The man had no idea how much trouble that weather had caused him! "Indeed," he said brusquely, trying to force back the impulse to grab Mr. Bennet's arms and tell him his daughter had spent the last two nights sleeping in his arms. Then he would have no choice but to return to Longbourn and formally propose to Elizabeth, who would have to accept him this time. But Elizabeth did not want that, and he could not destroy Georgiana's prospects. The damage to his own name was something he no longer cared about. "Pray give my regards to your family. Good day, sir."

Somehow he managed to step past Mr. Bennet and into the safety of the livery. It took a moment for his eyes to adjust to the dim interior after the sunlight reflecting on snow, and even longer for his heart to stop racing.

An elderly man came from the back of the office, wiping gnarled hands on his leather apron. "Anything I can help you with today, sir?"

He handed the man his card. "I need a horse to travel to London." If whatever old hack they gave him could actually be called a horse.

The fellow squinted at his card. "You that fellow who was visiting Mr. Bingley at Netherfield?"

As if it were any business of his! "Yes."

Rubbing his chin, he said, "You can have a horse, but it won't be what you're used to. The good posting stables, they're in Ware."

"And I am here. Anything that can get me to Town will do. My own horse bolted in the storm. If anyone reports finding a blood bay, 16 hands, with tooled saddlebags, send to me at that address, and I will make it worth your while."

"Oh, so that's *your* horse, then! He is right here. Came charging into town two days back, nearly ran over a little boy and broke the wheel on the grocer's cart."

Destroying everything in sight. "That would be Mercury." He had chosen to ride the half-trained horse from London in hopes the challenge would keep his mind from Elizabeth Bennet. Instead, the miscreant had thrown him straight at her feet.

"He were hard to catch. Didn't like the snow, that one."

"So I observed. Hence the bolting." Darcy dug out his remaining silver, saving one coin for some decent food, and dropped the remainder on the counter. "For your trouble, and for the grocer's cart."

The man's eyes widened. "Thank ye, sir. I'll bring your horse around front right away, soon as I've saddled him."

"Very good." The sooner he left Meryton, the better. Otherwise he might not be able to resist the urge to return to Elizabeth.

Mr. Bennet was the next arrival at Longbourn, but to Elizabeth's surprise, he was alone. "Where are my mother and sisters?" she asked anxiously. It had never crossed her mind any of her family could have been lost in the blizzard.

Her father snorted. "At your aunt Phillips's house, which I have been sharing with all of them. The constant chatter was torture! I escaped at the first possible opportunity, even if it meant fighting my way through the snowdrifts. I was far less frightened of the snow than of another discussion of lace and gowns."

"But they are well?"

"They are in fine fettle. Since no one could leave the town, it has been one long celebration since the storm began. Dancing and prattling, cards and games — I thought I should lose my wits. No, they are perfectly well, and plan to return once the snow on the roads has been trampled down. I, for one, hope that will be none too soon. I am looking forward to locking myself in my library for quite some time."

"I shall not disturb you!" she said with a laugh, but in truth she was glad of the opportunity to be alone.

Her heart was too heavy to pretend all was well for long.

Her reprieve proved briefer than she expected. Only a few hours later, Nell came to tell her Mr. Bennet was asking for her in the library.

She went to the library with trepidation. Could he have discovered the truth?

"You wished to speak to me?" Elizabeth stood in front of her father's desk.

"Yes, Lizzy. I wished to ask you about your whereabouts during the storm. The gossip among the servants has it you were not here."

Elizabeth took a deep breath. "That is correct. I went out walking after the wedding and was caught in the storm, so I took shelter in a cottage until it passed."

He removed his spectacles and set them on the blotter. "What cottage would that be?"

"The tenants were away, so I do not know their name. It is a small cottage just north of the Hatfield road, perhaps two miles past the tavern."

"I believe I know it – a tiny wattle-and-daub one set back from the road?"

"The very one."

"And you went into this stranger's empty house alone?"

"There was little choice, sir, unless I preferred to freeze to death. It was not a comfortable lodging, but it provided the shelter I needed." Hopefully he would not notice she had said nothing about being alone.

"I see. And then you returned here after the storm ended."

"Yes."

Mr. Bennet sat back in his chair. "When I returned from Meryton, I was apparently not the first to travel the road to Longbourn since the snow. There was a set of footprints heading toward the town."

"That is hardly surprising." Her heart hammered.

"What is surprising, though, is that when I passed the lane which runs to the Hatfield road, it appeared two people had walked there. One turned toward Longbourn House, and the other toward Meryton – an odd route to choose in the snow, since it is far from direct. I assume the footprints coming toward the house were yours, but I wonder who might have been accompanying you along the lane."

She had not once considered that their tracks might betray them. How had she missed it? Her best bet would be to tell as much of the truth as possible, since that way she was less likely to be caught out. "I met Mr. Darcy on the Hatfield road, and he was kind enough to escort me most of the way here. He said something about going to the livery stable in Meryton as his horse ran off in the storm."

"Yet you said nothing of meeting him to me."

Elizabeth attempted a laugh. "Should I have advertised that I had been alone with a wealthy gentleman? He did me a courtesy, and I do not wish to repay it by making my mother claim he somehow compromised me as we fought our way through the snowdrifts, which would have been quite a feat. If you do not believe me…"

"Oh, I believe you, my dear, if for no other reason than that I crossed paths with Mr. Darcy myself in Meryton."

Elizabeth had never wished so hard for the ability to stop a blush from rising in her cheeks. In an effort to sound indifferent, she said, "Oh? Did you speak to him?"

"Nothing beyond wishing one another a good day. He did not mention meeting you."

Here she was on safer ground. "You would be the last person he would wish to tell he had been walking alone with me! Can you imagine the degradation it would be to him if he were forced to make me an offer?" Bile rose in the back of her throat.

Her father chuckled. "I seriously doubt he would consider you worth the trouble. If you were compromised by him, that would be your problem, not his. What an unpleasant fellow he is! I am sorry you were forced to walk with him. I hope his pride recovers from the experience."

If only she could tell her father he was not like that at all – and that he did indeed think her worth the trouble. But those were things she must keep locked up inside forever, along with her memories of the last few days and an empty ache in her heart.

The snow was already beginning to melt when the remainder of the Bennet family returned the following day. Mary looked drawn, and Kitty's red eyes were a stark contrast to Lydia's excited demeanor.

"I declare, the road to Meryton has never

seemed longer!" Mrs. Bennet cried as soon as she entered Longbourn House. "I thought we might freeze to death at any moment, and you would find our bodies in the hedgerows after the thaw. What is this world coming to? I have never known such a winter!"

"At least not since last year," Elizabeth murmured to Mary, then she spoke more loudly. "I am glad to see all of you safely home."

Lydia cried, "We had such fun, Lizzy! I declare, I feel sorry for you, stuck here all alone while we were dancing and playing cards in town. It was a marvelous adventure! And you will never believe what happened! Such excitement! Yesterday…"

Mary said in a peremptory manner, "That is enough, Lydia. Let us speak of it no more now."

"Why should I not speak of it? It cannot be kept secret. Half the town already knows, and why should Lizzy be the last to find out?"

Kitty made a small sound, covered her mouth with her hand, and ran out of the room still wearing her pelisse. The sound of footsteps pounding up the stairs followed her departure.

"*That* is why you should say nothing," said Mary severely. "Kitty is distraught enough as it is."

Now worried, Elizabeth said, "Did something happen to Kitty?"

Lydia bounced up on her toes. "No, not to her. She is just being silly. It is Maria Lucas. I venture to guess you did not expect to hear *that* name! She disappeared from the wedding breakfast, and no one saw her until yesterday when she was found walking down High Street, weeping and clutching her torn dress to hold it together. She is quite ruined, of course."

Elizabeth closed her eyes. She had hoped Maria might somehow avoid discovery. "Poor girl."

"She is a fool. If she had only had the sense to return directly to Lucas Lodge and avoid being seen, no one might have known anything had happened. But she had to make a show of it. Now her mother will not speak to her, and Sir William Lucas will not speak to anyone at all. I imagine they will have to send her away."

"How did she come to leave the wedding breakfast?" Elizabeth addressed her question to Mary. It was something which had been troubling her.

"No one knows. She, Kitty and Lydia were flirting with the officers, and that is the last anyone saw of her."

Lydia, apparently cross at being cut out of the conversation, said, "She drank too much rum punch and became quite silly. She wanted Denny to notice her instead of me for once. Well, apparently he did. *I* never have any trouble handling the officers; I do not know why *she* could not stop them. She is such a child!"

Elizabeth refrained from pointing out Maria was almost a year older than Lydia, albeit far more innocent – or she had been. "I do not wish to hear any more of this from you, Lydia. I feel sorry for poor Maria. She has been very ill used."

Mrs. Bennet removed her bonnet and replaced it with her cap. "There is no need to carry on, Lizzy. It is no harm to you, and at least I will not have to listen to Lady Lucas boast of having a daughter married or of Charlotte being mistress of this house someday. My daughters may have failed to marry, but at least none of you have been disgraced."

Ignoring her mother, Elizabeth tugged at Mary's arm. "Come, you must be dying to put on some clean clothes. How long have you been wearing that dress?"

Mary followed her sister upstairs with a grimace. "I do not even wish to think of it!"

Chapter 9

DARCY REACHED LONDON in a vile humor. Mercury had shied at every unexpected sight en route, and there had been quite a few to choose from. Even with few travelers venturing out on the snowy roads, there were wagons stuck in ditches, carriages with their wheels sunk in drifts, and the hooves of any passing horse kicked up flying snow. He should have stopped at an inn to warm himself before continuing, but his desire to reach home kept him riding far longer than was comfortable or even sensible. At least the depth of the snow decreased as he approached the city. Apparently London had been spared the worst of the storm.

His butler had met him at the door with a look of profound relief. "Welcome back, sir. May I say, on behalf of all the staff, that we are happy to see you returned to us in good health?"

"Was my sister concerned?" That had not even crossed his mind, even though Georgiana always fretted herself over everything.

The butler coughed. "I believe Mrs. Annesley took the liberty of telling Miss Darcy we had received word you would not return until the weather cleared."

"Very good. I will want tea, brandy, and hot water for a bath. And something to eat. You may inform my sister I am back, and will see her once I am presentable." He hid Elizabeth's hair ribbon in his fist before giving up his greatcoat.

"Yes, sir."

Naturally, Crewe was already laying out fresh clothes for him. His valet often seemed to have an almost preternatural ability to foresee his actions.

Pursing his lips, Crewe ran a practiced eye over Darcy's apparel, but said nothing. That was a bad sign.

Tiredly, Darcy said, "Yes, I *have* been sleeping in these clothes for two nights, and on a straw pallet in front of a sooty fire, no less."

Crewe nodded an acknowledgment, then deftly assisted him in removing the tight top coat. The valet held out the coat to examine it. "And with a white animal, I take it, along with someone with long, curly chestnut hair," he said under his breath.

"What did you say?" Darcy demanded, fighting an urge to snatch the coat from Crewe.

"Nothing, sir. I will arrange for a suitable disposal."

"No. Do not dispose of any of it."

Crewe wrinkled his nose. "It will not be possible to return it to an acceptable state to be worn in public, sir."

"Nevertheless, I wish to keep it."

"Even the shirt? The soot stains will never come out."

"The shirt as well." For some reason it seemed

crucial not to lose those clothes, even if he never wore them again. Elizabeth had slept in his arms while he wore them.

"As you wish, sir." It was clear Crewe's wishes lay quite elsewhere.

Darcy frowned at the plate of food in front of him. Why should his appetite desert him now, after he had been longing for a warm meal for days? He was finally shaved and tidy, comfortably clad in clean clothes, though Crewe thought he had lost his mind.

Warm, clean, with servants to do his every bidding – he should be pleased. But how could he feel content when Elizabeth's absence was so palpable? How long would this torture continue? He needed to forget Elizabeth Bennet, and the sooner the better. Not that he had ever succeeded in that endeavor in the past.

The butler approached him with a bow. "Mr. Stanton is awaiting your pleasure in the study, sir.'"

It was not as if he was going to eat anything more in any case, so Darcy pushed back his chair. "I will see him now."

His man of business awaited him, dressed as always in a sober black which made him seem to fade into the woodwork.

"Thank you for coming so promptly," said Darcy, settling himself behind his desk. "I have a task I wish to see accomplished, but it needs to be done quickly and may require several days of your time. Would you be available for that?"

Stanton bobbed his head. "I can clear my

schedule for you, naturally."

"Good. I need you to go to Meryton again. Your first task is to ascertain whether there is any gossip about a young lady named Maria Lucas, the daughter of Sir William Lucas. In all likelihood, she has been ruined. If that is the case, you must find an officer in the militia regiment who is willing to marry her in exchange for a sum of money and the purchase of a commission in a regiment far from Meryton. One who will not be unkind to her, of course." He picked up a paper. "I have written all the particulars of the matter here for you."

Stanton took the list and perused it. "Ah. Mr. Wickham again, I see."

"Of course."

"I foresee no difficulties with that. I assume you wish this to be handled with the greatest discretion?"

"Yes." Darcy cleared his throat. "At our last meeting, you informed me Wickham was keeping company with Miss Elizabeth Bennet. She is no longer at any risk from him, and is aware of my interest in the matter of Miss Lucas. Should you require any further information about that situation, she may be able to provide it. I have written a letter which explains this to her. I hope you will have the opportunity to give it to her." He pushed the sealed envelope across the desk, watching the other man's expression closely.

If Stanton had any reaction to this unusual request, he hid it well. "That should not be difficult."

"Also, I would like to know if there is any unusual talk in the town regarding Miss Bennet."

"Very well, sir. And if there is gossip, what course of action should I undertake? The same as for…" He paused to consult the paper. "…Miss Lucas?"

Darcy's throat was tight. "No. Inform me of it immediately, but do nothing." He had to know the outcome, just in case Elizabeth chose not to inform him. Elizabeth. He rubbed the ribbon in his pocket between his fingers.

In Meryton Elizabeth found her way blocked by a nondescript gentleman.

He removed his hat. "Pardon me, miss, but might I impose upon you for directions to the Furnham farm?"

Taken aback by this approach from a perfect stranger, she pointed to her left. "It is just beyond the next curve in the road."

His next words were all in a rush, in a voice too quiet to be overheard. "Pray continue to point as I speak. My name is Stanton, and I was sent by Mr. Darcy to repair the unfortunate situation of a young lady. He told me if I could not obtain the local information I needed, I should approach you with my questions. Is there a time and place we could speak together? I pray you to recall you are supposed to be giving me directions."

Her breath caught in her throat. Darcy had not forgotten his promise to help Maria Lucas – and by extension, he had not forgotten *her*. "I… Yes, beyond the next curve, and you will pass a large oak, then two fields separated by a footpath with a stile. I would show you the way, but I must finish my errands here, and that will take half an hour or more."

"Very good," he said quietly. "By the stile, in half an hour or more." He replaced his hat and spoke loudly. "Thank you kindly, miss, for the directions and for taking the time to help a stranger."

As he walked away, Elizabeth stared after him, her pulses racing. What was wrong with her, that just hearing Darcy's name was enough to send her into a tizzy of the sort Lydia was known for? Willing herself to appear calm, she turned back toward the milliner's shop. Half an hour. No matter how many errands she had, it would be hard to wait so long.

She hurried through her shopping, but made every attempt to appear relaxed as she walked down the road towards the Furnham farm.

Mr. Stanton leaned against the dry stone fence beside the stile. "I thank you for joining me, Miss Bennet."

"If there is some manner in which I can be of assistance, I would be happy to do so. The young lady in question is suffering greatly."

"So I understand. My goal, if I may be direct, is to find her a husband, and then arrange for them to move far away from here. However, the first task is proving more challenging than I had anticipated."

Elizabeth raised an eyebrow. "Finding her a husband under these circumstances cannot be easy."

He smiled. "Ordinarily, a heavy purse is sufficient enticement to convince a man to wed almost any woman, but the gentlemen who were, ah, involved in her disgrace are too busy strutting themselves to think of the future. Were they not so engaged with telling one another what fine fellows they are for ruining a young girl's future, I might have had a chance. In this case, I cannot see any of them as good candidates for the role of husband, and Mr. Darcy made it plain he would prefer a husband who would treat her well. That is where I hoped for your assistance."

"A husband who would treat her well?" The image of what she had seen at the tavern flashed before her, leaving a sick taste in her mouth. "None of those involved would meet that description."

"I am glad you concur. My question is this: are there any officers in the militia who might be suitable and trustworthy? Preferably ones who would not mind leaving the regiment behind."

To think only a fortnight ago she would have characterized Mr. Wickham as such a man! She shivered, suddenly struck by how many of the militia officers were not the kind of men she would care to marry. "Let me see...Captain Carter seems an upstanding sort, although a flirt, but he has strong ties to Colonel Forster and might not wish to leave. Mr. Pratt – he is an ensign – might work. He is quite young, but so is Miss Lucas. Or..." She paused to think. There must be at least a few officers who were not flirts or skirt-chasers. "Mr. Chamberlayne might suit the purpose. Some of the officers mock him for his slight stature, so he might be happy to leave. He seems to prefer the company of young women to that of his fellow officers."

"Chamberlayne, Pratt, Carter. I will start with those." He made a note in a small notebook. "Your assistance has been invaluable, Miss Bennet, but I must not keep you. Mr. Darcy would be most displeased if I drew any untoward attention to you."

She could not help smiling, more from the pleasure of speaking to someone to whom she did not have to pretend a lack of knowledge of Darcy. If only she could do more than speak of him – but she should be grateful for what she had. "Pray tell Mr. Darcy I am grateful for his attention to this matter. I hope you are successful in your mission. It will make an enormous difference to poor Miss Lucas."

"Oh, I shall be successful, one way or another. I have no intention of disappointing Mr. Darcy. That reminds me..." He rummaged in his pocket and produced a letter. "He asked me to give you this. In case there should be a reply, I will return to this spot in two days' time." Was it skill or lack of knowledge which allowed him to appear so nonchalant about her compromising situation in receiving a letter from a single gentleman? Perhaps it was just tact.

Her heart hammered as she took it, wishing she could press it to her chest. But it was dangerous enough to have someone aware she was receiving correspondence from Darcy. Presumably he must have great faith in Stanton's discretion to have entrusted him with such an errand, but it would not do that have him report back that she had acted like a lovesick girl.

She hardly heard Mr. Stanton bidding her

farewell. What could Darcy have to say to warrant the risk of writing to her? She could not possibly wait until she was home to read it. Caressing the fine parchment, she slipped her finger under the red wax seal.

> *My dear Miss Elizabeth,*
>
> *By now Stanton will no doubt have explained why he is in Meryton, but I wish to reassure you he is quite trustworthy. I have employed him on many occasions over the years and have full confidence in him. I hope it did not cause you undue worry to have a stranger approach you. He has dealt with this sort of situation many times in the past.*
>
> *I hope there have been no repercussions to you from the blizzard, and I would still like to hear from you if there should be any difficulties. It has been something of a worry to me since I left Meryton.*
>
> *I hope you have been enjoying the smooth floors and warm food at Longbourn. I find myself noting whenever a fire is burning low, and must battle the temptation to pile it high. My servants would be very mystified should I do so!*
>
> *Yours, &c.,*
>
> *Fitzwilliam Darcy*

She ran her fingertip over his signature. He wrote in a fine, close hand, showing the same attention to detail in his penmanship as he had paid to the fire. For some reason it made her want to cry.

Should she write back? It was not as if she had anything of importance to report, and surely she could not say how she missed him. But he had taken the trouble to make arrangements to allow her to respond, so would it not be rude to say nothing? Perhaps she could write about Snowball's voracious appetite and what Cook had told her about the proper way to make onion soup.

Her lips curved up. Yes, she would write to him, if only for the pleasure of thinking about him.

Chapter 10

GEORGIANA'S FINGERS WERE moving ever so slightly as if she were playing an invisible pianoforte on her lap. It was a certain sign she was nervous. Darcy ran through the last day in his mind, looking for anything that might have caused her anxiety, but nothing out of the ordinary had happened.

He signaled the footman with his eyes to leave the room. Sometimes Georgiana could even be timid about servants. As the footman closed the double doors behind him, Darcy said, "Is anything troubling you?"

She froze. "No, not at all." Her fingers began moving. "Well, perhaps. May I ask you a question?" Her voice was trembling ever so slightly.

"Of course, at any time." He tried to sound warm and encouraging, the way Elizabeth did.

"I..." She swallowed hard. "Someone said my mother is not dead."

Damnation! He had hoped to postpone this discussion until just before she came out, when he could no longer hide the truth from her, and to have Richard by his side when he did it. "Who told you that?" he said, hoping to gain a little time.

Georgiana looked down in her lap. After a moment, she said in a voice just under a whisper, "Mr. Wickham."

Darcy sat bolt upright. "You have seen him?" he demanded.

He could have kicked himself when he saw how she cringed. "No. He told me last summer, in Ramsgate."

And she was only now asking him about it? Had she been so frightened of his anger at Wickham that she hid a question of this magnitude for months? Apparently so. Damn Wickham!

He pressed his palms together and tapped his chin. What should he say? Would this forever ruin any trust she had in him? His mouth dry, he said, "It was our father's wish that you be told she was dead, and I have tried to honor that." Tap, tap, tap. "But it is true; she is still alive."

Tears sprang to Georgiana's eyes. "Why was I not told?"

"He did not wish you to see her because he feared her influence over you, and it seemed simpler if you believed she was dead. So he sent her away, and then, after a decent interval, told everyone at Pemberley she had died in a riding accident. Only a very few of us knew the truth."

"But you did know."

"Yes."

"I wish *I* had known. It might have been easier than being...motherless." She burst into tears.

He moved beside her and put his arm around her shoulders. "I am sorry this is so painful."

After a few gasping sobs, she asked, "But *why* was she sent away?"

The question had been bound to come. "It was a complicated situation. She...Perhaps it would be best if Richard told you this part. I am... not unbiased." His tongue had tied itself into a knot, just as it always did when he attempted to speak of his stepmother – except to Elizabeth Bennet. For some reason it had felt comforting to talk to her about it.

Georgiana gulped back another sob. "Can you tell me about her?"

It was tempting to refuse, but she needed comfort, not dismissal. "She was very young when she married our father, little older than you are now, and about to enter her first Season. She was sorry to miss the excitement of it, but her father was glad to be spared the expense of it." She had been angry to be exiled, as she saw it, to Pemberley while her new husband, nearly old enough to be her father, remained in London. It was strange to think of her as Georgiana's age; she had seemed like an adult to him when he was a boy, but in truth she had been just a girl.

"Where is she now?"

"She married a country squire in Devon as soon as our father died, and I know nothing of her life since then. She does not move in the same circles we do." For which he thanked God daily.

"Could I meet her?"

"I think that would be a poor idea, and I doubt

Richard would agree to it."

"I see," she whispered, then fled the room.

Lady Matlock delicately set down her teacup. "You may, perchance, be wondering about why I am here."

Darcy had sat through nearly half an hour of small talk wondering that very thing. "You are not in the habit of paying calls on me, but I assume you have your reasons."

His aunt folded her hands in her lap. "I need to know what is troubling Richard."

"Richard? He seemed out of spirits after his return from Portugal, but I attributed it to his wound. He sounded happier when I saw him a few days ago, telling me he was going to Tattersalls to look at horses."

Her fine brows drew together. "That was his father's idea. He hoped a new horse would cheer him, so he offered to take Richard and buy him a new mount. Apparently everything was going well, and Richard had shown interest in several horses, when suddenly he announced he was leaving. He refused to return to Matlock House with his father, and instead disappeared for two days. I assumed he was most likely with you, and was about to send for you when he appeared on the doorstep, disheveled and stinking of gin. Since then, he has left each day soon after rising and not returned until near dawn, always in the same condition."

Three days, and she was only now telling him? "Where does he go?"

"He does not tell me."

His aunt always was perfectly aware of every detail that occurred involving any of her family. When he was a boy, it had looked suspiciously like witchcraft. "I did not ask if he had told you where he went," he said carefully.

Her perfectly composed features suddenly seemed to droop with weariness. "Gaming hells, and once a prizefight."

Gaming hells? *Richard*? "He has always avoided those places in the past."

"So I had believed."

"Has he said anything of note?"

"As little as possible, and his only explanation for leaving Tattersalls was that he was displeased by the horses. His man will say nothing, even under threat of dismissal."

It must be something serious. "I will see what I can do."

Darcy finally caught up with his cousin in one of the less savory gaming hells of St. James, full of stale air and the smell of too much liquor. Through the haze of smoke, he made out Richard's figure sitting bent over at one of the card tables and fought his way to his side. When Richard failed to look up, Darcy put his hand on his cousin's shoulder.

Richard looked up at him blearily. "Darcy, what are you doing here? Sit down, sit down. We will be starting a new game shortly. I am about to win a pile of blunt."

"I am here to see you, not to play. Will you come with me?"

His cousin's eyes darted around the room. "Why not talk here? Plenty to drink and good company."

"Not the sort of company I am looking for, and I prefer some privacy."

Richard looked down at his cards and licked his lips. "I will call on you tomorrow, then." He threw back a glass of what appeared to be port.

This was not like Richard at all. It was time to play his trump card. "Richard, I need your help."

Richard dropped his cards on the table. "Good God, what is the matter?"

Darcy glanced uncomfortably at the crowd around the table, several of whom were now staring at him. "Not here. Come back to Darcy House with me, and I will tell you there."

His cousin pushed himself out of his chair, which seemed to take more effort than the action should require. Just how foxed was he? He kept an eye on Richard as he wove his way to the door through the crush of gentlemen.

Finally they reached the street. Richard came to a halt as Darcy tossed a coin to a ragged boy holding a torch.

"Where to, sir?" the boy asked in a thick Cockney accent.

Darcy placed his hand on Richard's arm, urging him along. "Upper Brook Street. Darcy House."

Richard blinked at him in the torchlight. "No

carriage?"

"It is not far to walk, and will help you sober up." There was no one else in the world Darcy would be so direct with, but this was Richard, who knew him better than anyone else. He could say anything to Richard.

"Am not foxed," muttered Richard, but he shuffled along without complaint.

Darcy shortened his stride as they turned up Albemarle Street. "I thought you despised the gaming hells."

"I do. But they are..." Richard waved his hand about vaguely. "Distracting."

"There are many other distracting things."

"I have not seen *you* at any of them. Why have you been avoiding me? Is it because of what I have done?"

This was worrisome. "I have no idea what you have done, and I have not been avoiding you."

"I come back from Portugal, you spend one evening with me, then disappear. I call that avoiding me." Richard staggered as he hit an uneven bit of cobblestones.

Darcy counted backwards in his head. Richard was right. "Very well. I *have* been avoiding you, but only because I have been avoiding *everyone*. I have been preoccupied and uninterested in company." Preoccupied with Elizabeth Bennet and wanting no company but hers.

"Why?"

Apparently there were some things he could not

say to Richard after all. "No good reason." That much was true, anyway. "Thinking about last summer and Ramsgate."

"Ah, when will you accept you cannot control everything? You did your best, and all's well that ends well. Except, of course, for a certain blackguard remaining alive. Had I not been in Portugal..." He stopped short, then shook his head violently and increased his pace, his shoulders hunched.

He had never seen Richard behave like this. Had something happened to him in Portugal? If only the cold air could chase all the drink out of him!

"Do not dawdle. It is not safe." Richard glanced over his shoulder, his eyes darting from side to side.

"Not safe? What do you mean?"

Richard nodded sagely. "Footpads. In the trees."

"Richard, this is Berkeley Square. We are in no danger here."

"You never know. Did they tell you what I did?"

"Your mother told me you were going to gaming hells, yes."

"Not that! My horse. Ramses."

Darcy decided to keep Richard far from the brandy bottle when they reached Darcy House. "What about Ramses?"

"I killed him. Shot him dead."

Despite himself, Darcy was shocked. Richard had raised Ramses from a colt, and loved him. "Was he injured?"

Richard nodded heavily. "The damned Frogs.

Dug holes to trip up the cavalry and covered them up. Broke his leg. I had to do it. I had to, I really did."

"Of course you did," Darcy said soothingly. "If his leg was broken, there was nothing else you could do."

"He trusted me. He looked at me while I shot him." Richard halted and doubled over, retching.

Drunken gentlemen casting up their accounts were hardly an unusual site late at night in fashionable parts of London, but Darcy would never have expected to see Richard be one of them. Lady Matlock had, as always, been correct. Something was very wrong. He waited until his cousin straightened and wiped his mouth with his handkerchief. "Come, we are practically there," he said gently.

"I still see him, every time I close my eyes." Richard's voice was dull.

"Hence the need for distraction?"

"I did not tell you the worst of it. Men lay all around me, dead and dying, screaming with pain, and all I cared about was my horse. How can I call myself an honorable man after that?"

"You could not stop being honorable if you tried, Richard, or you would not be so distressed by it. You should never have been on a battlefield in the first place." Why, oh, why had Lord Matlock refused to listen all those times Darcy had told him Richard was ill-suited for the army? This was bound to happen, sooner or later. Richard had never been able to bear watching anyone be hurt.

His cousin straightened his shoulders. "It was

my duty. It *is* my duty."

And there was the crux of it. Richard would always be miserable in the army, but he would never leave it, not while his father told him his duty lay there.

Richard rubbed his hand over his eyes. "I should not be saying any of these things."

"It goes no further. Remember —together against all enemies, against all odds?" It had been a solemn boyhood oath, though they had made a joke of it in recent years, but it still held true. It was why he could count on Richard, no matter how foxed he might be, to drop everything when he said he needed help – and why he knew nothing would give Richard more purpose.

"Against all enemies." Richard essayed a wan smile.

"Against all odds." Darcy clapped him on the shoulder.

A short time later they were settled in Darcy's study, Richard gingerly sipping hot coffee. "So, you need my help. Is it Georgiana?"

"No, not precisely." Darcy drew the letter out of a drawer in the writing desk and held it out to his cousin. "*She* is back."

Richard's brows flew up. "Not..."

"Yes. *Her*. She wants to see Georgiana."

"Absolutely not. Under no circumstances." Richard opened the letter and began to read it. He snorted at one point. " 'I can understand you might hold the past against me.' She is good at stating the obvious."

"She writes an excellent letter, and there is nothing at all objectionable in it – except that *she* wrote it."

"And that she is coming to London and wishes to see Georgiana, which is *not* going to happen."

"Even though Georgiana has asked to see her?"

"What? You told Georgiana?"

"No, but she found out recently her mother was alive, and asked me if she could meet her. I said no, but of course I had no reason to think *she* had any interest in Georgiana. Now it turns out she does, so perhaps we should allow them to meet. Carefully supervised, of course."

"What could possibly be the benefit?"

Darcy shrugged. "Relieving Georgiana's curiosity, I suppose."

"At the expense of exposing her to whatever ploy that woman has in mind? I think not. I know you hate to disappoint your sister in any way, but this is not the time to give in to her. What would your father say?"

He scuffed his boots on the rug. "I think we both know the answer to that."

"Well, then." Richard folded the letter and stuffed it in his pocket.

"What are you doing?" demanded Darcy.

"I think I should be the one to respond. She cannot charm me, and I am Georgiana's guardian as well. Yes, I know; you are always the one to be in charge. But this once, you are not the right person to handle this. I can be more direct with her."

"I can be blunt as well."

Richard crossed his arms and glared.

"Oh, very well," said Darcy ungraciously. "If you must." He did not want Richard to guess how relieved he was not to have to write to her. His hand would probably refuse to hold the pen.

"I will tell her she is not to come near Georgiana, and should she come to London, I expect her to keep a good distance from Darcy House or anywhere Georgiana is likely to go."

"What makes you think she would listen to you?"

Richard laughed dryly. "She is afraid of my father."

"Like everyone else."

His cousin smiled. "Yes, like everyone else. I might as well put it to use."

"The question is *why* she is suddenly so interested in Georgiana. I think I shall send Stanton to make some inquiries. Perhaps he can discover what it is she is really seeking from me."

Richard snorted again. "Money. What else? Most likely she had got herself into debt and hopes you will rescue her."

"That could be. After my father's death, I discovered he had been paying her an allowance, a generous one, and he left instructions I was to continue it unless she remarried. That was only a matter of weeks, of course, just long enough to call the bans, so the question never arose." Her letter to the family solicitor informing him of her remarriage had arrived a month to the day after his father's death. How odd that she had bothered to inform him, since likely he would have never have found out and would have kept paying the allowance, but her reasoning had always been a mystery to him.

"Naturally. She would not have left without a fuss unless he made it worth her while. Women are so mercenary."

Not all women. Not Elizabeth Bennet, who had refused to marry him despite his riches.

Elizabeth held out the dish of chicken scraps. "It is food," she coaxed. "You like food."

Snowball's furry white form emerged from behind a bale of hay. With a dubious expression, she took the tiniest bite, appeared to consider the matter, and then wolfed down the rest.

"Better than boiled turnip, is it not?" Elizabeth stroked her soft fur, now well groomed and no longer matted. Snowball rubbed against her hand and purred. "Well, I am happy to see you as well, but we must decide what to do with you. Perhaps the people who live in the cottage are wondering what happened to their little cat." While she was growing increasingly attached to Snowball and would be happy to have her continue to live in the Longbourn stables, this question had been troubling her more each day. But she was oddly reluctant to return to the cottage and to put faces to the unknown owners. "I suppose there is nothing for it but to send someone to ask, perhaps with a gift of dried venison."

The cat washed her face delicately, then

bumped up against Elizabeth's leg and circled around her.

"Yes, I know who you are looking for!" said Elizabeth with a laugh. "Your favorite person is not here, I fear."

No matter how much she might wish otherwise.

⁂

"Lizzy! I declare, that girl will be the death of me. Lizzy!" Mrs. Bennet's shrill voice echoed through the house.

In the stillroom, Elizabeth made a face at Mary. "I wonder what I did this time," she said with a laugh. She untied her apron and hung it over a chair back. "Yes, mama, I am coming." Had she been seen receiving the letter from Mr. Stanton? She had best concoct an acceptable explanation quickly.

In the sitting room, her mother reclined on the fainting couch, fanning herself vigorously despite the chilly air. Her sister, Mrs. Phillips, hovered over her.

"There you are," cried Mrs. Bennet, waving a handkerchief through the air. "What do you say to *that*?"

Elizabeth glanced around the room, but nothing seemed out of place. "To what are you referring?"

"Lord save me, to *this*!" Mrs. Bennet shook the handkerchief once more.

"Your handkerchief?" Puzzled, Elizabeth reached out to take it.

"Not *my* handkerchief, young lady!"

Indeed it was not her mother's, nor hers, for that matter. It was a man's handkerchief using a finer linen than her father employed, with a large stain in the middle. Then she saw the initials in the corner and froze. It was *his*. She had pressed it against his bleeding head.

"I see you recognize it! What do you have to say for yourself now?"

Elizabeth wished she could clutch the handkerchief to her, as if it contained the essence of Mr. Darcy. "It… It is a man's handkerchief. That is all I know. Where did you come by it?"

"I should think *you* could guess! Oh, my poor nerves! How could you do this to me?"

Her aunt Phillips said, "Did you not ask Nell to take a basket of food to the cottage where you took shelter during the storm? They were bewildered to receive it, saying you had left a pile of silver already, far more than they deserved."

"A pile of *silver!*" interrupted Mrs. Bennet, wiping her brow.

"And they gave Nell this handkerchief, saying you must have left it behind," Mrs. Phillips said triumphantly.

"Well, obviously they were mistaken, since it is not mine." Elizabeth's heart started to race. If only Nell had thought to bring the handkerchief directly to her instead! This was not a discussion to have in front of her aunt, who was even more inclined to gossip than her mother, and had less reason to protect her.

"Then someone else must have been with you, for it was found *after* you stayed there. Oh, my nerves! Alone with a man for three days! Lizzy, how could you do this to us? It would have been better had you frozen to death alone in the snow!"

A charming sentiment indeed! "Someone must have been confused. But wait, let me see that again." She did not need to examine the handkerchief, but she did need the time to collect her wits. "Oh, I remember now! I found this by the side of the road and picked it up, planning to return it to its owner later. But I forgot all about it in the storm, and must have left it behind. All we need do is to find the gentleman it belongs to."

Mrs. Bennet frowned suspiciously, then squinted to examine the handkerchief. "FD. I know no one with those initials," she said fretfully.

"Nor I." Mrs. Phillips crossed her arms over her chest.

Just then Mr. Bennet passed beside Elizabeth and plucked the handkerchief from his wife's hands. "It is obvious," he said dismissively. "Fitzwilliam Darcy. He was stranded here during the storm. No point in returning it, though; I doubt he would notice its absence among all his possessions. Now that is resolved, Lizzy, I require your assistance in the library."

This brisk behavior was so unlike her father's usual indifference that Elizabeth followed him without a word, leaving her mother in mid-sentence of a new complaint.

Once the door of the library was closed, Mr. Bennet sank into his favorite chair. "So, you met him on the road, did you?" he said coolly.

Elizabeth's shoulders tightened. "No, he was stranded with me, but it seemed better if no one knew that."

"Including your own father? Well, never mind that. What did he do to you?" His voice was weary.

"Nothing. He was injured and confused after a fall. I tended to his injury. You can still see the bloodstain on that handkerchief."

"Or was that a different sort of blood?"

Her cheeks grew hot. "Father! I give you my word that the only blood came from Mr. Darcy's head. He was injured, and I have never been handsome enough to tempt him, as you know. Why would you think anything had happened?" She pushed the memory of what Darcy had told her to the back of her mind.

Her father looked down at his hands. "He is a man unaccustomed to a lack of entertainment or to be denied anything he wants, and in circumstances like that, men will often settle for what is available."

For some reason, his doubt infuriated her. "Well, some men might, but this one did not. All he did was to keep the fire lit so we did not freeze."

His eyes narrowed. "And what did *you* do?"

"Tried to stay warm, talked to him, and attempted to make soup. It was not a complete success, so it was fortunate we were both very hungry and disinclined to turn up our noses at anything." She smiled, hoping to distract him with humor.

"Three days alone with a man, and you expect me to believe *nothing* happened?"

"Do you think I would throw myself at an injured man?"

Bile rose in the back of her throat. "He did not seem injured to me when I saw him in Meryton, when presumably he had already walked several miles through the snow."

"I could almost believe you *want* me to say he compromised me!"

"Only if it is true."

She huffed and looked up at the ceiling. "Nothing happened between us beyond ordinary conversation." The last thing she wanted was for her father to confront Mr. Darcy.

He observed her closely for a minute, then removed his spectacles and sighed. "Very well. I hope for your sake that no word of this gets out."

At least this time she could tell the truth. "I hope so, too."

Chapter 11

UNFORTUNATELY, HER HOPES were in vain.

"I am so sorry, Miss Lizzy," whispered Nell as she took Elizabeth's pelisse at the door.

So even the servants had already heard. Elizabeth should have known Lydia and Kitty would tell everyone in earshot about what had happened in town. But she had not been able to face the walk home in their company, not after the mortifying way the townspeople had treated her, so she had gone off on her own and taken the long way back, and her sisters had returned to Longbourn first.

Her mother's piercing wail came from the sitting room. "He must be made to marry her!"

Elizabeth winced. "I will be in my room," she told Nell. "There is no need to tell anyone I have returned."

"Yes, miss. Shall I bring you a cup of tea?"

At least Nell was being kind to her, which is more than she could say for her own sisters. Lydia had laughed at her discomfort, and Kitty had not known where to look. She could not expect sympathy from her mother. If only Jane were not far away in London! It was a sad state when only the maid seemed concerned for her well-being. "That would be most welcome."

She tiptoed up the stairs, skipping the third one from the top which always creaked loudly. A few more steps and she would be safe. Once she had quietly closed the door behind her, she could let down her guard.

Sinking down on the bed, she let loose the tears she had been holding back for hours. Never before had she been the subject of malicious whispers and comments, and she had not known how much it would hurt to see people she had considered friends shunning her. And all of it based on hearsay and the evidence of a handkerchief! Her stomach churned anew.

But crying would solve nothing. She rinsed her face in the basin, then sat at the vanity, staring into the mirror at her red-rimmed eyes.

What should she do? Ignoring the gossip was not an option; her very presence would keep adding fuel to the fire. Repeating her story about finding the handkerchief on the road might convince a few people, but enough would still choose to believe the worst. She could leave Meryton, but some might see that as a proof of her guilt.

Then there was the option that frightened her most of all – writing to Mr. Darcy. She had never intended to act on the option he had given her, but that was when she thought discovery, if it ever occurred, could be laughed off.

There was no other choice. Half of the townsfolk in Meryton had failed to meet her eyes, and she could hear the whispers that followed her. No, she had no option but to write to him because of the scandal. It was not *just* that she desperately wanted to see him.

But what should she say? She tapped the end of the quill against her nose as she thought, then dipped the point in the inkwell.

Dear Mr. Darcy,

As you may have surmised, I have a powerful dislike of being proven wrong, but I try to balance it by openly admitting my failings when they occur. You were correct about the consequences I would face, and I was incorrect.

That much was simple, but how should she proceed from there? 'Pray come marry me as quickly as possible' hardly seemed the sort of thing one could say in a letter.

She was rescued from her dilemma by a knock at the door. She slid the letter under a fresh sheet of paper before opening the door. Her welcoming look faded when she realized it was not Nell with the tea as she had expected, but her father, lines of worry etched between his eyes. Wordlessly she held the door open for him.

He sighed deeply as he sat down beside her bed. "Well, Lizzy, it seems your little escapade with Mr. Darcy has become general knowledge. Your mother is demanding that I do something about it."

Elizabeth bit her lip. "There is no need. Mr.

Darcy told me he would marry me if anyone discovered I had been with him."

Her father blinked. "He said he would *marry* you? You must have misunderstood him."

Stung, she said, "I did not misunderstand. He said it several times. All I need to do is to write to him, and I am certain he will do what is right."

He shook his head, then removed his spectacles and began to polish them with his handkerchief. Finally he said tiredly, "Lizzy, my dear, of *course* he said he would marry you. Why would he not say that? If he told you he would *not* marry you, you might have cried, or pleaded, or been angry with him, and he could not escape you until the storm was over. So he said what he thought would keep you calm and pleasant, knowing there were no witnesses and it would be his word against yours if it ever came up."

Could it be true? Her stomach roiled. "No, that is not how it was. He offered to marry me regardless of discovery, and kept bringing it up, even after I refused him."

"You refused *Mr. Darcy*? That is my brave Lizzy! But still, I assure you, he did not mean it. If he kept asking you, it was only in the hope you would allow him liberties. Every gentleman knows this trick. Men laugh about it all the time, how often they have done it and how it is the best way to... well, to have their way. Believe me, I *know*."

She looked hard at him. He *did* know. He might not be able to speak for Mr. Darcy, but he was telling her the truth for himself. *He* had done it; told women he would marry them without meaning a word of it, hoping only to take advantage of them. Certain things suddenly began to make more sense to her. "Perhaps many men would, but I believe Mr. Darcy meant what he said. I will write to him, and then we will see."

Her father snorted. "Do not be ridiculous! If he were even to bother to read such a letter, he would laugh at it. Why should such a proud, unpleasant man care about your reputation?"

She could hardly say it was because she believed him to be honorable, not when it meant accusing her own father of dishonor. "I think he will care." Despite her best efforts, her voice shook a little.

"Sometimes you can be as foolish as your sisters! Very well, write your letter if you must, and I will send it for you, but we will tell no one about it. It is one thing to provide sport for our neighbors, but quite another to allow our family to become a laughingstock for asking for the impossible."

Her throat grew tight. "Then how am I to convince everyone in Meryton that I am innocent? I cannot just ignore the problem!"

He pinched the bridge of his nose. "No, of course not. I have a different solution; I have already written to your uncle Gardiner, asking him to permit you to join Jane in London. If you are not here, the talk will fade soon enough."

"If I leave, it will look as if I have something to hide, and it will be even worse when I return!"

"You underestimate how short the memory of

fools can be. Your scandal will be forgotten as soon as
the next one comes along." He must have been able to
tell she did not believe him, for he added, "As for
anyone who might still care, such squeamish people
who cannot bear to be connected with a little absurdity
are not worth a regret."

She shook her head. "I doubt it is that simple."
Her father only wanted the easiest possible way out of
his dilemma with her mother, not a solution to the
problem, but why should she bother to argue? Mr.
Darcy would answer her letter, and on her next visit to
Meryton, she would be Mrs. Darcy.

He slapped his hands on his thighs, then rose to
his feet. "In any case, you will be off to London as soon
as I receive a reply from your uncle. I hope you will not
have to stay there long; with both you and Jane away, I
shall not hear a word of sense from one week to the
next."

"Very well. I will go to London." It was
probably for the best; it would be easier for Mr. Darcy
to approach her there.

Her father kissed her cheek. "I knew you were
not quite as silly as your sisters."

The jest which he had made so often now
rankled. "Indeed," she said coolly, and closed the door
behind him.

At least the problem of what to tell Mr. Darcy
was solved. She sat down again at her writing desk, and
as soon as her hand stopped trembling, she wrote:

Owing to the unpleasant nature of the gossip, I

will be leaving Meryton in the next few days to visit my aunt and uncle, Mr. and Mrs. Gardiner, who live on Gracechurch Street in London. It would perhaps be best to communicate with me there rather than to have your sudden appearance here create even more talk.

Most sincerely yours,

E.B.

Once the ink was dry, she folded and sealed it, then wrote the address on the outside. When he had told her where he lived, she had resolved not to remember it, but it had stayed with her anyway.

For the first time in weeks, a sense of peace came over Elizabeth. It was done.

When Elizabeth presented her father with her letter to Mr. Darcy, she asked, "Are you still willing to send it for me?"

He harrumphed and straightened his spectacles. "In fact, I have decided to do better. I intend to deliver it to him myself and await his answer. He will know I cannot fight him, but perhaps it might shame him into doing what he ought. I doubt it, but your mother is convinced it is worth attempting."

"*You* are going to London?" It was hard to convince her father to stir himself to go as far as Meryton. His willingness to travel so far and actually speak to Mr. Darcy was so uncharacteristic and showed such concern for her that Elizabeth's anger toward him abruptly melted away.

He curled his lip. "Yes, *I* am going to London,

fool that I am!"

She stepped around his desk and kissed his cheek. "Thank you, papa. I think you will be pleased with his response, and I am glad you will have the opportunity to become better acquainted."

Mr. Bennet did not look convinced. "Well, we shall see."

⁂

Just before they climbed the steps to the house of Mr. and Mrs. Gardiner, Mr. Bennet stopped Elizabeth with a hand on her arm. "Remember, not a word to anyone of my business with Mr. Darcy."

It was at least the fourth time he had reminded her of this during their journey. "I do not see why they should not know, but if you insist, I will say nothing. *Now* may we go in?"

The warm reception Elizabeth received from her aunt and uncle provided a much needed respite from the waves of disapproval which had followed her as she waited for the stagecoach in Meryton. Even though the Gardiners already knew about the scandal, the worry they might disapprove of her persisted until she could see from their smiles it was not the case. Jane's embrace nearly brought her to tears.

The rough and tumble welcome from her young cousins made for happy moments as well. Elizabeth was a favorite with the Gardiner children owing to her willingness to join them in their games.

"That is quite enough," admonished Mrs. Gardiner. "Lizzy has had a long journey, and she will not be playing with you tonight. Now, off to the nursery with you."

This edict was met by some grumbling, but after a little assistance from their nurse, the children managed to comply with their mother's instructions.

"Now, you must be in need of refreshments. We have laid out some food in the sitting room for you."

Elizabeth hung back to allow her father to go first, and said quietly to her aunt, "You are not angry with me, then?"

Mrs. Gardiner put an affectionate arm around her niece. "If I discovered you had left an injured man to die on the roadside, *then* I should be cross with you. I fail to see how you could have behaved differently, and if you say nothing untoward happened, then I believe you."

Somehow this statement of trust made hiding anything more difficult. "I cannot say *nothing* happened. We had to huddle together for warmth. There was very little firewood, you see."

The corners of Mrs. Gardiner's mouth twitched. "Well, that is a very different story, since clearly it would be *much* better for you to freeze and have your family find both your dead bodies than to do what was necessary to ensure your survival! Really, Lizzy, I cannot see why you did not preserve every evidence of propriety even at the cost of your own life."

A giggle escaped Elizabeth. "I suppose that would have been rather silly."

Jane's cheeks were pink. "No one blames you, Lizzy."

Elizabeth thanked her for the sentiment, even though her sister's blushes showed her discomfort with Elizabeth's actions. It was nothing to fret over, though. Soon enough Mr. Darcy would know what had happened and they would be married. Even Jane's delicate sensibilities would be satisfied then.

Elizabeth had assumed her father would visit Mr. Darcy the day after their arrival in London, but he seemed disinclined to stir from Gracechurch Street. Finally, after three days, she waited until she found him alone reading the newspaper. "When do you plan to call on Mr. Darcy?" she asked, her mouth dry.

"What, in such a hurry to discover he has deceived you?"

"Or that he has *not* deceived me. I promised to contact him, and if you do not intend to call on him, I will send him a letter as I originally planned."

He folded the newspaper and set it aside. "Lizzy, what has become of your sense of humor? Your Mr. Darcy seems to have had an unfortunate influence over it. I have already told you what will happen when I speak to him, and while I am in no hurry to have him laugh in my face, I will go tomorrow. Are you satisfied?"

But the next two days brought rain, so he delayed yet again, until Elizabeth could hardly bear to be in same room with him. All she wanted was an end to the uncertainty. No matter how many times she reminded herself Darcy was not like her father, the niggling doubt had taken root.

Night was falling when Mr. Bennet finally returned. He looked calm, and a tremulous smile grew on Elizabeth's face. She had been right. Her father had been mistaken. She was not surprised when he made no effort to speak to her alone immediately, since he always disliked admitting to being in the wrong.

She found her chance just before dinner. "May I have a moment of your time?"

He raised an eyebrow. "If you wish."

She ushered him into the small sitting room and closed the door. "Well?" Her heart was pounding.

Her father sank down in the upholstered wing chair. "It was much as I told you it would be, although I give him credit; he did not laugh when he read your letter."

Was he teasing her? "I did not think he would. What did he say?"

"That he was sorry the situation had caused difficulties for you, but unfortunately marriage was not an option. As I told you he would."

Bile rose in the back of her throat. Could it be true? Surely he would not have dismissed her father with nothing, not after the extent to which he had helped Maria Lucas! "Is that all he said?"

"He offered to settle a small amount of money on you, or alternatively to locate a man willing to marry you. And pay him for the privilege, presumably. So I grant you, I did underestimate him in thinking he would not care at all, but he still has no intention of marrying you."

So Mr. Darcy wanted to marry her off to

someone, as he had arranged to marry Maria Lucas to Chamberlayne. What a fool she had been! Elizabeth bit her lip till it hurt, fighting to keep tears back, tears of pain and humiliation. "And does he plan to find a husband for me, then?" she choked out.

Her father waved his hand. "I told him we would manage on our own, and he would have to find another way to assuage his conscience. So that is done, and you are well rid of him. Truly, I would not wish to see you married to that disagreeable fellow and in his debt."

"So I see. Well, then, if you will excuse me, I must see if Jane requires any assistance." It was a very weak excuse, but she might lose her wits if she had to keep looking at her father's smirk. She needed to be alone, to think. Or perhaps just to cry.

That night, Elizabeth crept out of the bed she shared with Jane and tiptoed downstairs to the dark sitting room where she could let her tears fall freely. No matter how good a face she put on during the day, it was time to face the truth.

Mr. Darcy was not going to come to her rescue. Why would he, after all? Marriage to her offered him nothing. *His* reputation was unblemished, and why should he care what the people of a country town in Hertfordshire thought of him? He had no reason to tie himself to a woman so far beneath him. Either he had not meant his offer in the first place, or more likely a little time and distance had reminded him of the gulf that lay between them, not to mention all the disadvantages to him of such a match.

Oh, why had she believed him? Why had she allowed herself to be seduced into caring for him, into thinking he cared about her? Most likely he had simply not wished to deal with her hostility during their involuntary confinement together, and a few kisses had broken up the monotony of the days. What a fool she had been!

She pressed the heels of her hands into her eyes as she struggled to muffle the sobs wrenching through her. How could she have allowed herself to make such a terrible mistake? She had known the sort of man he was from his behavior during his stay at Netherfield, and Mr. Wickham had even warned her about him. But all it took was a few sweet words and she had tumbled straight into his hands, all her misgivings forgotten. And all these weeks she had been *missing* him and longing for his presence!

Had he been relieved when her father left without further demands, or did he have a moment of wistful regret when he thought of her? She would never know. After everything that had passed between them – everything she *believed* to have been there – he was only willing to undertake the same efforts for her sake that he had for Maria Lucas, whom he did not even know. He had not even sent her a message through her father. Now all she could do was to cry and pound her fists against her thighs until the pain drowned out the ache inside her.

The next day Mr. Bennet left for Longbourn

and Elizabeth began the rest of her life without Mr. Darcy. If she was paler than normal or seemed to pick at her food, these were belied by the smiles and teasing she forced herself to produce. She had no intention of humiliating herself even further by confessing her foolish expectations to Jane or her aunt.

She thought she had Jane fooled; after all, Jane was still focused on her own disappointed hopes of Mr. Bingley. But Mrs. Gardiner cast sharp looks in her direction from time to time, so Elizabeth attempted to smile even more brightly.

A few days later, her uncle brought home one of his employees for dinner. Mr. Hartshorne had seemed quite taken with Elizabeth on one of her previous visits to London, though it had been understood nothing more than that was possible. After all, she was a gentleman's daughter and he was employed in trade.

Elizabeth was as pleased to see him now as she was likely to be to see anyone, which was only a very little, but he was a distraction from her thoughts. At least until she noticed the glances he was exchanging with her uncle and the oddly almost triumphant smile he wore when he looked at her, and she realized they must have been discussing her and her newly limited options.

Just as Mr. Darcy had paid Chamberlayne to marry Maria Lucas, Mr. Gardiner had brought home Mr. Hartshorne. Bile rose in Elizabeth's throat, and she had to excuse herself to regain her composure. In the small room she shared with Jane, she stared at her wavy reflection in the aging mirror.

There were still more bitter facts she had to face. She could not return to Longbourn without facing a scandal and harming her sisters' hopes for the future, and she could not stay with the Gardiners forever. If Mr. Hartshorne was willing to consider her, she ought to be grateful. After all, at least she knew he had admired her when he had nothing to gain from it and she had enjoyed his company, and that was more than most other men could offer. If Mr. Darcy was being practical about his marriage options, then so must she.

Even if the idea of marrying Mr. Harshorne made her stomach ache.

She blew out a deep breath and pinched her cheeks to bring color to them before she returned to the dining room, her lips forced into a smile.

Darcy strode to the study with a spring in his step. He had not expected Stanton back so quickly, or rather he had not dared to hope for a response from Elizabeth so soon. It was not as if he had anything of importance to say to her, certainly nothing to justify the risk of a secret correspondence, but the pleasure of maintaining even this slight connection to her was worth it.

Stanton usually waited for him in the leather chair beyond his desk, but today he stood just inside the door, his face unreadable.

Darcy motioned him to the chair. "Well? Was your errand successful?"

"Miss Lucas is married and off to Norfolk with her new husband, and Mr. Wickham is safely in

Marshalsea Prison for inability to pay his debts." Stanton tossed a bundle of paper onto Darcy's desk. "These are from his creditors. He will not be released unless you receive payment for these."

"Excellent." After what he had done to poor Miss Lucas, Wickham deserved to rot in prison, and it would have the added benefit of keeping him far from Elizabeth. "Were you able to deliver the letter to Miss Elizabeth?"

"No, sir, I was not." Stanton held out the familiar envelope, its seal intact, but did not meet Darcy's eyes. "The young lady is not in Meryton."

Not in Meryton? She had said nothing in her recent letter about plans to travel. "Were you able to ascertain where she is?"

Stanton shook his head, his gaze still lowered. "No, sir. The locals seem ignorant of her whereabouts, saying only she was sent away somewhere. The servants at Longbourn are close-mouthed and resentful of questions when it comes to Miss Elizabeth, although they are happy enough to gossip about her younger sisters. Her sisters are sufficiently indiscreet that most likely I could obtain the information from one of them, but I thought I should inform you of these events first."

So this was more serious than a journey for pleasure. The room suddenly seemed colder than it had a minute before. "You say she was sent away? Why?"

Stanton finally raised his eyes to meet Darcy's, his face still expressionless. "It has become general knowledge that she had an assignation with a gentleman during a recent spell of inclement weather."

Darcy's throat felt thick as he faced Stanton's accusing gaze. "Blast it! When was this discovered?" And why had she not informed him?

"Over a fortnight ago."

So there had been more than enough time for her to contact him, but she had not done so, although he had made his wishes perfectly clear. Why had she chosen disgrace over honorable marriage to him? It made no sense. His stomach churned. The first thing was to find her - but he had no idea where to begin looking.

Colorlessly, Stanton said, "Shall I return to Meryton in the morning to seek further information, sir?"

"Yes. You... No. I will take care of this myself from here." He reached into a desk drawer for a bank note. Stanton took it from him, but with a hesitation which might almost have been reluctance. Was Stanton expressing disapproval of *him*? Darcy could almost read it in his face. "There is another matter I would like you to look into. My father's second wife, now remarried, lives in Devon. I would like to know anything you can discover about her, her reputation, her behavior, her plans, and most especially if she has been saying anything about my sister. Here is the direction." He handed it to Stanton.

Stanton's eyes flickered over it. "I know the town. I checked on her several times at your father's behest."

Darcy attempted to hide his surprise. "Will she recognize you?"

"I doubt it."

"What did you find when you went there?"

"There was little to discover. She had set up a household in a small house on her family's estate and was active in paying visits in the neighborhood. Your father asked me particularly to check on whether any gentlemen showed her particular attention, and as far as I could discern, she took great care never to be alone with any gentleman, though she was on friendly terms with several of them." He folded the paper and placed it in his coat pocket. "Will there be anything else?"

"No, that will be all."

Stanton bowed and departed, closing the study door behind him.

Darcy paced to the window, staring blindly out into the garden. Devil take it, why had Elizabeth not agreed to do the sensible thing in the first place? Then neither of their good names would have been besmirched. But to be fair, she had not had to work hard to persuade him. Had he realized then how much he would miss her, he would have insisted on marriage, regardless of the need for it.

Yes, that was it. In the morning he would do what he should have done in the first place — ride to Meryton and speak to Mr. Bennet. He and Elizabeth would be married as soon as possible.

Suddenly he could breathe easily again.

Darcy chose back roads to reach Longbourn, not wishing to draw any unnecessary attention to his visit. Presumably there was quite enough talk about him already in Meryton, and he had no desire to be subjected to more accusatory looks, especially when he had done everything that could be expected of a gentleman. The fact that his accusers were unaware of this did not make him any more comfortable.

The Longbourn manservant who responded to his arrival was badly in need of training, judging from his shocked expression when he recognized Darcy. Not that he expected better from the staff at Longbourn; it was hardly a well-run household. Darcy handed him his card with a curt instruction to give it to Mr. Bennet.

Waiting inside the small entrance hall, he winced at the shrill voice of Mrs. Bennet echoing from the sitting room. She was one more thing he would prefer to avoid. He stayed as close to the door as possible. Where was that servant? He tapped his foot on the scuffed tile floor.

Finally he was shown into Mr. Bennet's library, a small room which would have been pleasing enough were it not for the piles of books left strewn about. At Pemberley, books were returned to the shelves when not in use.

Mr. Bennet slowly rose to his feet. "Mr. Darcy," he said mildly. "This is quite a surprise."

"I cannot imagine why, unless your daughter thought word of her situation would not reach London."

"Has she contacted you, then? I cannot imagine your usual circles have the least interest in the events in Meryton."

"I have heard nothing from her." He certainly

was not going to explain why he had sent Stanton to Meryton. "If you forbade her from contacting me, she has been obedient to your wishes."

A dry smile twisted Mr. Bennet's lips. "I saw no reason to forbid her anything. It would have made no difference, and it was rather too late to begin."

"If you are insinuating something, pray be more direct."

"My Lizzy can put on a polite mask, but she is not talented at disguise. I cannot claim to know what happened between the two of you during those three days, but I do know she was *not* telling me the truth when she said *nothing* had happened."

Darcy folded his hands behind his back where he would not be tempted to use them. "I suggested marriage at the time, but she demurred, believing a scandal could be avoided. I asked her to contact me should any difficulties arise. Since she has not done so, it falls to me to find her and take the necessary steps to protect her reputation. This would be much simpler if I knew where she was, and I had hoped you would be able to assist me with that."

Mr. Bennet placed his hands on the desk in front of him, then slowly lowered himself into his chair. "Do you mean to say you *proposed* to Lizzy?"

Darcy stared at him. "Of course I did. What gentleman would not?" Suddenly Mr. Bennet's attitude made sense. In the absence of that knowledge, it was perfectly natural he would be hostile. "I assumed you were aware of that. Perhaps you thought my purpose today was to ask your permission to marry your daughter, which I will do if you wish, though it strikes me as a mere formality under the circumstances. None of us have a choice in the matter."

The older man pushed up his spectacles. "Apparently Lizzy believes *she* has a choice."

"If you will be so kind as to tell me where I may find her, perhaps we can resolve this matter."

Mr. Bennet gazed at him for a minute, then inexplicably smiled. "If, as you say, you proposed to her, and if, again as you say, you told her to contact you if there were difficulties, then I can only conclude Lizzy has made a decision she does not wish to marry you. I will respect her decision, so under the circumstances I feel unable to share her whereabouts with you."

"I believe there may be a misunderstanding. I do not believe Miss Elizabeth is opposed to the idea."

"You may believe what you like if it gives you comfort, but it will not change reality."

Good God, what was wrong with the man? Darcy could barely keep his voice even as he said, "If you prefer your entire family to suffer the effects of this 'decision,' there is nothing I can do to dissuade you. Should either you or she think better of it, I can be reached at my London address. Good day, Mr. Bennet." He stalked out of Longbourn and rode off before he gave into the temptation to say a great deal more.

Darcy flipped the unopened letter back and forth between his hands, wishing he could consign it to the flames unread. First Mr. Bennet's insults, and now he had to deal with this. Grimly he slipped his thumb under the seal and snapped it open.

Dear Mr. Darcy,

I have, as instructed, gathered information on Mrs. Dawley, previously Mrs. Darcy. She appears to be respected in her neighborhood. She and her husband are fond of society and entertain frequently. She has two sons under the age of four. Her husband is a portly fellow, who is considered most amiable and is well liked. The only criticisms I heard leveled at Mrs. Dawley were that she was occasionally frivolous and should not dress in green so often as it does not flatter her complexion. She is accounted a good mother to her boys. The servants have no unusual complaints about her or Mr. Dawley, and generally believe they are reasonable masters. The Dawleys travel to Manchester or London on occasion, but own no house in town and so spend most of their time on their estate.

There have been no suggestions of impropriety about Mrs. Dawley's behavior. Her previous marriage seems to be generally known, along with the fact she lived separately from her husband. Among those who knew her at the time, she seemed well pleased with her situation, with no evidence of missing her husband, only the daughter she had left behind. At first it was assumed her husband had sent her away for infidelity, but as she showed little interest in flirtations, most of the local people now assume she must have interfered with her husband's pleasures too often. Although Mr. Dawley had shown interest in her for some years, she did not permit him to call upon her until her husband's death. She did not observe a mourning period for him.

I will be back in London on Thursday and can give you a full report at that time.

Yours, &c.,

W. Stanton

Darcy did not know what he had expected, but it had not been this. A country squire's wife, fond of society, somewhat frivolous, but generally respected and well-liked? It did not sound anything like the moody woman he recalled from the last time he had seen her. Could Stanton possibly have found the wrong woman? No, he had been given the name and direction, and the story of her first husband was consistent. Perhaps he had not dug deeply enough.

Chapter 12

IN THE OVER-GILDED sitting room in Rosings Park, Richard Fitzwilliam stretched out his legs. "What of our cousin, Anne? I hope her absence does not indicate ill health."

Thank heaven for Richard! Darcy would not make it through two days with Lady Catherine without Richard's ability to speak calmly to her. Especially in her sitting room, where the painfully vivid turquoise wallpaper made his eyes ache.

"Anne's health is much improved. Darcy, you will be quite pleased when you see her."

He ignored the implication that Anne's health would matter particularly to him. Lady Catherine knew his feelings on the matter. "I am glad she is in good health."

"I am very pleased with her physician, Mr. Graves. He is most diligent and particular in his care for her. He comes to see her every week even when she is in good health, since he says it helps him understand better how to help her at other times. He went as far as to join us when we travelled to Ramsgate and took Anne for a walk along the promenade, saying it would be good for her spirits to have the opportunity to walk out with a gentleman like any other lady, and she did look much better on her return. He has also given me a most useful tonic for my gout."

And no doubt Mr. Graves also enjoyed the payments he received every week. If his remedy for gout were truly effective, presumably Lady Catherine would not require the assistance of two footmen to walk even a short distance.

Richard said, "He is fortunate to have so generous a patron as you."

"He is cognizant of his good fortune, I assure you, as is the clergyman I appointed to the Hunsford living. I am most pleased with my choice. Mr. Collins is one of those rare men who know their station and appreciate the condescension of their superiors. He is always happy to receive my advice."

"It sounds as if you could not have chosen a more grateful recipient for your attentions." Richard winked at Darcy.

"He has benefitted greatly from my advice. Why, just a few months ago, at my recommendation, Mr. Collins took a wife, a good, sensible one. All rectors should be married, I told him. It sets a good example to their flock. Darcy, his wife claims to have met you."

"I find that unlikely. Perhaps she was mistaken." He was hardly listening. Mention of the obsequious clergyman had brought his thoughts back to Elizabeth. Where could she be hiding?

"No, I am certain of it. She met you in Hertfordshire. I have a most particular memory of her saying as much."

Hertfordshire? He caught his breath. No, of course it could not be Elizabeth. Her father would have told him had he married her off. "What is her name?"

Lady Catherine smiled triumphantly. "She was Miss Lucas. I remember it quite distinctly, for she told me her father's name. He was knighted, which was fortunate for her, since Mr. Collins had my most particular instructions to marry a gentlewoman for my sake."

Could it be? Elizabeth had said her friend had married a fool and moved away. If Mrs. Collins was indeed the former Charlotte Lucas and Elizabeth's particular friend, surely she would know where Elizabeth was to be found. She had a practical mind. She must have, to marry that fool Collins for his prospects. But wait – Elizabeth had said she was to visit her friend. Could he possibly be so fortunate? He cleared his throat. "It must be difficult for her to be so far from her family and friends. Or do they visit her?"

Lady Catherine curled her lip. "There was to be a visit, but it had to be cancelled at the last minute, something about her sister being ill. I was quite cross, for I could see no reason for them to stay away. Dr. Graves could have seen her if she were ill."

His heart slowed to a normal rhythm. Perhaps Miss Lucas – Mrs. Collins – might have the information he needed. But the momentary hope of seeing Elizabeth so soon left a bitter residue when it vanished. Why, oh why, had she not contacted him as he had asked her to?

Darcy resolved to call on Mrs. Collins at the first possible opportunity.

"Is she such a friend you cannot stay away?" asked Colonel Fitzwilliam. "I have never seen you so eager to pay a call."

Darcy deliberately slowed his brisk stride. "I am eager to be free of our aunt's company; that is all."

But his cousin gave him an odd glance, clearly unsatisfied, and announced his intention to join Darcy in his visit to the parsonage.

Mrs. Collins greeted the two cousins with all courtesy, but Darcy thought he could detect a slight narrowing of her eyes when she looked his way. So she knew about what had happened with Elizabeth, or at least some of it. Had she heard the rumors? Or had Elizabeth said something about him in a letter to her? If her dislike of him came from Elizabeth's criticism, then he would have no choice but to accept Mr. Bennet's opinion that Elizabeth wanted nothing to do with him.

That thought was too difficult to bear.

He had to find out. "Mrs. Collins, I hope your family in Hertfordshire is in good health."

"They are tolerably well, I thank you." Her tone was cool, almost dismissive.

"Does your father continue to enjoy the hunt?"

"That is unlikely to change, unless it should come to pass that every animal and bird should flee the environs."

He could remember nothing about her mother, but he had to find something to say to keep the conversation on Meryton. Otherwise he could not ask about Elizabeth. "Your mother is also well?"

Mrs. Collins's eyebrows rose slightly. ""She has been quite busy. You would not have heard the news. Shortly after my own wedding, my younger sister became engaged and was married soon afterwards. Marrying off two daughters in as many months has kept my mother well occupied."

Darcy wondered how she would react if he told her he probably knew more about her sister's marriage than she did. "I hope your sister will be very happy. Is the fortunate gentleman one I might have met during my stay at Netherfield?"

"Your paths might have crossed. He was Lieutenant Chamberlayne of the militia, now Captain."

"I believe I recall him. He seemed an amiable fellow."

"I barely knew him myself, but it seems he is kind to my sister."

He certainly ought to be kind; he was being paid well for it. "Do you hear from any of your friends in Meryton?"

Now her eyes definitely narrowed. No doubt she had an excellent idea of precisely which friend he was curious about. Mrs. Collins, like Elizabeth, was not a fool.

"A few, though I have not been here long. Lizzy Bennet has been a regular correspondent, of course. Perhaps you might remember her." Her words seemed to have sharp edges.

"I remember her quite well." Day and night, for

that matter. "How is Miss Elizabeth?"

Her smile was completely devoid of warmth. "She is in good health."

"I am glad to hear it." A poor excuse for an answer when he wanted to encourage her to say more. If only Richard were not there! His cousin, he was certain, was not missing a word of this exchange. "Pray give my regards to your parents when you write them next, and to Miss Elizabeth as well."

"I will be happy to do so, sir." Her tone indicated precisely the opposite. "Pardon me, Colonel Fitzwilliam. It is inexcusably rude of us to discuss people with whom you have no acquaintance. Lizzy is my dearest friend from Hertfordshire, as well as Mr. Collins's cousin."

"A double connection, then," said Richard.

"Were It not for her, I would never have met my husband. Now it will be her turn, as she is to be married soon as well. Perhaps she already is; I have not heard from her for over a fortnight. Are you quite well, Mr. Darcy? You look suddenly pale." Her words might as well have been knives.

He was not at all well. A drenching in icy water could not have had a more shocking impact. If his stomach had churned before, it was nothing to this, when every muscle in his body seemed to clench in protest. "Married? That is very sudden." He had to force the words out.

"It seems to be the fashion these days. Or did you think no man would want her?"

Out of the corner of his eye, Darcy saw Richard

sitting forward at this. "Nothing of the sort. I simply had no idea she was thinking of marriage."

Mrs. Collins shrugged. "It is the usual story. She had no intention of marrying now, but someone began to spread rumors about her – quite unfounded, I assure you – and it turned into a scandal. So she will marry soon and the gossip will die a natural death."

Richard shook his head sympathetically. "It is very sad. Sometimes I do not know how young ladies tolerate it – the knowledge that all it takes is one malicious person to ruin their reputations. I am sorry for your friend, and I hope her marriage will prove tolerable."

Tolerable! She could have married *him* and been Mistress of Pemberley, and Richard hoped her marriage would be *tolerable*! It had been one thing when he thought she might have hoped to go back to her old life once the scandal had passed, but to marry another man? What was wrong with her? She had been happy enough with his company during the storm – not to mention his kisses – but now for some reason she seemed to have returned to her old ill opinion of him.

Had Wickham said something to her to poison her mind against him? He would strangle the blackguard with his own hands! But it made no sense. After seeing the scene at the tavern where Wickham had taken advantage of Miss Lucas, Elizabeth surely would not credit any of his lies.

Perhaps it was her father, who seemed to hold something against him. Had he influenced Elizabeth somehow? Or was it that unequal marriage nonsense she had spoken of during the storm?

He flexed his hands. If only he could *do* something! A fierce bout of fencing or a wild ride across the countryside would help, but all he could do was to sit quietly until he could decently make an excuse to leave. That was hardly satisfactory when he wanted to break the window panes, tear down the shutters and smash them into kindling. Kindling. Lighting a fire. Elizabeth. Devil take it – she would drive him out of his mind!

It was a miracle Darcy managed to stay awake throughout Mr. Collins's intolerably dull sermon the following day. Not that he was listening to it, of course. His mind was fully occupied with strategies for cornering Mrs. Collins after the service.

A near sleepless night of torturing himself with images of Elizabeth in another man's arms was enough. His feelings for her would not go away; he knew that now. Not while at some basic level he would always belong to her. By the time the clock had chimed three o'clock, he had been castigating himself for failing to seduce her while they had been stranded. That would have resolved all these problems.

She had responded to him; of that much he was certain She was not indifferent to him, and had sent a friendly letter to him via Stanton. So why had she chosen not to write to him now? Much more of this and that question would be indelibly etched inside his skull, along with the other question of why he had allowed her to walk away from him in the first place.

What a fool he had been, thinking of duty and what society wanted! All it had taken was discovering Elizabeth might already be married to someone else, and all the duty in the world turned into dry ashes. Why had he not realized it earlier?

But Mrs. Collins had only said she *might* be married already, so he would pray she was not. There was no time to delay though, not when every day was another risk of losing her forever to another man. He had to find her first.

Finally the sermon came to its long-winded end. Darcy went through the rest of the service automatically. Mrs. Collins was in the pew behind his, so he would need to exit quickly in order to prevent her from avoiding him. Once he knew where Elizabeth was, he would leave Rosings today despite his exhaustion. He could sleep after he had somehow convinced Elizabeth to marry him. How he would manage that when he had been unable to do so in three days alone with her in the storm was not to be considered. Somehow he would accomplish it or die trying. He could picture her amused look, asking him to explain precisely how one might die trying to propose to a woman. All he knew was a life barren of Elizabeth would be a kind of death.

The congregation was rising now. Darcy had taken care to sit at the end of the family pew to facilitate his escape. If he had to wait for Lady Catherine to move her painfully gouty legs, he would lose his chance. He set out purposefully toward his quarry, who was already making for the church door, no doubt trying to escape him.

He caught up with her on the church steps. "Mrs. Collins! A moment, I pray you."

She hesitated, clearly wishing to refuse, but unwilling to appear so uncivil to her patron's nephew in public. It was what he had counted on. "Mr. Darcy."

"Where is Miss Elizabeth Bennet?" Wonderful – such an eloquent opening! What had happened to 'good day' and all the usual pleasantries? Desperation had stolen them away.

Her eyebrows rose fractionally. "I cannot tell you."

"Cannot or *will* not?"

"Very well then; I *will* not tell you."

"Mrs. Collins, this is of the utmost importance."

"To you it may be, but to me, retaining my friend's trust is of greater importance. I hope you will find it in your heart to forgive me." The look she gave him said she would not care in the slightest if he never forgave her.

"I mean her no harm. I pray you, Mrs. Collins, to assist me." How infuriating it was to be forced to plead with her!

"Pray pardon me. My place is by my husband." She turned from him.

"Wait!" He could not allow her to get away. "Would you at least write her and tell her I wish to speak to her – as soon as possible?" The parishioners were beginning to pour out of the church, and soon they would be surrounded.

There it was again – that narrowing of her eyes. "I will *consider* it. Good *day*, Mr. Darcy."

As he strode away, he cursed all stubborn women. Richard would have to escort Lady Catherine in the coach on his own. Darcy could not bear another half hour in company, not now.

Chapter 13

DINNERS AT ROSINGS were hardly an event to anticipate with pleasure, but Darcy made certain to be downstairs early on Monday evening. Lady Catherine had mentioned in passing at breakfast that Mr. and Mrs. Collins would be dining with them. "I try to invite them every Monday since Dr. Graves dines with us after he sees Anne. That way he has someone of his own station in life to converse with. I am extremely attentive to these matters."

Darcy did not care about the reason as long as it brought Mrs. Collins within his reach again, but Richard must have been puzzled, for he said, "Anne's doctor stays for dinner? Did you not say he lives in London?"

"Of course he does. I would never allow an ignorant country doctor to care for my daughter! But his treatments for my gout take several hours, and he prefers to see how Anne improves after a day of the plasters he gives her, so he stays the night. He has his own room here."

Richard's sidelong glance at Darcy spoke volumes of his opinion of a doctor who created such a lucrative opportunity for himself. No doubt Lady Catherine must pay him extremely well to spend so much time at Rosings, money which could be better spent repairing the horribly rutted roads on the estate. But naturally Lady Catherine would never agree to fix them until they were impassible.

When Darcy entered the blindingly gaudy sitting room, he was surprised to discover Anne was already there, dressed in an attractive pink gown and the full-length gloves she always wore even in the warmest weather. She was accompanied by a woman about her own age as well as Dr. Graves, whose handsome appearance no doubt explained Lady Catherine's interest in his protracted treatments. Anne usually did not join them until just before dinner was served, no doubt to conserve her strength. Perhaps she felt bolder with Dr. Graves present to attend to her.

Anne introduced her companion as Miss Holmes. "Her brother is rector of one of the neighboring parishes, and Miss Holmes is kind enough to stay with me when Mrs. Jenkinson visits her son in Maidstone." It was more than Anne usually said to him in the course of an entire evening.

Perhaps it was the influence of Miss Holmes, who appeared to have a livelier temperament than Mrs. Jenkinson. She was bold enough to look him in the face and say, "So, you are the famous Mr. Darcy of whom I have heard so much."

He bowed silently, in no mood to encourage flirting.

"And I see you are as taciturn as I have been

told! Well, I shall leave you to yourself, then." She turned pointedly to Dr. Graves and asked him a question about London.

Where was Mrs. Collins? He ground his teeth with frustration when a new arrival proved to be Mr. and Mrs. King from a neighboring estate. Odd; very few of the neighbors chose to accept invitations from Lady Catherine. But he had not met this couple before, so perhaps they were new to the area.

He dismissed them from his mind as Mrs. Collins finally entered on her husband's arm. He immediately made his way towards her, but the presence of Mr. Collins prevented him from asking her again about Elizabeth. Instead, he was forced to listen to a quarter hour of obsequious flattery from the annoying man, while Mrs. Collins actively avoided saying a word to him.

Darcy was ready to throttle Mr. Collins by the time dinner was announced. Mrs. Collins's look of relief at the prospect of being separated from him by the length of the table did not improve his mood in the slightest.

At least the dinner conversation was better than usual, as he was seated by Mrs. King, who proved to be well-read and witty, much as he imagined Elizabeth might be in twenty years. When she mentioned her recent return to Kent, he said, "Perhaps that is why we have not met before, even though I come here at Easter each year."

"Oh, we have been away for some years. My husband served as the ambassador to the Viceroyalty of

Peru, and of course I could not resist the opportunity to travel to the other side of the world with him."

He would cross the ocean to be with Elizabeth, but she would not even speak to him. "Did you enjoy it?" he asked dully.

"Oh, yes. It is another world, so unlike our England it is almost impossible to describe. The raw beauty of the jungle alone is worth the voyage. And the indigenous people – they are so mysterious. No one ever truly knows them."

From her other side, Richard said, "That sounds like something from a novel."

She tapped his arm with her fan. "I will tell you a secret, young man. I wrote one, and I have just received my first copy from the publisher."

"I will be certain to read it," said Darcy. He could see Elizabeth making a similar resolution. Would she find travel stimulating? Perhaps not all the way to Peru, but he could take her to Italy and Greece. If only he could *find* her! He glared at the oblivious Mrs. Collins. He *had* to find a way to speak to her.

Instead, of course, he had to remain with the other gentlemen after dinner while the ladies withdrew. He listened with half his attention as Richard drew out Mr. King on the subject of his travels.

"The voyage was the hardest part. I was seasick the entire way, but my bold Jocelyn stood in the bow with the spray in her face."

Richard laughed. "I have only had the misfortune to sail to Portugal, and wild horses could not drag me on a ship again! I have never felt so ill in my life, stuffed in the hold with dozens of soldiers. I was ready to kiss the ground when I disembarked."

It was good to hear Richard speaking of anything during his campaigning days without any evidence of distress. True, the voyage hardly counted, but he had seen his cousin go white from a mere mention of the Peninsular War. Perhaps time was easing his memories.

When they rejoined the ladies, Darcy found Mrs. Collins firmly fixed beside her husband, and apparently not inclined to even look in his direction. He bided his time until she left her husband's side to return her teacup, but before he could even lift a foot to move in her direction, Dr. Graves stepped in front of him.

"Mr. Darcy, this is a fortunate happenstance," said the doctor. "I had hoped to find the opportunity to speak to you this evening."

Darcy's hands tightened into fists. Over Dr. Graves' shoulder, he saw Mrs. Collins setting down her teacup with a polite word to Anne, but then Lady Catherine gestured to her and proceeded to engage her in vigorous conversation. He had missed his chance.

He glared at Dr. Graves. "Yes?" He had no intention of appearing welcoming to the man, who was no doubt hoping for his patronage.

"As you may know, Miss de Bourgh has been under my care for the last two years. I have recommended repeatedly to her mother that Miss de Bourgh would benefit from exposure to a different environment and wider social circle."

Darcy held up his hand. "You may tell my aunt you did your best to convince me Anne's very health depends upon my marrying her and taking her away, but that I proved obdurate. She will be unsurprised, I promise you."

"You quite mistake my meaning. Lady Catherine did not ask me to speak to you, and I have not the least interest in whom you plan to marry. However, owing to her ladyship's plans, you are in a unique position to convince her to allow her daughter to pay a visit, perhaps to your sister, or to anyone else you deem suitable. I am certain it would prove beneficial to your *cousin*." He placed an emphasis on his final word, as if to remind Darcy of his responsibilities.

Darcy's lip curled. What was the man hoping to gain from this? "How kind of you to take such an interest in your patient. However, such an invitation would only encourage Lady Catherine in her schemes, and might raise Anne's expectations only to suffer a later disappointment. *That* would hardly be beneficial to her health."

Dr. Grave smiled. "I assure you, Mr. Darcy, Miss de Bourgh has made clear to me she has no, ah, *expectations* of you whatsoever; and should Lady Catherine insist upon her marrying you, she would refuse. You need have no fears in that regard."

Darcy's eyes swiveled toward Anne, who was giggling behind her hand in response to something Miss Holmes was saying. Could it be true? He had always assumed Anne shared her mother's desire for a match between them, but he had never discussed it with her.

Or anything else, for that matter. He always avoided showing any interest in Anne lest her mother start in on her ridiculous ideas again.

Just then Lady Catherine said, "What is that you are saying, Darcy? What is it you are talking of? What are you telling Dr. Graves? Let me hear what it is."

He gritted his teeth. "We are speaking of the value of travel in maintaining health."

"Of travel! Then pray speak aloud. It is of all subjects my delight. I must have my share in the conversation, if you are speaking of travel. There are few people in England, I suppose, who have more true interest in travel than myself. If I had the opportunity to travel that young men do, I should have seen all of Europe."

Dr. Graves turned to his patroness. He said smoothly, "Perhaps some day Miss de Bourgh will have the chance to travel. I was just telling Mr. Darcy of the remarkable improvement she has shown this year."

"Indeed, she is much better; I could not concur more. Thanks to her current regimen and the tonic I give her every day, her health is continually improving. I have told Mrs. Collins she would benefit from taking the tonic as well."

The doctor's smile seemed to slip a little at the mention of the tonic. "Yes, I brought you several new bottles of it, made precisely to your recipe by the finest herbalists in London."

Lady Catherine waved this aside. "Darcy, I am certain you must be able to see how much stronger

Anne has become. She is quite ready to take on the management of Pemberley."

Darcy ignored her last comment, but dutifully turned to examine Anne. Astonishingly, she *did* appear to be in better health than in past years. Her cheeks had some color in them instead of the ghostly pallor she had sported for years. When had he last seen her swoon? Not since his arrival, unless she had hidden it well. Once it had been a daily occurrence.

Her smile, another thing which had been in short supply for years, make her look almost pretty. But that was very new; even last night she had worn her usual cross expression. Perhaps the presence of the lively Miss Holmes instead of sour Mrs. Jenkinson had improved her spirits.

"I am glad to know she is in better health," said Darcy icily. "Some day, after all, she will need to manage *Rosings*." It was better than a direct contradiction which would lead to a scene unpleasant to them all, but his aunt was perfectly capable of hearing only what she chose.

"That as well," she said with a decisive nod, and turned back to Mrs. Collins.

Darcy frowned at Dr. Graves. "You see?"

The doctor eyed him, then said slowly. "I do see. I see an elderly lady who cannot move without pain and has little time left in this life, with no power whatsoever to force two young people in their prime to marry. All she has is words."

"No power over me, perhaps, but she could disinherit Anne. The estate does not pass automatically to her."

"That is true; she would hate to lose Rosings, but being disinherited is not the end of the world."

The man clearly did not understand the bond between a family and its birthright. Anne would no more give up Rosings than he would surrender Pemberley.

"Again? You are going to the parsonage *again*?" Richard stared at him in disbelief.

"There is no reason why I should not." Darcy did not meet his cousin's eyes.

Richard counted on his fingers. "You called on them yesterday after seeing them at dinner the day before and at the church the day before *that*. The parson is a fool and his wife does not even like you. I've seen those looks she gives you! And she is plain to boot, so I hope you are not interested in her, or I will have to question your taste indeed."

"For God's sake, Richard! She is a pleasant person, and there is nowhere else I can go to avoid our aunt."

"You." Richard shook his finger at Darcy. "You are up to something, and attempting to keep it secret from me."

"Clearly you must be very bored, since you are chasing after phantoms!"

"And what *did* you do in Hertfordshire, anyway, to earn her dislike? If she can tolerate her ridiculous husband's company on a daily basis, *you* must have truly offended her."

"If my doings are of such great interest to you, perhaps you should set spies on me." Darcy jammed his hat on his head. "Good *day*, Richard."

His cousin's laughter followed him. "Never fear, I will not attempt to follow you to your little assignation this time. I would hate to see you forced to employ base stratagems to talk to her. The parson's wife, of all things!"

Darcy ignored him.

Mrs. Collins welcomed him to her sitting room with a resigned look. "You are very persistent, Mr. Darcy." At least she did not sound annoyed.

He decided to meet her bluntness head on. "You are my only conduit to Miss Elizabeth."

"Nonsense. You could simply ride to Longbourn and ask her father where she is. But of course that interest might lead to questions you do not wish to answer and expectations you do not wish to meet." The barbs were back.

"I have already tried that, and he refused to tell me. I also attempted to call on her sister in London, but she had already departed from town."

Clearly he had surprised her. "Interesting. I had not heard Jane was planning to leave town, but no matter." She eyed him with calculation. "But if her father will not reveal her whereabouts to you, why should I?"

He should have said nothing, but her clear implication of dishonorable intentions on his part had stung. "He has some agenda of his own. He said if

Elizabeth wanted me to know where she was, she would have told me herself. He did not suggest how she might have been able to accomplish that feat."

Mrs. Collins smothered a giggle. "That is Mr. Bennet for you. Always inclined to do whatever is least expected.'

"I do not find it amusing."

"I suppose not. Forgive me; I was not laughing at you, but at Mr. Bennet's mischief."

He accepted her apology with a nod. "May I inquire if you wrote to Miss Elizabeth?" He had been unable to ask her the previous day owing to the presence of both Richard and Mr. Collins, and it had been gnawing at him."

"I did, but even if she replied to me the instant she received it and rushed her reply to the post, I could not possibly hear anything before tomorrow. I could hardly justify sending it express, after all."

Darcy counted days in his head. "She cannot be too far away if a letter can get there in a day."

She laughed aloud. "Very well, now you may be certain she is somewhere in Southern England. You should have no trouble tracking her down with that information." For once her response did not seem to have an edge.

After gazing at her for a brief moment, Darcy allowed himself a slight smile. "I have to begin somewhere."

"There is every reason to believe she will not reply immediately. She has many other things to do besides writing to me, and it might be weeks before I hear anything."

How well he knew it! That was one of the thoughts which had haunted him, along with the temptation of telling Mrs. Collins what he had done for her sister in an effort to convince her to reveal Elizabeth's hiding place. "Unfortunately, there is little I can do about that," he said through gritted teeth.

"Well, I shall not put you through the trial of having to call here every day in hope of news. We should have a signal. I know – if I hear from Lizzy, I will leave a handkerchief half way out this window. If you do not see a handkerchief, then I have not received a letter. Will that suit?"

"What if your maid sees the handkerchief and removes it."

"Then I shall put it back and instruct her to leave it there." This time she definitely did smile.

For the next few days, Darcy found excuses to pass the parsonage frequently, even during a succession of rain. Once he called on Mrs. Collins simply to reassure himself he had not missed the handkerchief. Apart from discovering that lady had given over her hostility towards him in favor of being amused by his desperation, he learned nothing.

It was intolerable. Any one of these days might put Elizabeth beyond his reach forever. She could be marrying another and spending their first night together as man and wife. Those images tortured him, yet he was helpless to do anything about them. He was at Mrs. Collins's mercy.

Finally he could bear it no longer. Fortune, in the guise of his aunt, was to bring the Collinses to Rosings for dinner, where the group setting could allow more opportunities for private discourse. He could only hope Mrs. Collins would take pity on him this time and reveal Elizabeth's whereabouts. If that did not work, he would throw his scruples to the wind and send for Stanton. It was beyond improper to send someone to spy on the Bennet household, to ferret secrets from the servants and to attempt to charm the information out of Elizabeth's heedless younger sisters, but he was desperate.

His new resolve inured him to Lady Catherine's stream of advice and Richard's teasing as they awaited their guests. Finally Mr. and Mrs. Collins were announced. Precisely on time, of course, but Darcy felt as if he had been waiting for hours.

And then he saw her.

Elizabeth Bennet floated into the room behind Mrs. Collins, wearing that teasing smile he loved so much. Mrs. Collins introduced her to Lady Catherine as the dear friend from Hertfordshire she had mentioned to her ladyship a few days previously. Richard had already put himself forward for his share of the introductions by the time Darcy's feet had unfrozen from the floor.

He stepped toward her tentatively, as if she might disappear if he moved too quickly. She had not noticed him yet.

Mrs. Collins said, "And of course you are already acquainted with Mr. Darcy."

The color drained from Elizabeth's face as she turned to look at him. She took a step backwards, her eyes wide. Then, remembering herself, she gave the slightest of curtseys and said coldly, "Indeed, I am acquainted with him." Then she turned her back to him.

This must be what it felt like to take a bullet in the chest, a stabbing pain spreading in waves and threatening to engulf him. It was the one possibility he had not truly believed to be possible, that, as Mr. Bennet had said, she wanted nothing to do with him.

She was standing stiffly; he could tell that even from his position behind her. This meeting must have taken her as much by surprise as it had him. Why had Mrs. Collins chosen not to warn her friend of his presence? He wondered under what pretense she had lured Elizabeth here.

Perhaps her reaction was nothing more than shock and dismay over meeting him so publicly. She would not wish to draw attention to their connection. That must be it. Why would she suddenly despise him when two months ago she had been lying sweetly in his arms and returning his kisses with a burgeoning passion? It made no sense.

Determined, he strode forward and took the vacant seat closest to her. She made no acknowledgment of his presence, continuing to attend to Lady Catherine's current recitation of her great wisdom. He waited until his aunt's attention turned to Anne, then said to Elizabeth, "I hope your journey was not a difficult one."

Slowly she turned her face toward him, her expression sober. "My *journey* went smoothly." She did not need to add that her arrival was not as happy.

He could not help himself. "I do not understand," he said urgently. "Why are you upset with me? Did I do something? I assure you, if I have offended you, it was not purposeful."

She bit her lip. "It is not so much what you did as what you did *not* do."

"What do you mean?"

Crossing her arms, she asked, "Did you receive my letter?"

What did that have to do with anything? She had not seemed angry in the letter Stanton had brought him. "Yes."

"And you spoke to my father?"

So she already knew he had traveled to Longbourn. "Yes."

She drew in a sharp breath, her eyes blinking rapidly. "You do not even try to deny it," she whispered. "Then there is nothing left to say." She turned back toward Lady Catherine in an obvious dismissal.

His hands were trembling. What had happened to his sweet Elizabeth? He could think of nothing in her letter to account for any distress, much less something of this magnitude. Fearing his agitation would be visible, he rose and crossed to the window where he could ignore the rest of the company as he wrestled with this unexpected agony.

He heard footsteps behind him but did not

turn. They were not her footsteps; he would have recognized them. "Go away," he said.

Richard held out a glass of brandy. He must have gone to the dining room to fetch it. "You looked like you needed this," he said quietly. "Now I will leave you in peace."

Darcy stared down at the glass, then took a long sip of it, letting it rush past his tongue so it burned his throat. This was going to be the longest evening of his life.

"Darcy! You are not attending to what I am saying," snapped Lady Catherine.

"My apologies. My thoughts were wandering." Wandering straight to the parsonage along with the just-departed guests.

Richard said, "He is tired, and it is my fault. I sent him the wrong direction on his ride today and it took him hours to return."

Why had his cousin concocted that little story? Not that it mattered. The only thing that did matter was discovering why Elizabeth had changed so drastically towards him.

It did not help that his gut wrenched every time he remembered her cold looks. He had tried twice more to approach her after dinner, but fared no better, unless one counted the stilted polite conversation when others were watching.

"I *said*, do you not think Anne was in very good looks tonight?"

Fortunately, no thought was required for his

response. He knew better than to agree with any compliment to Anne unless he wished for a resumption of the discussion of their fictional engagement. "Pardon me, madam. I did not notice, but no doubt you are correct." He had said some variation on this hundreds of times.

What could he possibly have done to offend Elizabeth so badly? He had never seen her behave in such a cold manner to anyone, even if she had no fondness for them. Had she attempted to brush him off, or said something witty, then turned away, he could believe her to be indifferent to him or to hold him in some dislike. But she was not indifferent. She was furious.

Richard silently replaced his empty brandy snifter with a full one. That was the third time his cousin had given him brandy this evening. Obviously *he* realized something was wrong, even if their aunt did not. Richard might tease him mercilessly over minor issues, but when it came to a real problem, he was as steady as the Rock of Gibraltar.

How soon could he decently make his excuses? He needed to examine Elizabeth's letter. There had been no reason to bring it to Kent, but like Elizabeth's hair ribbon, he found it impossible to leave it behind. Now he was grateful for the impulse that made him bring it.

He had to find out what in it was the cause of Elizabeth's disturbance of spirits. Obviously he must have missed something despite his repeated perusals of the letter. He would find out what was amiss, and he would fix it. That was all there was to it.

Chapter 14

WHEN A LIGHT knock sounded on Elizabeth's door, she knew who it must be. "Come in, Charlotte," she said resignedly.

Her friend – or perhaps she should call her a former friend – slipped through the door. Clad in a nightgown and cap, she looked younger than her eight and twenty years. "I thought it only fair to give you the opportunity to berate me in private. I did not miss the looks you have been casting in my direction all evening."

"And you deserved them! Charlotte, I *cannot* believe you did this to me! Could you not have allowed me to make my own decision on whether I wished to see him, or at the very least *warned* me? That was one of the worst moments of my life!"

"Would you have come, had I told you he was here? Or agreed to meet him?"

"No, I would not! And it should have been *my* decision!"

"Had I thought you would be reasonable on the subject, I would have told you. But your letters made it clear you never wished to hear his name again. I was not happy to see him here either, but it soon became clear to me there is some sort of misunderstanding here. And completely apart from your wishes, not to mention those of your father, he deserves the opportunity to state his case to you."

"Or do you take his side because he is Lady Catherine de Bourgh's nephew?"

"Lizzy Bennet, that is quite uncalled for! If you knew Lady Catherine in the slightest you would be aware the *last* thing she would desire would be to give Darcy the opportunity to marry anyone beside her daughter."

"He has no intention of marrying me. And if not for Lady Catherine's sake, then *why?* And pray do not tell me how fortunate I am to have earned the attentions of such an eligible man."

"Very well, although it is true." Charlotte paused and sat down on the bed. "If you truly wish to know, the reason I sent for you is because he is quite violently in love with you, and his inability to find you was causing him a great deal of pain. If you do not wish to marry him, all you need do is say so. There is no reason to make him suffer for lack of an answer."

"Did you not hear a word I said? He does not wish to marry me, and I told him quite clearly where to find me. He *chose* not to find me."

Charlotte rubbed her hands over her face. "This is where I cannot agree. I have watched him for more than a week, and he has been at his wit's end, begging me to reveal your location, and when I refused, pleading with me to write to you and tell you he wished to speak to you. I cannot believe a man of such pride would go through such an act if he already had the answer. Why would he be so worried about the scandal if he did not care about you? If he did not want to marry you, why did he go to Longbourn and ask your father where he could find you? An odd step indeed for a man with no interest in matrimony!"

Elizabeth clenched her hands into fists. "I do not believe it. He did not go to Longbourn. My father would have said something to me. But that is not the most damning part. How could he even know of the scandal if he did not speak to my father in London and receive my letter from him? He is not in contact with any of our circle. They would not even know how to reach him."

"Are you certain of that?"

"Yes!" She was not, in fact, completely certain, but Charlotte seemed to have missed the point that, whatever game Darcy might be playing now, he had not come to her assistance.

"He says he went to your uncle's house as well and asked to speak to your sister, only to be told she had left London."

Shaking her head, Elizabeth said, "That is ridiculous. Jane is still there. *I* was there. He has made up the entire story. I do not know why he is playing this game, or what it is he wants. Surely he knows I would never agree to anything less than marriage."

"If you would simply talk to him, perhaps *you* could discover the answers! Lizzy, do not let your stubbornness stand in the way of your future happiness.

You did not see his face when I told him you were contemplating marriage in the near future."

"Oh, pray tell me you did not! How can I ever face him? I cannot bear having him know a husband had to be found for me. It is humiliating!"

More gently Charlotte said, "Have you agreed to marry him?"

Elizabeth blew out a long breath. "I told him I would give him my answer on my return, but we both know I have little choice in the matter."

"Do you think you could be happy with him?"

She shrugged. "I do not know. He is amiable enough, but the way he looks at me makes me nervous. As if I were a possession he was clever enough to obtain, and that he knows he has the upper hand because I have to marry. I do not like the idea of being in his power, but I see little choice."

"You may have a choice. Will you listen to Mr. Darcy?"

"You do not know what you are asking, Charlotte. I will not be his fool again."

"Well, I know better than to press you when your mind is made up, but I think you are making a mistake. But he was not the only reason I wished to speak to you."

"What else?" Elizabeth said wearily.

The words began to tumble out of Charlotte's mouth. "Truly, Lizzy, you cannot know how glad I am that you have come, quite apart from the matter of Mr. Darcy. I have longed not only to see you, but to hear more of what happened to Maria. All I have had is tidbits of information in letters from my mother, and no doubt most of the worst left out, and it is difficult not to know the entire story."

Elizabeth spread her fingers on her knees. Just what she did not want to think about – Mr. Darcy's efforts on Maria's behalf. "I do not know how much I can tell you, as I left Longbourn only a fortnight after you did."

"But you were there, during the worst of it. What happened?"

"I did not see her myself, though I heard from several people how she appeared on High Street after the blizzard, disheveled and in deep distress. Your mother kept her secluded at Lucas Lodge after that, even after Mr. Chamberlayne offered for her. It did nothing to quell the gossip, since he had been stranded in town with everyone else, and so it was well known he was not among those who compromised her. I was glad for Maria's sake when I heard he was to be transferred to Norfolk."

Charlotte's brow furrowed. "Poor Maria! It is such a strange case, and I cannot make it out at all. My mother wrote that Chamberlayne must have been in love with her all along, but I had never seen him show the least interest in her. He was always amiable, but he never flirted with her. He told Maria openly he had been given money and a promotion in exchange for offering for her, and she assumes it was our father who did it, though he denies it. Had it been him, he would have owned it to us privately, but it does not seem the sort of thing he would do. His idea was to send Maria away. But who else could it have been? I even suspected your father, but I doubt he could spare the funds."

Elizabeth was not about to reveal the answer to that question, not with Charlotte already taking Mr. Darcy's side. *I have cleaned up George Wickham's messes more times than I can count, but I can do nothing for her if I do not know her name.* "It would not have been my father. Whoever it may be, I am grateful he did it, and I hope Maria will be able to find happiness in her marriage." Even if her gratitude was grudging.

"She misses home terribly and finds Norfolk depressing. I try to write her as often as I can to ease her loneliness. It seems all of her friends from Meryton have broken off the connection."

"Even Kitty? I am sorry to hear that." Elizabeth had been fortunate, since her closest confidantes had been Jane and Charlotte, and neither of them had cast her off when the rumors began. She would have to speak to Kitty about writing to Maria. "Is her husband treating her well?"

"Apparently so, and that raises an even more curious question. I have no reason to think Chamberlayne would have been unkind in any case, but it seems whoever arranged for his proposal also agreed he will receive fifty pounds per year so long as Maria is happy and well-treated. And *that* is something my father certainly would not think to do."

Mr. Darcy must take the task of cleaning up Wickham's problems very seriously indeed – and had considered the possibility that a man bribed to marry Maria could easily desert or mistreat her. But if he did so much for Maria, whom he did not even know, why had he not honored his word to her?

The pain in her palms made her realize she was digging her fingernails into them. She would never understand Mr. Darcy. And despite her sympathy with Charlotte's concern over Maria, she would not be in a hurry to forgive Charlotte for putting her in this position.

In the morning, Elizabeth opened the wardrobe and stared at her trunk. It would not take long to pack it, since she had not fully unpacked it the day before owing to the need to be prompt for dinner at Rosings. Had she known whom she would discover there, she would have asked to remain at the parsonage instead.

The worst part was how her heart and her body kept betraying her. When she had realized Mr. Darcy was in the same room, her first impulse had been to throw herself into his arms. The urge to be near him, to touch him, gnawed at her all evening. And her heart wanted nothing more than to forgive him, to believe this had all been a terrible mistake and he was still willing to marry her. And according to Charlotte, he was.

But even if it were true, being willing was a long way from wanting to marry her. Now matters between them were even more unequal than during the snowstorm, because she had been fool enough to fall in love with him. If she did marry him, all the power would be his, and she would be devastated when his interest wandered from her, as inevitably it would.

Her father had been faithful to her mother, but that had been more a matter of his lethargy than anything else. Finding a mistress was too much work for him to be willing to undertake it. It would be no trouble at all for Mr. Darcy; all he would need was to crook his finger and women would come running to him.

Elizabeth bent forward over her knees as nausea roiled her innards. No, willingness to marry was not enough, tempting as it might be to accept the scraps he would offer.

And *why* was he suddenly willing, anyway? He admitted to receiving her letter and speaking to her father, but had done nothing about it. Then, on his arrival at Rosings, he became suddenly anxious to see her, but not anxious enough to travel to Cheapside to do it. Charlotte's argument fell apart there. He had received her letter so he knew where she was. Had it been merely for his convenience he had wanted her brought here? For that matter, if it was beneath his dignity to go to Gracechurch Street, why had he not tried to send for her himself long before he saw Charlotte?

Charlotte. That must be the answer. As long as he felt safe from gossip tainting his good name, he had not pursued her. Then he had come to Rosings and discovered there was someone who could expose his behavior; a woman whose husband could not be kept quiet for an hour with a leather gag, much less for the rest of his life, a woman who had nearly lost a sister to scandal and would thus be doubly protective of her friend in the same situation. From his point of view, Charlotte would have every reason to expose him. And abruptly he had reverted to wanting to marry her. *Willing* in this case meant *barely willing*.

Poor Charlotte, knowing nothing of her father's call on Mr. Darcy, had misinterpreted his distress as violent love when it was nothing more than fear for his good name. And Charlotte claimed she was not romantic!

Elizabeth picked up her brush and began tugging it through her hair, wishing it were as easy to make a decision as it was to yank the brush through a tangle. It hurt for a minute, and then it was done. But what was she to do about the tangle which was Mr. Darcy? And why did she have to remember how he had combed out her hair in the cottage, then kissed her neck?"

Her first impulse, leaving Kent, was not a solution. As long as he feared his secret would be exposed, he would come after her. Charlotte had been right about one thing, though, which was she had to tell him her choice directly. If he proposed and she refused, no one could say he had not done the honorable thing. Then she could return to London, but she still would not be free. She would have to marry Mr. Hartshorne to quell the scandal. He would never break her heart, but he also could not provide her a home in her beloved countryside. She would be trapped in London forever, with only an occasional excursion to remind her of what she had lost.

Or she could accept Mr. Darcy's proposal and

face the heartbreak of a lifetime with a man who had no respect for her, but at least it would be a life of ease and provide the freedom to travel. He presumably would not care if she wished to stay at Longbourn when he was in London. In fact, he might be happier that way, free of the responsibility of a wife who was an embarrassment to him.

If only she did not care for him! Or was that, perhaps, something she could change? She had fallen in love with the man she thought him to be on those three days, and now she knew more of his flaws. Could she convince her heart not to hold him so dear? Perhaps if she could look at it as an arranged marriage, it would be tolerable.

But even in an arranged marriage, some mutual respect was necessary. Perhaps the first step would be to convince him to tell her the truth. Hearing from his own lips he had intended to abandon her just might be enough to convince her traitorous heart and body he was nothing but an ordinary man, as selfish as any other.

Darcy hoped to escape to the parsonage and Elizabeth early the next morning, so he breakfasted in his room to avoid having to deal with his aunt. Apparently he did not walk past the sitting room quickly enough, though, since Lady Catherine snapped, "Darcy, there you are! I especially wished to speak to you this morning. Why were you not at breakfast?"

Resignedly he stepped just inside the sitting room. Richard was already there, wearing a long-suffering expression. Darcy said, "I beg your pardon. I did not realize you had plans." And if her plans included him, he had no intention of cooperating with them. Not today.

"Well, you are here now. You know what I wish to discuss."

"Actually, I have not the slightest idea."

She narrowed her eyes. "Do not be coy. It is far past time for you to announce your engagement."

Darcy stiffened. How had she discovered about Elizabeth? Had she arranged for someone to watch his every move? But it made no sense. She should be horrified by his desire to marry a country nobody. Unless... "Are you by chance referring to your daughter?"

"Of course I am speaking of Anne!"

Why did she have to choose this moment for their annual argument? "We have discussed this before, and my views have not changed. I have no intention of marrying my cousin, either now or in the future. I hope I have made myself perfectly clear."

"Nonsense. You have been promised to her since you were in your cradle. I have stood by while you sowed your wild oats and learned to manage Pemberley, but now it is time. Anne is 27 years old. You cannot afford to wait until she is past her childbearing years."

"Then you must find some other man for her to marry. It will not be me. I do not feel bound by any agreement to which I was not party, and I will not marry to please you or anyone else – as I have said many times before."

"Your mother would have something to say about that, young man! She would be ashamed of you."

"Perhaps she would, but I would give her the same answer. As it happens, I have already chosen the lady I intend to wed, and it is not your daughter. By this time next year, I will be married, and we will be spared having this discussion ever again. I wish you good day." He turned to leave.

"Stop right there, young man! You owe me this." She all but hissed the words.

He looked back at her incredulously. "I owe you no such thing."

"Your father was supposed to marry *me*. It was all arranged. Pemberley should have been mine, but at the last minute, he chose Anne in my stead."

"I have heard this story a thousand times. I am not responsible for decisions made by my father before I was even conceived."

She pushed herself up from her chair, her arms trembling as they supported her. "They all promised me! My father, your father, and Anne – that if I had a daughter, she would marry their son, and my grandchildren would have Pemberley."

"May I point out that my father obviously did not feel himself bound to honor the betrothal set up by *his* parents? Why should I feel obligated to do something my father would not?" His hands tightened into fists.

"It is not the same at all! He still married into the family. If I had two daughters, and you wanted the younger one instead of the elder, I would accept that.

But Anne is all I have."

"I am very sorry for your disappointment, and that my father and grandfather made promises they were not in a position to keep, but it makes no difference. I honor you as my aunt, but I *will not* marry your daughter, and that is the end of it." He stalked away, ignoring her as she furiously called his name.

Richard followed at his heels. "That was certainly unpleasant. I suggest we absent ourselves from the premises until our aunt reverts to her usual level of irritability."

Darcy did not slacken his pace toward the front door. "I am going to pay a call at the parsonage. You may exercise Bucephalus if you wish." With any luck, Richard would prefer a long ride to the prospect of spending time with Mr. and Mrs. Collins.

"Trying to rid yourself of me, are you? You must be planning another assignation with Mrs. Collins."

"Richard, for the last time, I am *not* having assignations with Mrs. Collins."

"It is so pleasantly simple to annoy you, cousin! Have you really promised yourself to another woman, or was that simply an attempt to put a final end to the discussion of marrying Anne?"

Trust Richard to remember that bit and gnaw at it like a bulldog! It could hardly remain secret long, though, especially if Richard insisted on trailing after him constantly. "I am not at present engaged, but I have fixed my mind on the lady I wish to marry."

"And you do not wish to tell me who she is, it

seems! Does she know of her good fortune yet, or are you planning to surprise her with the news? If you have been courting anyone, I have failed to notice it. Do I know her?"

"Do you plan to question me until you are able to narrow down the possibilities from every lady in England?"

"You must admit it would be amusing, and would pass the time far better than playing cards with our dear cousin whom you have just jilted."

"Not you as well! You know I have never said I would marry Anne. In fact, I have denied it repeatedly."

"Does Anne know that?"

Darcy stopped in his tracks. "I do not know. I have never done her the discourtesy of saying so to her face, but she must have heard it by now."

"For her sake, I hope that is the case. If she has believed her mother's fairy stories, she may be in for a rude shock."

Why must he think about Anne's sentiments right now, when every instinct was urging him toward the parsonage and Elizabeth? He had been champing at the bit since the previous day, trying to recall her every look and word, and to read into them what she was thinking. But it was hopeless. He had never understood why Elizabeth made the choices she did.

"I will deal with Anne when I must. For now, I am off to pay my call. I will return before dinner."

"Oh, no, cousin! I am going with you. You are up to some mischief, and I intend to discover what it is."

"No, you intend to be a nuisance and drive me to distraction. That is what you mean," grumbled Darcy.

"Oh, well put!" said his cousin.

Chapter 15

DARCY'S IMPATIENCE TO SEE Elizabeth grew greater as they approached the parsonage. He could still hardly believe she was truly there. Even his skin prickled with awareness at the thought of her.

Richard's voice flowed past him, making him aware his cousin had been speaking for some time. "I beg your pardon. I was woolgathering and missed what you said."

His cousin laughed. "That much was obvious. I was merely wondering what our aunt is doing now, and whether we should expect her to swoop down on us like a Valkyrie from Valhalla."

"Heaven forfend," said Darcy dryly. "She is quite formidable enough without the addition of supernatural powers."

They turned up the path to the parsonage in greater accord, Darcy all but counting the seconds.

In the parsonage sitting room, Colonel Fitzwilliam so quickly engaged Charlotte in a conversation that Elizabeth strongly suspected the maneuver had been planned by his cousin. Mr. Darcy's immediate approach to her seemed only to confirm it. Well, she had no intention of giving him the satisfaction of knowing he had the power to hurt her. She made a point of not looking at him when he sat next to her.

Without preliminaries, he said in a low, pained voice, "Do you think I did not do enough for your friend's sister? Was the man chosen for her unsuitable?"

It was so startlingly unexpected she forgot her resolve and looked at him. "No, he was suitable." That must sound remarkably ungrateful after his extraordinary efforts for Maria Lucas, so she added, "You were very generous, and I thank you for that." It would do; she had said it as ungraciously as possible, but at least she had said it, and that debt was paid.

"Then why? I know I have failed to understand your intentions on various occasions, but I have read through your letter dozens of time, and for the life of me I cannot find anything to explain why you would want nothing to do with me." He unfolded a sheet of paper and pushed it into her hand. "Show me what is wrong. I deserve that much."

It was the first letter she had written him, the one sent via his man Mr. Stanton, full of teasing about onion soup and thanks for his kindness to Maria. Why had he brought it with him to Rosings? She folded it slowly and handed it back to him. "Not that letter," she said flatly. Her anger kept her from bursting into tears. "The one my father gave to you."

"But your father gave me no letter." He sounded genuinely bewildered.

For a moment hope soared in her, but then she remembered what Charlotte had told her. "I might even have believed you did not receive it, but I have evidence enough to know not to believe what you say. If the letter did not reach you, how did you discover there was a scandal?"

His brows drew together. "Stanton told me. He discovered it when he traveled to Meryton to make the final settlements for Miss Lucas. Is that what the letter was about? I have been losing sleep for weeks over why you never contacted me as you promised."

She shook her head. "That is not all. Charlotte told me you claim to have called at my uncle's house and been told Jane had left for the country. Unfortunately for you, I happen to know that was untrue. Jane is still there, even as we speak."

He held his hands out palm up. "I have no explanation. I *did* call at your uncle's house and sent in my card to Miss Bennet. Shortly afterwards, your uncle came out and told me she had returned to Longbourn. I do not know why he did that, but I am telling you the truth."

"So you accuse my uncle of lying? What would he stand to gain by it? No, Mr. Darcy, I am afraid I cannot credit your story." But she could also not keep her composure much longer, so she stood quickly, her skirts rustling, and moved a chair so she could sit as close as possible to Charlotte. He would not dare to attempt a private conversation there.

She tried to focus on the conversation between Charlotte and the colonel, if for no other reason than to avoid thinking about the man sitting across the room. She could feel the weight of his eyes on her.

The colonel said, "Your husband seems inordinately proud of his garden."

Charlotte smiled demurely. "I encourage him in that. The fresh air is good for his health."

"Indeed, it is good for all of us. Miss Bennet, your friend was telling me you are a great walker. There are many fine walks to explore in the area."

"How delightful. You must know it well." It was not much of a response, but it was something.

"I explore when I can. I am very partial to Kentish scenery, which is fortunate for me as I was recently stationed at Folkestone. It proved a most pleasing location."

Charlotte said, "I know little of Folkestone except it is by the sea."

"Our encampment is actually at the top of the cliffs overlooking the channel. The winter winds there are fierce, but the view over the water is unmatched. I often walk along the beaches there as well."

"I have heard sea air is most invigorating." Charlotte glanced at Elizabeth.

"I hope you will be able to experience it yourself soon," said the colonel. "We are not far from the coast here."

Elizabeth jumped when Darcy spoke. "Miss Elizabeth has also never seen the sea."

She swallowed hard. "Alas, unless you refer to a sea of snow, it is true."

Richard rubbed his hands together. "We must do something about that, then. Darcy, do you think it would it be possible to arrange an outing? Folkestone is but ten miles hence."

Elizabeth prayed he would say no. A day in a carriage with him would be unbearable.

"My carriage is at your service." There was no animation in his voice.

Charlotte glanced sidelong at Elizabeth. "That is a generous offer, Mr. Darcy."

Why was he playing the part of the injured party? Was she supposed to take pity on him and tell him she understood why he had refused to marry her? He would be in for a surprise if he hoped for that. Why was he pursuing her anyway? If only he could simply leave her alone!

"Miss Elizabeth." Darcy cleared his throat. "I was surprised to discover you bear more of a resemblance to your uncle than to either of your parents. I was struck by it when I met him. He has the same dark hair, though his is straight and has gone full silver at the temples. He is tall, although not so tall as Richard. But it is in his face I could truly see the resemblance. The shape is similar, especially around the chin, but the most notable thing was his eyes. I did not appreciate it until he removed his spectacles, but his eyes have the same tip-tilted shape as yours, although his are not as dark. Like yours, his face shows a tendency toward laughter, even when he is discussing a serious matter. He wore a blue waistcoat embroidered with entwining vines. It made me wonder if he enjoyed nature as much as you do." His voice was frighteningly level.

Colonel Fitzwilliam laughed. "Why, you are becoming an artist in your old age, Darcy! I have never known you to take so much notice of details of someone's appearance."

Darcy did not look at him, his eyes still fixed on her. "I have always noticed these things. I simply do not usually bore people with such a recitation unless there is a purpose. I could also mention the flowerpots with daffodils on each side of the doorway, while the window boxes had a mixture of blue and yellow flowers."

Elizabeth drew in a shaky breath. So he *had* been to Gracechurch Street and met her uncle – and she had accused him of lying. He could not have imagined all those details. But it still made no sense. Why would her uncle send him away when Jane was there – or could it be he wished to prevent him from discovering Elizabeth was there as well as Jane? Her uncle was an honest man, but he would not be above concocting a polite story to safeguard one of his relations. Except she had not wished to be safeguarded from Mr. Darcy. She had been longing for him. Could it also be true he had not received her letter? Had her father lied to her?

Over the pounding of her heart, she said, "I withdraw my accusation. I will grant you have met my uncle and seen his house."

Darcy nodded once, slowly. "And the rest?"

How could she answer with Charlotte and the colonel staring at them, as well they might with this extraordinary discussion? Her stomach turned somersaults, while fear and a dizzying hope warred within her. "I...I do not know."

Charlotte interposed hastily, "I have never visited your uncle's house, but I know you always enjoy visiting it, Lizzy."

She could not bear to look at Mr. Darcy's stern face, so she dropped her gaze to her folded hands. "Yes, I do. They have been very welcoming to me," she said softly. "The window boxes have forget-me-nots and violas."

Darcy made a sound which was almost a cough. When Elizabeth peeked at him he was looking questioningly at Charlotte, who shrugged lightly.

The sudden high-pitched scream of an animal in pain put a halt to the conversation. Charlotte, looking relieved at the interruption, jumped to her feet and peered out the window. "What do you suppose it was? I cannot see anything."

Colonel Fitzwilliam's face was pale. "It was a horse. I am certain of it."

"We have no stables here," said Charlotte.

Darcy strode to join her at the window. "It must be a traveler, then. Did you hear which direction it came from?"

Charlotte shook her head. "I am not certain. But wait – it looks as if someone is coming down the road. We shall know soon enough."

Darcy looked back at Colonel Fitzwilliam. "It might not have been a horse. It could have been a child."

"It was a horse. I have heard enough horses scream in battle to know whereof I speak. It is not a sound one forgets."

"He is coming here. I will…"

But the maid was ahead of whatever Charlotte was planning. There was no knock, so she must have opened the door to him right away, and brought the visitor to her mistress.

He was a child of no more than ten, panting heavily. "You must come quickly. 'Tis a terrible accident!" He leaned forward, his hands on the front of his thighs, gasping for breath.

"Where?" asked Darcy.

"At the bend in the road, by the stream. 'Tis very bad."

"Come, Richard," said Darcy. "Ladies, pray excuse us."

They were out the door before Elizabeth could even think to say farewell. "Should we go after them, do you think?" she asked Charlotte.

Her friend was already pulling on her gloves. "I must, but you may remain here if you wish."

She could not let Mr. Darcy go without any further explanation. "No, I will come with you. Perhaps I can help somehow."

On the road in front of the parsonage, the gentlemen were already far ahead of them, traveling at a run. Elizabeth wished she could do the same, but Charlotte was the rector's wife and had to set an example. Still, their pace was quick.

Charlotte said, "This was bound to happen

sooner or later. The stream bank has been undercut for some time and the lane crumbling at the edge. Mr. Darcy said he had spoken to Lady Catherine about the need to repair it, but she has been unwilling to spend the money. I hope this will be enough to make her see differently."

"Why is it Mr. Darcy's business to care for the roads here?"

"He advises her on estate matters, though I expect she rarely follows his advice. She has strong opinions of her own. I suspect she only asks him do it because of her hopes he will one day marry her daughter."

The words were enough to shock Elizabeth. "Oh, yes, Mr. Collins told me something of that once."

With a glance of keen observation, Charlotte said, "There is nothing to it, Lizzy. I have seen the two of them together and he has no interest in her. And surely you cannot now doubt he has strong feelings for you."

"I do not see..."

"Oh, dear God!" cried Charlotte. "That is Lady Catherine's carriage!" She kilted up her skirts and began to run.

Elizabeth hurried after her. A large, ornate carriage lay on its side half way in the stream, its side shattered in. Two horses scrabbled wildly just above it, their reins a tangled mess, as Darcy and Colonel Fitzwilliam struggled to hold them back.

Darcy spotted them first and raised his voice. "Mrs. Collins, could you assist Lady Catherine? We cannot let these horses loose."

"Of course." With no attention to propriety, Charlotte half-slid down the bank and approached the carriage from the back where she would be safe from the crazed horses. She had to struggle to unlatch the carriage door at its unnatural angle. "Lady Catherine? It is Mrs. Collins. May I assist you out?"

Elizabeth could not hear the words of the reply, just the annoyance of the tone.

"Very well, I will climb in." Somehow Charlotte managed to scramble on top of the fallen coach and then lowered herself inside.

Elizabeth saw then why the gentlemen were holding back the horses. Just beyond them lay a man in livery, curled up on the ground and moaning. She hurried to his side and crouched beside him. The clear mark of a horse's hoof showed on his face. "Are you able to move?" she asked him.

"I cannot," he whispered. "Oh, dear God, how it hurts!"

She looked up at Darcy. "He cannot move."

"Ask him if he has a pistol or a rifle."

She bent close to his face again and repeated the question, odd as it might be.

"On… on the bench."

She relayed the words to Darcy.

He frowned, then said, "I am sorry to ask this of you, Elizabeth, but I cannot let go of this horse. Could you attempt to find it for me?"

"Yes." It was easier to say than do. After circling around the wildly kicking horses, she had to hold onto a sapling to climb down the bank, but it was simple from there. The pistol was on the bench, just as the coachman had said it would be. She reached out for the strap holding the holster, but stopped when she heard Darcy's worried voice.

"Be careful, Elizabeth! It is most likely loaded, and possibly cocked."

With somewhat greater care, she unbuckled the strap and gently lifted the pistol, holster and all. She did not want her fingers anywhere near the trigger. Holding it in both hands, she carried it over to Darcy. Only then did it occur to her to wonder why he wanted it.

His eyes shone. "I thank you. And now I must ask you to stand back and look away."

Those were instructions she had no hesitation in following, closing her eyes for good measure.

Darcy said quietly, "I am sorry, Richard. It would have to be done anyway. His leg is broken."

"Just do it," his cousin snapped.

The crack of the pistol echoed in the crisp air, the smell of burnt gunpowder incongruously reminding Elizabeth of when she as a child would run to meet her father on his return from a hunting expedition. But the simple days of childhood were far behind her.

Suddenly she realized she had heard nothing from Charlotte since she entered the carriage. Keeping her eyes away from the fallen horse, she hurried past the colonel, who still held the head of the living horse while Darcy sawed through the entangling reins with a knife. "Charlotte, do you need assistance?"

"Not now." Her friend's voice was oddly heavy. Then Charlotte's drawn face appeared through the open door of the coach. "Lady Catherine is dead."

Chapter 16

IN THE SHOCKED silence following Charlotte's announcement, Elizabeth numbly returned to the injured coachman. His injuries seemed to be internal apart from scrapes and bruises, so there was little she could do for him beyond speaking gently and telling him help would be there soon, but it seemed better than nothing.

Mr. Darcy had approached the overturned carriage and was speaking urgently but quietly to Charlotte as Colonel Fitzwilliam attempted to calm the remaining horse. It seemed like an eternity before two beefy farmers hurried up to the coach.

Darcy said, "No, leave it. Take care of the coachman first. There is nothing you can do for Lady Catherine now."

Elizabeth stood back to allow the men to pick up the coachman and carry him off to a nearby farmhouse. The jolting movement made him howl with pain.

Then Darcy was by her side. He took her hand in his, and she did not resist. After this nightmarish scene, she was glad of the comfort, and he must need it even more than she did. He had lost his aunt, while Lady Catherine had been nothing to her apart from the object of Mr. Collins's fawning. If only she could embrace him! But there were too many people watching, and he was presuming already by holding her hand and standing so close to her.

"Would you assist me with something?" he said in her ear.

"Of course. Anything." After the words had already left her mouth, she realized how unwise they might have been.

He chuckled softly. "And just when I cannot take advantage of it. Do not fret. I am only asking you to spend some time talking to Richard."

"Colonel Fitzwilliam?" She tilted her head to one side. Why would he be asking this as a favor?

"Yes. He needs someone to distract him. Talk to him about anything – Longbourn, your favorite birds, some place you visited in London – as long as it has nothing to do with war, guns, death or horses. Keep talking even if he seems not to be listening. I will explain later."

She recalled the frozen look on the Colonel's face after Darcy had shot the horse. "No need to explain. I have met soldiers before who are still fighting old battles."

He tightened his grip on her hand. "Thank you. I must stay here until everything is taken care of, but he should not. Take him away from here – perhaps to the parsonage? He should not have to inform Anne of her mother's death."

"I will."

"And Elizabeth?" His voice deepened.

"Yes?"

"When there is time, will you permit me to call on you?"

She let out a long breath she had not realized she was holding. "Yes. Yes, I will."

He closed his eyes for a brief moment, then opened them. "Thank you." With apparent reluctance he released her hand. It was just as well; she did not need her reputation ruined in Kent as well as Hertfordshire.

How could everything have changed so quickly?

Colonel Fitzwilliam stood beside the tethered horse, one booted foot scuffing the ground. He looked up at Elizabeth's approach, but his smile did not reach his eyes.

"Colonel, might I impose upon you to escort me back to the parsonage? I am feeling quite faint, and I prefer not to attempt to make my way there alone." Looking as if she was on the verge of swooning was not among Elizabeth's talents, but she did her best.

His shoulders straightened and he offered her his arm. "It would be my pleasure, Miss Bennet."

On the short walk she managed to ask a number of questions about the immediate area and his previous visits to Kent. Once they reached the parsonage, she realized the problem with using faintness as her excuse when he suggested she rest for a while.

Thinking quickly, she said, "I would rather not. It would only make my mind turn to what happened. If you do not object, conversation about other things distracts me better than anything else. Mr. Darcy has told me of his cousins with whom he lived for a time as a child. Were you part of that family?"

"Yes, that was my family. He lived with us, then I lived with him and his father for a time."

"Then you must be the cousin who learnt to light fires in a cave."

He bowed his head in acknowledgment. "Indeed I was. I hope Darcy did not tell you how long it took us to figure out the obvious."

"I believe he skipped that part and focused more on your successes than your failures."

"How very generous of him! Tell me, how do you come to know Darcy?"

"We met when he visited Hertfordshire, and stayed not far from my own home."

"And you conversed enough to discuss our old cave haunt, did you? You must know him rather well, then."

Elizabeth's throat constricted. "Not well, but we conversed on several occasions. During one of them he told me about his family – his stepmother, his adventures living with you, his sister. That sort of thing."

The colonel's smile seemed to freeze in place. "Darcy told you about his stepmother?"

"I am sorry; should I not have mentioned her?"

"Not at all. It is simply that Darcy never speaks of her if he can avoid it, so I was rather surprised."

She needed to take care before she revealed just

how much she and Darcy had shared. "Only in passing, as part of his explanation of how your father came to take him in for his safety. He said very little about her."

Colonel Fitzwilliam tugged at his cravat. "He told you about what she did?" he asked disbelievingly.

"Just a mention of it. It was quite insignificant."

"If Darcy so much as alluded to it, it was far from insignificant. I have never known him to speak of that, even to me."

Was it true? "I must have caught him at an unusually loquacious moment, then. I am sure it signifies nothing. I only recall it because of my surprise when he said he had liked his stepmother. She did not sound at all likeable to me."

The colonel was looking at her oddly. "I barely knew her, but Darcy loved her. At least until he came to live with us. You say you met Darcy in Hertfordshire?"

This at least was safer ground. "His friend, Mr. Bingley, had just taken a lease on a house a few miles from my own, and Mr. Darcy was his guest there."

"That would be the same time he first met Mrs. Collins, then."

"Yes, she was another neighbor. Mr. Darcy and I both attended gatherings at her father's house, Lucas Lodge." That was good – putting Charlotte in the center of the story distracted from her own role in it. "She met Mr. Collins, my cousin, around the same time. I was very sorry to lose her from the neighborhood."

"How fortunate you can visit her here, then." He watched her carefully.

The sound of the front door closing precluded any need to answer. Mr. Collins's sturdy form appeared in the doorway, his hat in his hand.

"What is all this nonsense? People running back and forth, no maid at the door. And where is my wife?" Then his tone changed suddenly from annoyance to servility. "I beg your pardon, Colonel Fitzwilliam; I did not see you there. Pray permit me to welcome you to my humble abode. I hope my cousin Elizabeth has been seeing to your comfort. Cousin, surely you have not been alone with the colonel all this time?"

So the news had not reached him yet. Colonel Fitzwilliam had gone pale again. To spare him the pain of delivering the ill tidings, Elizabeth said, "I fear we have tragic and shocking news to impart. There has been a terrible accident. Lady Catherine's carriage overturned just up the road. The coachman was gravely injured; and I am very sorry to report Lady Catherine did not survive."

Mr. Collins, apparently unable to comprehend her words, said, "Lady Catherine? Oh, no, Cousin Elizabeth. You must have misunderstood. Nothing of the sort could possibly befall her."

"Indeed I wish it were so, but it is not. Colonel Fitzwilliam can vouch for my veracity. Charlotte was with Lady Catherine when she breathed her last, and she remains on the scene to offer what assistance and comfort she may, as befits a rector's wife."

His mouth fell open. "It cannot be! Not Lady Catherine!" His eyes bulged almost comically. He looked more bereft than either of Lady Catherine's nephews had.

"I am very sorry for your loss," she said.

"Where is she? I must go to her at once! Lady Catherine would be most displeased if I were not at her side."

Elizabeth refrained from pointing out Lady Catherine was beyond being displeased. "The carriage is just beyond the bend in the road. I imagine she may still be there."

"She cannot be permitted to remain out in the open! It is an insult to her dignity. I…"

He was interrupted by Charlotte's tired voice coming from behind him. "She is being borne to Rosings as we speak."

Mr. Collins spun around. "My dear Charlotte! Why, are you injured? You must take better care."

Charlotte looked down at her skirts. "The blood is not mine, but Lady Catherine's, poor lady."

"It is most unsuitable for a rector's wife to appear so in public!"

"Indeed it is," said Charlotte soothingly. "That is why I returned here as soon as I could be spared from her ladyship's side. But should you not be at Rosings? I am certain Miss de Bourgh will be in need of your comfort."

He clasped his hands together. "Oh, you are quite correct, my dear! I must go immediately. Pray excuse me, Colonel Fitzwilliam, Cousin Elizabeth, but duty calls!" He clapped his hat on his head and rushed off.

The colonel rose to his feet slowly. "I should

return as well, now that Mrs. Collins is here. On my family's behalf as well as my own, I thank you both for your timely assistance today." At least his color had improved again.

Elizabeth curtsied to him. "I am in your debt for your kindness in assisting me back."

"I am always at your service." He bowed and took his leave.

Charlotte mopped her forehead with her sleeve. "What a terrible day!"

Elizabeth took her arm. "Come, you must change into a clean dress. I will assist you."

"Thank you. Who knows when the maid will return?"

Elizabeth followed her friend as she trudged upstairs. Once in the bedroom, she could feel Charlotte trembling as she undid the small buttons down the back of her dress. "You must be exhausted. I cannot imagine what it was like for you to be with Lady Catherine at the end."

Charlotte stepped carefully out of the dress. "It could have been worse. At first she was simply cursing the driver and Mr. Darcy. I did not realize her injuries were serious until the very end."

"She said nothing of it?" That was a surprise; she would have expected Lady Catherine to be vocal about such things.

"Just that her leg hurt; but her legs are always paining her, so I thought it was just the uncomfortable position. I helped her raise her feet out of the water, and that was when I saw she was bleeding. One of the struts had pierced her leg just beneath her hip. It must have struck the great artery, for as soon as she moved, the blood shot out. What a terrible sight! She pressed her hand over it, but would not permit me to attempt to staunch the flow, but there was nothing I could have done for a wound so wide and deep in any case. She was gone so quickly! The water beneath her ran red, as if it had turned to blood." Charlotte shivered.

"I am sorry you had to witness such a thing."

Charlotte poured water into a basin and began scrubbing her hands fiercely. "I have never been susceptible to nightmares, but I suspect tonight may prove the exception!"

Would her own nightmares be of the accident or of that terrible moment when she realized she had falsely accused Mr. Darcy? Silently she handed Charlotte a linen towel to dry her hands.

Her friend hunted through the wardrobe with shaking hands and pulled out a simple dressing gown. "All I want now is to sit in front of the fire with a cup of tea, and I daresay you would benefit from the same."

"Tea and a fire sound lovely." But a chance to talk to Mr. Darcy would be even better. Unfortunately, under the circumstances it might be some time before she had an opportunity to do so.

Richard motioned to Darcy to follow him down the passageway and into his bedroom. Once they were both inside, Darcy closed the door and leaned back against it. "That was distinctly odd."

His cousin was already reaching for the brandy

decanter. "To say the least." His hand shook slightly as he poured two glasses.

Darcy accepted one, but unlike Richard, did not drink it immediately. "I had always been under the impression Anne was quite fond of her mother."

"It certainly appeared that way to me, though I could not understand it myself. Even so, I would not have thought she would *smile* when we told her of Lady Catherine's demise."

With a frown, Darcy said, "That odd question she asked – about whether we were teasing her. How could she imagine we would tease about such a thing?"

"I have no idea. I suppose we should be grateful she did not have a fit of the vapors, but she did not seem to care in the slightest. I cannot say I know Anne well. She has always preferred to speak to her companion instead of me, but apparently I know her even less than I thought."

Darcy took a sip of the brandy and let it slide down his throat. "I always avoided speaking to her. Even looking in her direction could set Lady Catherine off on the advantages of a match between us. But I admit I am shocked by Anne's behavior today."

Richard drained his glass at a pace unsuited for brandy, then filled it again. "Speaking of being shocked, I take it the lovely Miss Bennet is the young lady towards whom you have intentions."

Darcy frowned. "Did she tell you that?"

"Not at all. I could say it was because of that odd conversation about her uncle, or because you used her Christian name and held her hand at the carriage wreck. But I was uncertain until I learned you had told her the tale of your stepmother. *That* was as good as an announcement in the papers to my mind."

Of course. Elizabeth could not have known it was something he did not speak of. "I will not deny she is the woman I spoke of, but the matter is still undecided. As you saw earlier, we have yet to resolve certain matters."

"You are not certain you wish to marry her?" Richard asked sharply.

"*I* am certain, but I do not know what she wishes. We might have had the opportunity to sort it out today, but heaven only knows when that will happen now."

Richard nodded slowly, but the blankness had faded from his eyes, replaced by a thoughtful look.

The parsonage was quiet. Mr. Collins had not yet returned from Rosings Park. Charlotte was busy trimming her mourning clothes and sewing black armbands for the servants. Elizabeth had tried to help, but Charlotte had gently told her to read her book when it became clear she was too unsettled to keep her thoughts on any tasks.

Concentrating on her book, however, was impossible. All Elizabeth could think of was her interrupted conversation with Mr. Darcy.

If he had told the truth about calling at the Gardiners' house, then she had to also believe his claim that her father had not given him her letter. If only there had been enough time to ask him what her father had said to him!

Perhaps she should write her father and demand the truth. No, that would solve nothing. Even if her father admitted to it, it might take weeks before he bothered to respond to a letter. But there was someone whom she could ask about part of Mr. Darcy's story.

"Charlotte, is there somewhere I could write a letter?"

"Of course. There is a small desk in the back sitting room."

"Thank you." Glad for the excuse to escape Charlotte's sharp eyes, she hurried out.

There was paper and ink aplenty in the desk, though the quill needed sharpening. In her impatience, Elizabeth managed to split the pen when she attempted to mend it, but fortunately there was a second. This time she was more careful, and soon began to write.

Chapter 17

DARCY RUBBED HIS eyes with ink-stained fingers. Three letters done, which left only two dozen more. Thank God Richard was taking half of them. Anne had taken to her bed, but since she still showed no signs of distress, Darcy suspected it was nothing more than a ploy to avoid taking on her share of the work.

Knowing Elizabeth was just a short distance away at the parsonage was a constant distraction. He reached into his pocket to touch the worn ribbon. So much was left unresolved. How could she have thought he would lie to her? They had much to discuss, yet here he was, tied to a desk for the foreseeable future. But even if he were not, it would be inappropriate for him to leave a house of mourning to pay a social call. Lady Catherine would be delighted if she knew how much trouble she managed to cause even in death.

He checked the list the housekeeper had given him, then wrote the next name on a fresh sheet of paper. *I regret to inform you…*

Higgins knocked on the open door. "Mrs. Collins and Miss Bennet are calling. Shall I tell them you are not at home?"

That was what he *should* do. There was no time to waste on social calls, not with the stack of correspondence before him. But duty be damned! Why should he be forced to pay for Lady Catherine's failings? His breathing quickened. "Show them in, please."

The butler pursed his lips in an expression which had always meant he would be informing Lady Catherine of some unfortunate behavior on Darcy's part. Well, he could report it to Anne if he pleased. Had Higgins been employed at Pemberley, he would have been dismissed long ago for daring to judge his betters. "If that is what you wish, sir."

"If it were not what I wished, then why would I have said it?" snapped Darcy.

His back erect with offense, Higgins stalked off. Definitely dismissed without character! Darcy wished Anne joy with the staff she had inherited. Of course, she had never known anything else.

Mrs. Collins was dressed all in black, naturally, while Elizabeth seemed slightly muted in pale lavender. Half-mourning, even though she had only met his aunt once? It was respectful, certainly, but Darcy would have given a great deal to see her light up the room with color and laughter. Only one day and already he was weary of the funerary atmosphere. "Welcome, Mrs. Collins, Miss Bennet."

Mrs. Collins flashed a quick smile. "I know you must be very busy, so we will not trouble you with polite niceties. We came to pay our condolences, but also to see if we could be useful in any way."

If only he could ask for the thing which would

help most – to leave Elizabeth with him. "That is very kind of you, especially as we already imposed on you yesterday. I must again give you my thanks for your level-headed assistance at the scene of the accident."

Elizabeth's fine eyes were fixed on him. "It was the least we could do under the circumstances, and we would still be happy to be useful."

Just the sound of her voice soothed his nerves. It was too bad it would be inappropriate to ask for more of that.

Mrs. Collins's voice broke into his reverie. "It occurred to me Miss de Bourgh has no female relatives present to assist her in preparing the body, even if her health permits her to perform those duties. I would be glad to offer my services."

"Mrs. Collins, I must admit it would be a relief to me. My cousin has taken to her bed, leaving those duties to Mrs. Jenkinson. Since she cannot manage them on her own, the housekeeper has been assisting her, but I know my aunt would have preferred not to involve the servants directly in the preparations."

"I would be honored to be of assistance. Is there anything else? Lizzy has, of course, offered to assist with preparing the body as well, but as she only met Lady Catherine one time, I thought it would not be appropriate."

Elizabeth said, "Naturally I insisted on accompanying her here anyway in case I might be of use in some other manner." Her eyes seemed to send a different message, though. Or was it simply that he wanted so badly for her to have come to see *him*?

He locked gazes with her. "I am very glad you did so. Very glad, though I believe all other preparations are progressing well enough. Richard and I have nothing to complain of beyond excessive correspondence which will keep us busy most of the day."

Richard strode into the room. "And complain of it I shall! I feel as if I am back in the schoolroom. Good morning, ladies."

Mrs. Collins's brows drew together. "Is not Mr. Lymon available?"

Darcy scowled. "Lady Catherine's so-called secretary? I discovered this morning he is extremely gifted at the art of flattery, but cannot compose even the simplest letter without constant direction, and even then in barely adequate handwriting, certainly not suitable for formal correspondence."

Elizabeth's lips curved in a slight smile. "I am not a secretary, but I write a fair hand. If the letters are not of a personal nature, perhaps I could assist you."

He should not accept her offer. She was not part of the family yet, and he should not impose upon a gentlewoman to do a secretary's work. But it would give him an excuse to keep her by his side, and that was more precious to him than diamonds.

Thankfully, Richard seemed to have no such hesitations, "Miss Bennet, you must be an angel descended directly from heaven! I would be perpetually in your debt. Of course, Darcy can be a stern taskmaster, but I imagine you have ways to soothe the savage beast." He winked at Elizabeth.

Darcy said gravely, "If it would not be a great imposition, I would be most grateful for your assistance." She could not possibly imagine just how grateful he was.

On the following day, Mr. Collins did not return to the parsonage until dusk. "What a fine thing it is to return after a long day to my own humble abode! And what a day it has been! I daresay Lady Catherine would have been most pleased by it."

Charlotte set aside her work. "I am certain you led the funeral in an exemplary manner. Did you dine at Rosings, or shall we prepare something for you here?"

Mr. Collins puffed out his chest. "I did indeed dine at Rosings, and was invited to do so by no less a personage than Lord Matlock! His condescension almost equals that of Lady Catherine herself. I have no doubt he is universally acknowledged to be one of the greatest men in England."

Elizabeth hid a smile. She wondered how Mr. Collins would respond when he discovered she was to become Lord Matlock's niece. She could hardly credit it herself. The previous day they had no opportunity to speak privately, but Darcy's smiles and gentle touches on her arm as she had assisted him with his letters had assured her he did indeed intend to follow through on his long-ago promise to marry her. Even thinking of him made her want to hug herself.

Charlotte said, "That is an honor indeed! We watched as you and the other gentlemen in the funerary procession went past."

Elizabeth had only had eyes for Mr. Darcy. More than once she had seen him glance toward the parsonage. Had he been thinking of her?

Mr. Collins launched into a long soliloquy about the funeral service, including where each of the gentlemen stood by the graveside and their expressions during the crucial points of his prayer. "If I do say so myself, I believe it was one of my finest funerals! Lord Matlock seemed most impressed. He even said Lady Catherine had been fortunate to have me as a rector. Poor lady!"

Charlotte said soothingly, "It is a great loss to all of us, but most especially to you, since you knew her so well.

"It is true; I do feel it exceedingly. But I know she would be joyous tonight, for all of her plans will finally be realized! But I am going ahead of my story. After we adjourned to Rosings, the solicitor read Lady Catherine's will, which was, I imagine, quite a surprise to all the gentlemen. Lord Matlock clearly had not expected it." Mr. Collins rubbed his hands together.

"Why, what was so surprising? Did she not leave everything to Miss de Bourgh?"

"*That* was what everyone anticipated. But here is where Lady Catherine's true brilliance shines through! Miss de Bourgh will only receive her inheritance if she is married to Mr. Darcy within the year. If they do not wed, she will be left penniless, and Rosings will go to a distant cousin. Of course, Mr. Darcy could never permit his cousin to lose her inheritance, so Lady Catherine's dearest wish will soon be granted! Is that not the cleverest conceit you have ever heard, my dear?"

Elizabeth stared at him, her mouth dry. Could this be true? Mr. Darcy's sense of family responsibility was powerful. Had Lady Catherine after all managed to put a period to their plans from beyond the grave?

Charlotte shot her a concerned glance. "Most clever indeed. What did Mr. Darcy say when it was revealed?"

"Nothing at first, though he did not seem best pleased. Lord Matlock said he was certain Darcy knew his duty, and Mr. Darcy replied it was neither the time nor the place to discuss it. Once the solicitors were finished, he left and did not dine with the rest of us. No doubt he was already with Miss de Bourgh, who took dinner in her rooms."

Despite the hollow ache in her chest, Elizabeth could picture it – Darcy stalking off in a quiet rage to nurse his wounds in private. He must be furious at being placed in such a position. He could not have foreseen this any more than she had. Fate had played a cruel trick on them both.

"Lizzy, is your headache worse?" asked Charlotte. "Perhaps you should lie down and rest for a time."

"My headache? Oh, yes," said Elizabeth dully. "You are quite right. I shall go upstairs directly and rest."

If sobbing quietly into her pillow could be called resting, she rested for some time.

A letter from Gracechurch Street arrived at

Hunsford the following day while Charlotte was at Rosings with her husband. Elizabeth stared at it dully. Why bother to read it when the answers no longer made a difference? Her last hope had been that Mr. Darcy might contact her that morning. He must know Mr. Collins would have revealed the contents of the will. But no word had come.

With a sigh, she broke the seal on her aunt's letter.

> *My dearest Lizzy,*
>
> *As it happens, I do not need to apply to your uncle, as I am already aware of this matter. You had been here about a fortnight when Mr. Darcy called, asking to see our dear Jane. You and I were on an outing with the children when she received his card. Uncertain of the best course of action, especially since her acquaintance with him was too slender to warrant a call, she approached your uncle.*
>
> *In light of your situation, your uncle could only assume Mr. Darcy had called on Jane in order to discern your whereabouts. That he would take such a step rather than to approach your father suggested his interest was not an honorable one. Your uncle's first suggestion was for Jane to see him and tell him she was unsure where you were, and refer him to your father, but Jane doubted her ability to maintain such a deception. Your uncle, concerned you might return before Mr. Darcy departed, decided to direct him to Longbourn himself, and told Mr. Darcy Jane had already left us and was back at home. Mr. Darcy was clearly displeased by this intelligence, but made no quarrel with it.*

Afterwards, your uncle and I came to the conclusion it would be better for you remain unaware of the incident, as it could only cause you even more distress to discover Mr. Darcy planned to take advantage of your loss of reputation. If there have been unfortunate consequences of this decision, I am truly sorry. We made it with your best interests in mind.

So it *was* true. Not that she had really doubted it, at least not since the day of Lady Catherine's death, but it was different to know for certain – and just when it was too late.

If only her father had given him the letter, or the Gardiners told her of Mr. Darcy's visit, the one she had been so longing for, by now she would be firmly engaged, if not already married to him. Anger tightened her chest. The people who loved her had cost her the chance of happiness, and for the rest of her life, she would regret what she had lost. What she and Darcy had *both* lost, for she did not doubt he was feeling the same regrets for their lost future. How could her family have done this to her?

But the voice of her conscience could not be stilled. It was *her* fault as well. If she had accepted Mr. Darcy's proposal during the storm, or if she had gone with her father to call on Darcy, or even if she had told the Gardiners of her hopes and expectations, none of this would have happened. Her pride made her keep it a secret so no one could know of her disappointed hopes. Or if she had only listened to Mr. Darcy her first night in Kent, they might have reached an understanding then, and Lady Catherine would not have decided to race down a road to her death. No, her loss was at least as much her own fault, and she could blame no one but herself.

Now her punishment was upon her, and once more she must face facts. There was nothing to be gained by remaining in Kent except more heartbreak. It was hard enough to know Darcy must marry Miss de Bourgh without having to listen as he told her so. No, it would be better to leave with what few good memories remained intact – and before she weakened enough to hope for some limited contact with him.

But she could not leave him without a word. Setting down her letters, she crossed to the small writing desk and removed a sheet of paper. The quill did not need mending this time and the inkwell was full, so she had no excuse to delay. Taking a deep breath, she began to write.

Dear Mr. Darcy,

By now you will be aware I have left for London. Mr. Collins told me the terms of your aunt's will, and I fully understand your duty to your cousin must come ahead of the much more nebulous one to a woman in my position, especially one who has been as ungracious to you as I have during my stay in Kent. I would not expect you to make any other decision, so pray believe me when I say I understand.

As to my ungraciousness, I have received confirmation from London you did indeed call at my uncle's house as you said. Please accept my deepest apologies for disbelieving you.

She paused and tapped the quill against her lips. Should she leave it at that? There was so much more she wished to tell him, though it would serve no useful purpose. But there would never be anyone else she could unburden herself to, and she wanted him to know. He deserved it.

I would not have reacted so badly to seeing you had the previous months not been so painful. When the scandal first broke, I felt more relief than anything else because it gave me the excuse to write to you and accept your offer. I had not anticipated how much I would miss your companionship after the storm, nor understood how much my own sentiments towards you had changed. Once I wrote the letter my father was to give to you, I looked forward eagerly to reuniting with you.

I am still ignorant of what passed between you and my father, but when he told me he had met with you and you had no intention of marrying me, I had no reason not to believe him. I was devastated, though I could hardly blame you for it, but the distress it occasioned me was deep. The idea of never seeing you again was even more painful than the reality of dealing with my disgrace. I say these things not to cause you pain, but in the hope it may help you understand why I wanted nothing to do with you when I saw you again.

Eventually my grief turned to anger at being abandoned, as well as discovering you were not the man I believed you to be. I know now this was based on mistaken assumptions. When I saw you first at Rosings – Charlotte had given me no warning of your presence – I could only assume our meeting was mere happenstance, and likely an embarrassing reminder of an episode you would prefer to forget. I could not bear to face that, so I avoided you. When you confirmed you had received my letter, I lost my last sliver of hope you might be innocent of abandoning me. After that, I would not allow myself to hope, but I cannot express to you what a profound relief it was when you proved to me you had told the truth. It was a completely unexpected reprieve from a torment such as I hope never to experience again.

I wish I had the opportunity to tell you these things in person, but I believe we both understand it is better if we do not meet again. I plan to return to my uncle's house for the time being. Should you ever need to contact me, I will inform both Charlotte and my uncle they may give you my direction. As I do not understand my father's role in this, I plan to say nothing to him, but in any case, I do not foresee a future which would permit me to return to Longbourn.

I will only add, God bless you, and I hope your marriage to Miss de Bourgh may somehow bring you more happiness than you at present expect.

With deep & abiding affection & respect,
E. Bennet

Blinking back tears, she pushed the letter away and capped the inkwell before she gave into the temptation to bare her soul even more. She blotted her eyes fiercely with a handkerchief. This was not the time for to cry. There would be plenty of opportunity in London for tears. No, this was the time for action.

The first step was to pack her belongings. She pulled her trunk out of the wardrobe, yelping when it landed on her toes. How could an empty trunk weigh so much? She hopped to the chair on her good foot, then removed her slipper and sock. Her great toe was reddened and already beginning to swell, but she could move it easily enough she doubted there was any serious injury. Her toe appeared to disagree, given the discomfort caused by replacing her stocking.

She hobbled back to the wardrobe and glared at the trunk as she unlatched it and was met by a musty smell. Obviously it would need to air out before she packed it.

In any case, Charlotte was likely back from Rosings by now, and she might as well break the news to her. Walking on the heel of her injured foot made the trip down the stairs reasonably tolerable, although her toe continued to throb.

Charlotte was sorting through embroidery threads in her sitting room and humming under her breath. Her brows drew together when she spotted Elizabeth. "What is the matter, Lizzy?"

Elizabeth raised her foot a few inches. "I hurt my toe, but it is not serious. It will be better in an hour or two."

"That is not what I meant." Charlotte indicated her no doubt reddened eyes.

Bother it! She should have washed her face and waited for the evidence of tears to fade before she came down. "Just the usual," she said dismissively. "I have come to a decision that I will return to London tomorrow. I have written a letter of explanation to Mr. Darcy which I hope you will be kind enough to deliver to him on my behalf."

"Oh, but you cannot leave yet!" Charlotte sounded truly stricken.

Elizabeth closed her eyes for a moment to regain her composure. "I appreciate the sentiment, but you must understand I have no desire to be here when his engagement is announced."

"That is not what I meant. It is only that...oh, dear, it was meant to be a surprise, but I suppose I must tell you now. I had a long talk with Colonel Fitzwilliam, and he is planning to take us both to the seaside tomorrow. He has arranged for a carriage and rooms at an inn, and Miss de Bourgh has offered to let Mrs. Jenkinson come as our chaperone. She says Miss Holmes can stay with her just as easily and Mrs. Jenkinson would benefit from the sea air. The colonel is so excited about it, and I would feel terrible if we could not go after all the trouble he has taken to plan it."

Elizabeth wavered. It was a kind gesture on the colonel's part, and she wondered if he had guessed she would need some distraction. He certainly seemed to have suspicions about her history with Mr. Darcy. "I suppose I could wait until after that. After all, I would dearly love to see the sea." And perhaps it would give her time to regain some small bit of her spirits before returning to London.

Charlotte clapped her hands together.

"Wonderful! That is excellent news. Since now you know of the plans, you can help me decide what to bring. The colonel says it is colder at the seaside and the wind can be fierce, so we should be prepared for that."

The Earl of Matlock strode into the library. "Ah, Darcy. There you are. I want to talk to you about Anne."

"I do not intend to marry Anne."

"Now, there is no rush. With Anne in mourning, it will be half a year before she can marry you in any case. It would be best to take care of that as soon as possible, but that still gives you six months to enjoy your freedom."

"I am not marrying Anne at all. Not in six months, not ever." Darcy ostentatiously picked up a book and opened it.

There was an ominous silence, but Darcy refused to give Lord Matlock the satisfaction of looking up at him. Instead he slowly turned the pages, pretending to read.

"Darcy, no one wishes to see you forced into a marriage you do not want, but this is an unusual case. Your duty is absolutely clear."

"Lady Catherine knew she could count on you to say that. It was *her* duty to provide for her daughter."

"This is foolishness! Catherine was always obstinate and annoying, but she only wanted the best for Anne and for you. It is a good match on both sides, and Anne is family, so we know she is trustworthy. Still, I would support you in refusing her, but not at the cost of losing Rosings. It is an important asset."

"I do not need or want Rosings. Pemberley provides all I need."

"This is a duty to your family! We all benefit from the increased connections. And you know as well as I do that Pemberley needs an heir."

"My cousin John Darcy is Pemberley's heir."

"You would let Pemberley go to a distant cousin? Darcy, we sacrificed much to bring Pemberley into the Fitzwilliam fold, and it will all be wasted if you die without an heir. And think of poor Georgiana, thrust from her home!"

Darcy spoke through gritted teeth. "I have made certain Georgiana's dowry is untouchable and that she will have sufficient income for her lifetime. Richard helped with the arrangements, if you do not believe me."

Lord Matlock yanked the book from his hands, slammed it shut, and tossed it on the table. "Darcy, listen to me. Twenty years ago I took you into my home, at the cost of alienating not only your father but also *that woman's* very wealthy family. I barely knew you, but you were a Fitzwilliam, so I fought for the right to keep you safe. I have never asked anything from you in return. Tonight I am asking for something, asking for you to do your duty to our family in the same way I did for you. Marry Anne."

Darcy's hands clenched on the arms of the chair. This was the one appeal which could make him doubt himself. "I honor and respect you for all you have done for me and for your dedication to your family. I would do almost anything you asked, but I am sorry. I cannot do this." How fortunate it had proved that Elizabeth had been compromised by her actions in saving his life! Had it only been a matter of his love for her, he would have been hard pressed to deny his duty to his family and what he owed Lord Matlock merely for his own happiness. But Elizabeth *had* been compromised, so he had a competing duty to his honor, and his heart was grateful for it. But it would just create more problems if he told his uncle about Elizabeth. Family duty came ahead of honor to him.

His uncle's face grew red, and he smashed his fist onto the table. "Damn it, what is wrong with you? We stand to lose everything we have worked for in the last two generations! If we lose both Rosings and Pemberley, it will set us back decades. Do you know how hard I have worked all my life to regain our rightful position in society? And you will risk it over such a small thing?"

If only he had some brandy to ease his dry mouth! "Marriage is not a small thing, and you have not lost Pemberley. As for losing Rosings, Lady Catherine is at fault for that, not I."

"Do not speak ill of the dead!"

Richard poked his head in the door. "There you are, Darcy! Hiding from me?"

Lord Matlock pointed at him. "Out!" he roared.

With raised eyebrows and a deeply sympathetic look at Darcy, Richard backed away with an exaggerated tip-toeing movement. His father snorted at his retreating back and returned to his prey.

Charlotte opened the folded note and read it, then turned to the boy who had brought it. "Pray tell Colonel Fitzwilliam we shall expect him."

The boy nodded and hurried off. Charlotte read through the note again, frowning.

"Is something the matter?" Elizabeth asked.

"I do not know. Colonel Fitzwilliam would like to leave earlier than planned. He says, 'My father is in a towering rage, and unpleasant scenes at breakfast always trouble my delicate digestion.'" She laughed. "Only he would say such a thing! His delicate digestion, indeed!"

Chapter 18

ELIZABETH WAS AWAKE and ready early the next day. Disappointed love, she had decided, was a certain method to cure a tendency to lie abed in the morning. It was far better to arise and distract herself. Besides, she had longed to visit the seaside since she was a child, and she had no intention of moping for the entire journey.

Shortly after breakfast, an elegant closed carriage drawn by a four-in-hand pulled up in front of the parsonage. Apparently they were to be travelling in style. Elizabeth wondered if it was one of Lady Catherine's carriages or whether Mr. Darcy had loaned his for the occasion. The reminder of him made her swallow hard.

The coachman took their bags and strapped them firmly to the back while Colonel Fitzwilliam let down the steps. Elizabeth thought she saw him wink at Charlotte as he handed her in, and wondered if her friend was indulging in a brief flirtation with the good colonel. Certainly she had been in unusually high spirits when she returned from Rosings the previous day.

Elizabeth took the colonel's proffered hand and stepped up with care. She had bound her toes before putting on her half boots, but she still felt a sharp twinge of pain when she put weight on that foot, so she leaned against the side of the coach door with her other hand as she ducked to enter. It was not until Colonel Fitzwilliam closed the door and stepped past her that her eyes adjusted to the darkness, revealing another figure sitting in the shadows across from her. Her heart pounded when she saw Mr. Darcy's eyes resting on her, a slight smile playing on his face.

Charlotte said, "What a delightful surprise! I had not realized you would be joining us, Mr. Darcy."

Elizabeth did not miss the odd look the colonel cast at her friend. Charlotte must have known he was coming all along. How could she have done this *again*? This was the second time she had ambushed her this way. Elizabeth would definitely have words with Charlotte later.

Darcy said, "How could I stay behind when such a pleasant expedition was going forth?"

The colonel laughed. "He was simply jealous I would have all the lovely young ladies to myself!" He straightened his black armband which had gone askew.

Elizabeth looked more closely at Darcy. He was no longer wearing the requisite black mourning cravat and armbands the colonel sported. How odd, that he should decide to eschew mourning after only a few days! Even for an aunt, he would be expected to wear it for three months.

But she was glad he did not. Lady Catherine was the true source of their separation. Why should she do her the courtesy of mourning her loss? Darcy's choice was proof he too felt cheated by Lady Catherine.

For the first time in what felt like days, Elizabeth felt a genuine smile curl her lips. He wanted the same things she did, and there was no reason for them to be at odds. She could choose whether to spend the next two days brooding over the loss of him or enjoying this brief reprieve in his company, putting aside the pain the future would bring. Yes, she would take the gift of these two days, and later on, she could hold them close to her heart, along with her memories of the blizzard.

"Besides," said Darcy, "I would not wish to miss the expression on Miss Elizabeth's face when she catches her first glimpse of the sea – the one with water in it, that is."

The carriage jolted into motion. Although it was perhaps the best sprung coach Elizabeth had ever ridden in, the clatter of the wheels over the rough road drowned out any attempts at conversation. Public lanes were never so poorly maintained in Hertfordshire.

The colonel bellowed, "It is but a mile to the turnpike road, and it will be much better then."

Elizabeth did not mind, as the lack of discourse gave her an excuse to simply gaze at Mr. Darcy without any need to disguise her interest. After all, he sat directly opposite her. Had Charlotte planned that as well? Still, she might have felt self-conscious about watching him, were he not doing the self-same thing with every evidence of satisfaction.

It was odd. If he were in fact courting her, this display would be embarrassing. She could only indulge herself in this forwardness because she knew nothing could come of it. This time was somehow divorced from their everyday reality, much as the blizzard had been.

Colonel Fitzwilliam tapped Darcy's shoulder and leaned over to say something in his ear. Darcy raised an eyebrow before giving some sort of answer, then shifted his weight on the upholstered bench. He extended his leg until his booted foot rested on the floor just inches from Elizabeth's feet. No, not even that far, for she could feel it pressing against her foot through the layers of her petticoats.

He had done it deliberately; she was certain of it. Greatly daring, she allowed her own foot to press back, and was rewarded by a dizzying look of approval. Or perhaps it was simply the physical contact with him that dizzied her and sent odd sensations dancing up her legs and flutterings deep inside her. She risked a glance at the others, but they seemed to have noticed nothing.

It could barely even count as contact, after all, with so many layers between her foot and his – her stockings, the leather of her half boots, her shift, petticoat and skirt, his boots and stockings – yet it felt excruciatingly intimate, bringing back all the ways they had touched during those days at the cottage. Snuggling together for warmth, her body entwined with his as they slept, those astonishing and drugging kisses they had shared. The warmth of his breath against her ear when he said, *Sleep well, sweet Lizzy.* Goodness, her lips were tingling just from the recollection! Only a few days ago, the blizzard had seemed like the distant past, but now it might as well have been yesterday.

The carriage passed over a particularly large bump when it reached the turnpike road. The driver called out to the horses, and before Elizabeth had even recovered from the jolt, the carriage surged forward quickly enough she slid back an inch or two on the seat.

Thankfully, as the colonel had predicted, the racket subsided, though it continued to echo in her ears. It seemed almost preternaturally quiet, with nothing but the hoof beats of the running horses. Their speed was striking enough to draw Elizabeth's attention from Mr. Darcy as the scenery flew by and the trees beside the road seemed to blur.

Charlotte asked, "How far will we be travelling?"

"It is about twenty miles from here – two hours with Darcy's horses. At full speed, they can outrun a post coach."

Elizabeth laughed. "So fast? I have never ridden in a post coach, so this is very fast for me. But I am exposing the gaps in my experience and you will think me quite unsophisticated!" She wrinkled her nose at the colonel.

Darcy said quietly, "Your enthusiasm is endearing." His foot, which had been displaced by the jolting, pressed up against hers once more.

She should not be permitting this, but it was too sweet. Her reputation in Meryton was already in tatters, so this would make no difference, even if anyone discovered it. The only person with any possible right to object would be Mr. Hartshorne, and as soon as the thought of him crossed her mind, she knew with certainty she would not accept his proposal. It had been one thing to consider doing so when she thought herself spurned by Darcy; but feeling as she did for him, and knowing those sentiments were returned, at least to a degree, she could not marry another man, even when Darcy married Miss de Bourgh. She would have to think of another plan – but not until the day after tomorrow. For now she would live in the present.

Elizabeth clapped her hand to her bonnet and laughed with delight as the brisk sea wind threatened to tear it from her head. "Is it always so windy here?"

The colonel grinned at her. "Usually, and in the winter, it is much more so. Sometimes the wind makes it nearly impossible to walk."

"I had never imagined the waves would be so high, nor that I could smell the sea from this distance. I had always thought the white cliffs would be greyish, but they are truly white, are they not? And so tall!"

"When you are climbing up them, they seem even higher. There is a set of stairs carved into the cliff that goes down to the bottom. If you would like to walk on the beach, this would be a good time, as the tide is going out."

"Does the tide make such a difference to the beach?"

"Not in general, but here it does. If you follow the beach to the north just past the headland, there is a cove of remarkable beauty. The cliffs there are sheer, apart from a few caves. But you can only reach the cove when the tide is low, since the tip of the headland is submerged at high tide and the currents there are treacherous. It is not uncommon for visitors to be stranded in the cove until the tide goes out again." The colonel shaded his eyes with his hand. "It looks like you would have four hours or so – let us say three, to be on the safe side – before the tide would obstruct your way. It would be a pity for you to miss the cove."

Elizabeth rocked on her injured foot. The pain was manageable. "I would love to see it, if there is time enough."

Charlotte tightened her bonnet ribbons. "You should go, Lizzy, but I believe I will enjoy the view from here more. Going down the cliff sounds quite terrifying to me. Mrs. Jenkinson can keep me company." Since that lady had not even bothered to exit the carriage to view the sea, it seemed unlikely she would be interested in a walk on the beach.

The colonel turned to Darcy. "I have seen the cove many times before, so perhaps you could escort Miss Bennet, while I remain here with Mrs. Collins and Mrs. Jenkinson."

Alone with Mr. Darcy? It was one thing to flirt in a crowded carriage, but being alone together would mean they would have to converse, and there would be no happy endings in that. But she still longed for it – and could not refuse it.

Darcy held his arm out to her with a warm look. "Miss Elizabeth, I would be honored to explore this famous cove with you."

"A moment, Lizzy," said Charlotte. "With this

wind, you will need your pelisse."

"An excellent idea! I am chilled already." Elizabeth followed her to the carriage where the coachman produced the requested pelisse.

Charlotte pressed a full reticule into her hand. "Just a few biscuits in case you become hungry. That looks like a long walk."

"Thank you." Elizabeth put on the pelisse, then pinned the reticule to it. It had been a long time since breakfast.

On their return to the gentlemen, Elizabeth blushed at the sight of Darcy donning a very familiar greatcoat. Had it been only three months since she had felt its weight around her shoulders?

Darcy's eyes raked her from head to foot. "That is a very becoming pelisse, Miss Elizabeth." As if he had not seen it constantly for three days!

This walk seemed destined to raise many memories.

Although the cliff steps were neither overly steep nor uneven, Darcy took pleasure in the opportunity to offer Elizabeth his assistance whenever possible. The pressure of her hand on his provided a taste of the contact he had been craving, and he was sorry to relinquish it when they reached the shingle beach. Still, it was a joy to watch Elizabeth peering around her, taking in the scenery, touching the chalk cliff with her gloved fingertips, picking up and inspecting one of the flint pebbles making up the beach.

She turned her bewitching smile on him. "I had

not realized the waves would move so quickly. And the foam! Is it not beautiful?"

"Very beautiful," he agreed, admiring the sparkle in her eyes, as bright as the sunlight reflecting off the many-hued water.

"If the cove is more lovely than this, I cannot wait to see it!"

He gathered his courage. "Miss Elizabeth, may I be so bold as to ask you a question?"

"You may certainly ask; whether I shall answer will depend on the question." She sounded amused, but he could feel the sudden tension radiating from her.

"The second letter you wrote me, the one I never received. What did it say?"

Her smile faltered. "The general gist was that you had been correct about the consequences to my reputation from our little adventure. Then I spent quite some time dwelling on how very much I disliked having to admit I was wrong. I gave you the direction of my uncle's house in London, which is where my father sent me to avoid the gossip."

"You were *there*?" All that time he had been hunting for her and worrying, and she had been right under his nose? "I had persuaded Miss Bingley's coachman to give me the address, but I never even thought to ask for you, since all I knew was your sister was visiting them. Had I only known…"

"It would have done you no good. I have made inquiries, and the reason my uncle told you Jane was no longer there was to prevent you from discovering my presence. Apparently he assumed you planned to take advantage of my vulnerable position. It did not occur to him your intentions might be honorable."

Not honorable? How dare he think such a thing! And why had Elizabeth not told her uncle otherwise? But that was a question he dared not ask. "I had told your father I intended to marry you."

"When he called on you in London?"

Bewildered, he shook his head. "He never called on me in London; or if he did, I was out and he did not leave his card. I went to Longbourn to see him after Stanton reported your reputation had been compromised."

Elizabeth's eyes clouded, then she nodded. "You said you would marry me, and he still would not tell you where I was?"

It was painful even to revisit in memory. "He said you wished to have nothing to do with me."

"He *said* that? Oh, how dare he! He knew perfectly well I wished to see you, and that I needed to see you." Elizabeth looked down, her bonnet hiding her face, but he had already seen her troubled look.

He placed his hand over hers as it lay in the crook of his arm. "I am sorry he did so and for the pain it caused you, but that is past. It no longer matters."

Now she looked at him again, her eyes wide and stricken. "How can you say that? I know – and you must know I know – the terms of your aunt's will. Pray do not think I blame you; I understand you have been left with no choice. But pray do not suggest it does not *matter*!"

What in God's name did Lady Catherine's will

have to do with it? Cautiously he said, "I fear I do not understand."

She withdrew her hand from his arm and halted abruptly. "I know you must marry your cousin. I would prefer to return to the others now."

Bewildered, he caught her arms. "I do not know where you came upon that idea, but I have no intention of marrying Anne. How could I be here with you if I were planning to marry another?"

She kept her face averted. "I cannot believe you would allow her to lose her inheritance."

"Then you do not know me as well as you think. Had she been reduced to penury by some accident, I would feel a responsibility towards her, but her mother did this to her deliberately in an attempt to force my hand. When I first heard of her plans years ago, I informed her it would not work, and would only hurt her daughter. She seems to have decided I was bluffing. I do not bluff, nor do I submit to blackmail."

Elizabeth blinked rapidly a few times, then essayed a wan smile. "My father and my uncle should consider themselves fortunate. Had their delaying tactics created a permanent barrier between us, they would not have liked some of the things I would have to say to them."

It was an indirect answer, but it was an answer all the same. Darcy forced himself to peel his hands from her arms, and gestured down the beach. She took his arm again; that had to be a good sign.

He gathered his courage. "Speaking of barriers, when I first enquired of Mrs. Collins about you, she told me you were on the verge of matrimony." Even though she was here and with him, the words still tasted of poison.

"Oh, that. It is a somewhat embarrassing situation. My family deemed it necessary that I marry to deflect the scandal, so my uncle found a man willing to marry me, much as you found one for Maria Lucas. Charlotte's invitation to visit came at a fortuitous moment in that it permitted me to delay a final resolution." She shivered.

Darcy could not trust himself to speak.

"Is something the matter, Mr. Darcy?"

"Nothing at all, but I do have another question." Perhaps they could settle this for once and for all. He knew she would accept him, so why was his heart pounding? "Now that we have determined I am not engaged to Anne and you are not engaged to a man in London, may I presume you might now be willing to become engaged to me?"

She scuffed her half-boots in the stones underfoot, then looked up at him, her cheeks flushed. "I believe that would be a safe assumption."

"So you will marry me? Do me the great honor of becoming my wife?" Good God, he was practically stuttering!

A bright smile flashed across Elizabeth's face. "Yes."

"Thank God," he breathed, triumph filling him. If only he could kiss her! Perhaps he would be more fortunate than he deserved and the cove would be deserted. But it was enough to have her consent.

Finally!

The narrow pathway around the headland to the cove wound between boulders, requiring them to walk single file. The water was only a few feet beyond them, but presumably the tide would carry it further out.

Then they were around the headland and the beach opened up again, sheer white cliffs rising in a crescent around it. It would be impossible to build steps into these cliffs. At the far end of the cove, waves slapped against the base of the cliffs near two fisherman casting their lines. So much for the deserted cove.

"Oh, my." Elizabeth shaded her eyes as she looked up at the cliffs. "No wonder the colonel wanted us to come here. What an exhilarating sight!"

She was correct, but he was more interested in looking at her. The presence of the fishermen was disappointing; he was hungry to hold her in his arms. Later, he promised himself. Somehow he would find a way to be alone with Elizabeth today.

Elizabeth ran her hand along the fractured chalk of the cliff. "So imposing. It is a wonder the sea does not wash it all away."

"Chunks of it break off regularly." He picked up one of the rounded white rocks scattered among the darker flint of the shingle. "They are washed out to sea, and return like this."

"Over there – is that one of the caves your cousin mentioned?" She pointed to a hollow in the cliff.

"The cliffs are riddled with them. I gather they are popular with smugglers. Most are not deep, though."

"Would it be safe to look inside?"

How could he refuse her anything when her eyes sparkled like that? "I cannot see why not."

Together they picked their way across the shingle. It was not truly a cave, just a deep hollow in the cliff, but when they stood within it, it blocked the worst of the wind, making it seem suddenly quiet and still.

Out of the corner of his eye, Darcy saw the fishermen packing up their gear, sharing some joke which made the younger man roar with laughter. Were they in fact going to leave? Could he be so fortunate?

Apparently Elizabeth had also been watching them. "Good, they are gone! I do not think I could have remained proper another minute!"

Darcy's eyebrows shot up, but apparently her version of impropriety ran along different lines than his. She hurried off toward the water's edge, first at a trot, then stopping abruptly and continuing at a more sedate pace. He caught up to her in a few strides.

She halted when a wave curled towards her skirts, stopping just a few inches away. As it receded, she tugged off one of her gloves and stooped down. When the next wave came, she dipped her fingers in it, jerking them back in surprise, no doubt at the temperature. She looked up at him mischievously as she touched her forefinger to the tip of her tongue.

A surge of desire rushed through him, but somehow he managed to master it. "Salty?" he asked huskily.

"Oh, yes!" She jumped to her feet and gathered

up her skirt. Like a huntress, she began to chase the waves, stalking each one as it retreated, then racing back as the next one chased her. "Is it not glorious?"

How could he do anything but smile at her obvious delight? "Glorious indeed."

She halted, the light in her face dimming. "Am I shocking you?"

"Not at all." But she did not appear convinced, so he added, "I am trying to decide if I dare join you."

"Oh, do!" She held out her hand to him just as a gust of wind blew her bonnet back, leaving it hanging by its ribbons.

As if he could possibly stay away when her eyes were alight and her chestnut hair glistened in the sun! He grasped her hand. Almost immediately both of them had to jump back to avoid the next wave.

He had not laughed like this in years. Creeping forward after each wave, then rushing back, enjoying even Elizabeth's shriek when a wave almost caught them. Back and forth, back and forth.

A particularly large swell moved towards them. "Oh, dear!" cried Elizabeth through her laughter, gripping his hand more tightly as she turned to flee. The wave surged towards them, unstoppable. Even at a half-run, they would not make it.

He had been waiting for this. He swept her up in his arms, making her shriek once again. Water rushed around his boots as he straightened.

She linked her arms around his neck, her eyes dancing. "I did not know you also rescued damsels in distress, sir."

"Now you know, but I warn you, like the smugglers, I am not without my price. There is a ransom to be paid if you wish to be set free." The retreating wave tugged at his boots before releasing them.

Her eyes darkened. "And if I do *not* wish to be set free?"

Darcy swallowed hard, then said huskily, "There will be a ransom for that as well."

The tip of her tongue darted out to touch her upper lip, then retreated more quickly than the fastest wave. "Then I suppose I must pay."

"Indeed you must." To his delight, her lips met his halfway. Good God, she wanted this as much as he did! But he held himself back, sharing only the sweet pressure, until she sighed and opened herself to him.

His arms tightened around her as he accepted her invitation, exploring her mouth as he tried to express the fire within him and his aching longing for her. Time ceased to have meaning as the tides of desire raced through him.

Finally Elizabeth drew back, her breathing ragged. "You taste of salt," she informed him with a breathy laugh.

"So do you. Salt..." He dipped his head and kissed the tender spot just below her ear. "...And fresh apples..." His tongue traced her collarbone to the sensitive notch in the middle. "...And honey."

"All that?"

"All that and much more, every bit of it delicious." Hungrily he claimed her mouth again, and this time he could feel her arch upwards towards him.

He was barely aware of the ebb and flow of water beneath him, washing over his boots and then tugging at them. He was in no danger from the ocean's depths; he was drowning in Elizabeth's kisses. She trembled in his arms as he stroked his thumb against her skirted leg. He should thank heaven he was ankle deep in water, since it was likely the only thing holding him back from taking his need for her to the next stage.

In the meantime, supporting her body against his chest and the intoxication of her kisses was enough to make the world fade away, at least until a blast of icy water soaked his knees. With a yelp, he turned and strode back to the beach, clutching a laughing Elizabeth to him as the water trickled down his legs inside his boots. Stopping a safe distance from the water, he cast a dark look back at it. How had it become so deep? The tide was supposed to be going out, and he had not been kissing Elizabeth for *that* long. Not that he had been giving a single thought to time or tide, but still….

A thought struck him, and he twisted his head until he could see the headland, its base now submerged in waves.

Elizabeth followed his gaze. "I thought the tide was going out."

No question about it; the path was long gone. Damn Richard! "It seems my cousin was incorrect."

"Are we trapped here?"

"So it would seem, at least until the tide goes down again."

Her eyes widened. "How long will that take?"

"It is just over six hours between high and low tides, but it may be less than that, depending on how far above the low tide line the path is."

"Oh." She pulled her pelisse around her more tightly, then smiled. "Well, if we must be trapped here, at least we are already accustomed to being stranded in each other's company."

Any other young lady of his acquaintance would be having vapors. "Unfortunately, my fire-building skills will be less useful here." Hours stranded alone with Elizabeth. His mind whirled with the possibilities.

"Then it is good we both know other ways to keep warm." Her eyes lit up as she produced a reticule. "We shall not starve, at least. Charlotte thought to give me a bag of biscuits."

"Richard gave me a flask of wine. I am glad he insisted I wear my greatcoat if we are to be here for hours." A sudden suspicion crossed his mind. Richard had encouraged them to explore the cove. Mrs. Collins had suggested Elizabeth take her pelisse and gave her biscuits. It was almost as if they had *expected* them to be stranded. But why? Slowly he said, "They planned this. Richard knew perfectly well the tide was rising."

Her expression of perplexity was adorable. "They *planned* it?"

"Why else were they so careful to make certain we would be prepared to stay here a long time?"

"But what could be their purpose?"

"It makes no sense. The only reason a man and a woman are forced to be alone together is to compromise the lady, but Richard is well aware I intend to marry you, so that would be pointless."

"Charlotte thought as I did, that you would be forced to marry Miss de Bourgh. Perhaps it was her idea."

"No, I am certain Richard is involved somehow. First he insisted we had to make this trip now, despite being in mourning, and then, after consulting a book of tide charts, he said we had to leave earlier than planned." Perhaps Richard knew how badly he wished to be alone with Elizabeth, but surely there would be easier — and warmer - ways to accomplish that. But at least they were alone, and he intended to make the most of it. There might not be another opportunity for this much time alone again before their wedding. He held out his hand to her. "Come with me."

Darcy led Elizabeth back to the small cave in the cliff. Her face felt warmer now that she was out of the wind, but it was still chilly, so she was surprised to see Darcy removing his greatcoat. It made her smile, though, remembering how he had wrapped it around her during the blizzard. "Will you not be cold?"

He turned a devastating smile on her. "Not with you keeping me warm." He perched on a narrow ledge of chalk toward the back of the hollow, then held his hands out to her.

She ought to have refused, or at least to have hesitated, but she did neither. The brief time he had held her above the waves had only made her long even more to be in his arms. After all, they were to be married, were they not? She took his hands and let him draw her onto his lap.

He spread his greatcoat across both of them, just as he had in the cottage. She breathed in deeply, the remembered scent of spice and musk surrounding her once more. With a deep sigh, she leaned against his chest.

He chuckled. "It seems familiar, does it not?"

"It seems lovely." She tilted her head back to look up into his dark eyes.

Then his lips brushed hers, first gently, then with increasing hunger, filling her with heat and unspeakable longing to be even closer to him, to wipe out the memories of the lonely weeks when she had thought him lost to her. She linked her hands around his neck and gave herself over to his passion.

She was only half-aware of his tugging at the buttons of her pelisse until his hand slipped inside, molding against the side of her waist. Even through her dress, the warmth of his hand felt almost unbearably intimate, sending a wave of desire through her. It only intensified as his hand rose to her bodice and cupped her curves.

He released her lips, but did not move away. "Am I shocking you?" he breathed.

"A little."

He gave a throaty laugh. "That first morning in the cottage, I woke up to find my hand in that exact position. Fortunately I was able to remove it without waking you – not that I *wished* to remove it, mind you."

"I might have been rather shocked if you had not!"

"Or you might have decided you liked it, and we could have been married much sooner." He kissed her deeply, running his thumb across the top of her bodice, and a shock of pure pleasure followed his touch.

Elizabeth felt as if she were melting as a throbbing seemed to grow between her legs. Involuntarily she arched into his hand. She could not bear it if he stopped. "No."

"My sweetest, loveliest Elizabeth," he murmured.

Finally he pulled away. "We must stop, while I still can."

"Well, I no longer question whether you find me tempting!"

He groaned. "Far too tempting!"

Perhaps that would be enough; his desire and apparent enjoyment of her company. She could not credit Charlotte's claim that he was violently in love with her, but Charlotte did not understand how deep his sense of honor ran. She hoped it was deep enough for her to retain his affection once his passion was satisfied.

That was something she still needed to say. "I do appreciate your willingness to marry me under the circumstances. I know many men would have tried to avoid it."

He stiffened, then took her face between both his hands and looked deep into her eyes. "Do you truly believe I am marrying you only because it is the right thing to do?"

Embarrassed, she tried to shift her gaze, but

there was nowhere else to look. "Well, I do gather you will receive some pleasure out of it as well."

"*Some pleasure*? Elizabeth, there is nothing I want more than to marry you!"

She bit her lip. "That is very kind of you to say, but…"

"It is not *kind*. It is *true*!" He released her for a moment and rummaged in his pocket, finally producing what appeared to be a somewhat worn violet ribbon. "Do you recognize this?"

Should she recognize it? Then it came to her. "Is that one of the ribbons I was wearing during the blizzard?"

"I have carried it with me ever since, because I could not bear to let go of the last bit of you I had. I was longing for an excuse to contact you."

"Truly?"

"Truly. I know you have less choice than I in the matter of our marriage, but I hope to make you the happiest woman in the world."

"That is unfortunately beyond your power, for I am already the happiest woman alive!"

His face grew serious. "Are you? It seems like all you have done is to try to avoid marrying me."

She buried her face in his chest, clutching his waistcoat. "Yes," she said into the fabric. "I missed you terribly after the blizzard, and I was heartbroken when I thought you had abandoned me."

She felt him press kisses on her hair, her ear, her forehead, anywhere he could reach until she finally dared to lift her head. The gentle expression on his face was one she had never seen before.

"Thank you," he breathed. "I cannot tell you what a gift you have given me." His kiss was heartbreakingly tender.

Some time later, he said, "But I still fail to understand why your father does not seem favorably inclined towards the match, especially if he is aware you wished for it. The benefits are obvious."

Elizabeth exhaled heavily. "I suppose you will have to hear this story at some point, so I might as well tell you now."

"You need not tell me if you do not wish to."

"No, this is something you should know. When my father first met my mother, she was the beautiful and vivacious daughter of a local tradesman. I expect he intended it only as a flirtation, but they were caught together. My mother's family was not the equal of his, but was too prominent to ignore. Since he did enjoy her company, he proposed. It led to a rift in his family and to years of unhappiness on both their parts. He discovered unrestrained behavior is not the same thing as an adventurous spirit, vivaciousness does not imply wit, and beauty fades. He was, I gather, angry to discover how dearly he paid for a wife he could not respect and who embarrassed him regularly. He began to make cutting remarks, making fun of her, and she became more nervous and silly under the barrage."

"I would not behave that way, nor is there anything faulty in your behavior."

"How could my father admit you would handle an unequal marriage forced by circumstances any better than he has?"

"But the circumstances are not the same."

"I fail to see the difference."

"Well, I wanted to marry you even before the snowstorm. It simply gave me the excuse I needed to disregard my family's expectations."

She looked at him through her lashes. "You did? I had no idea."

"But I told you as much!"

"No, you said marrying me would not be a chore, not that it was something you actively wished for. I believed you were making the best of a bad situation, and would be relieved by my refusal.

"No," he said with a tender kiss. "I was not relieved. In fact, I was quite displeased, and considered telling your father the entire story so he could bring the issue to an end. But I still cared enough about society's approval, or thought I *ought* to care, that I did not. Instead, I returned to London and spent the next weeks fingering your ribbon and regretting that we had not been caught."

Elizabeth nuzzled into his shoulder. "I wish I had known that. It might have eased my fears."

"Your fears?"

"Of ending up like my mother. That was what prevented me from accepting you."

"But I never would have treated you so. It is not my way."

"I did not know you well enough to be certain of that. But that is, I imagine, the basis of my father's dislike of the idea – that you would end up with as little respect for me as he has for my mother."

"I wonder that he could not see the difference! When I came to him, nothing was motivating me beyond concern for you. The scandal in Meryton did not touch me in any way."

"How well I know it! When my father said you would not marry me, I thought that was why."

He stopped himself just in time from telling her she should have tried again to contact him. Her theory would have been true of all too many gentlemen, so he should not criticize. "Well, we are together now, despite my family and yours." And for that he would be eternally grateful.

Chapter 19

IT WAS NEARING dusk when Elizabeth and Darcy climbed the last steps to the top of the cliff. The carriage waited in the same place, but there was no sign of the rest of the party.

"Guilty consciences?" murmured Darcy.

The coachman jumped down from perch. "Begging your pardon, sir, Colonel Fitzwilliam and the ladies went to the inn, and instructed me to come back to wait for you."

"Perhaps they tired of the sea breezes," said Elizabeth brightly. "How fortunate for us we did not."

Darcy opened the carriage door and handed Elizabeth in. "I hope there is enough light for us to reach the inn as well. Otherwise we might be stranded, and we could not have that, could we?"

Elizabeth giggled.

"I took the precaution, sir, of bringing lanterns," said the coachman stoutly. "But the moon is bright, and my guess is we will do well enough without them."

Darcy said in Elizabeth's ear, "I have no objection to darkness; do you?"

She blushed fiercely.

⁓

"Oh, how delightfully warm it is here," said Elizabeth as they entered the inn, immediately holding her hands in front of the blazing hearth.

"There you are!" cried the colonel. "We were beginning to fear we would not see you until morning. Were you stranded by the tide, then?"

"Stranded, yes, but whether by the tide or treachery I cannot say," said Darcy deliberately.

Charlotte hurried to Elizabeth's side. "Poor Lizzy! You must be half frozen."

"I managed to find ways to stay warm." Elizabeth exchanged an amused look with Darcy. "But I am looking forward to hot food."

Colonel Fitzwilliam shifted from one foot to the other. "Dinner will be served at eight. I will tell them there will be two more for our party."

Darcy raised an eyebrow. "I hope there will be enough for us as well. All that fresh air has given me a remarkable appetite."

"I do hope they have onion soup," said Elizabeth. "I have been thinking of it all day." She handed her pelisse to a barmaid. Darcy's greatcoat and hat joined the pile in the barmaid's arms as she staggered up the stairs.

The colonel exchanged a glance with Charlotte as Darcy and Elizabeth joined them at a large oaken table. So apparently there *was* a conspiracy! "Well, Darcy, it seems you and Miss Elizabeth were alone together for some hours."

"Yes. It was quite enjoyable, I must say." Apparently Darcy was not above teasing his cousin.

Colonel Fitzwilliam cleared his throat. "I took Miss Elizabeth under my protection for the duration of this trip, and promised Mr. Collins I would guard her reputation as if she were my sister."

Darcy chuckled. "I suppose he has never met your sisters."

"Be serious, Darcy. This is a problem."

Good Lord! Was it possible the colonel and Charlotte had schemed to strand her with Darcy in order to force him to propose to her? This was irresistible. "Colonel, how very kind of you to be concerned about my reputation. I assure you, though, it is of very little importance since I was already compromised by Mr. Darcy several months ago, and much more thoroughly than this."

Colonel Fitzwilliam's jaw dropped, but he recovered quickly. "You were not under my protection then. Darcy, I know you feel bound to offer for Anne, but a matter of honor like this must take precedence over one of mere money and property."

Darcy's smirk faded. "Where did you get the idea I would offer for Anne now, after having refused to for so many years?"

"You are *not* offering for her? But she will lose Rosings!"

"I feel sorry for her loss, but it was Lady Catherine's choice, not mine. Because she is my cousin, I have a certain responsibility to her, and I plan to offer her a cottage at Pemberley and a small allowance. But I *never* considered marrying her out of pity."

"But everyone assumes...even my father thought...you said nothing when the will was read!"

Charlotte added soothingly, "It was a very general assumption. I certainly believed it."

Elizabeth elbowed Darcy. "See, it was *not* such a ridiculous thing to think."

The colonel shook his head. "I thought you felt obliged to offer for her, while your heart was set elsewhere."

"Is that why you staged this little drama? To give me a way out?"

Colonel Fitzwilliam coughed. "Well, yes, that was the general idea."

Charlotte covered her face in an attempt to stifle her laughter. "The best laid plans..."

Elizabeth shook her head at her friend. "I am developing a new appreciation for your ability for plotting, Charlotte!"

Colonel Fitzwilliam said, "Well, it shall be quite a celebration tonight. Say, Darcy, why did you never mention Georgiana would be joining us? What a surprise it was to discover her here!"

Darcy started. "*Georgiana* is here?"

Richard and Mrs. Collins exchanged glances. "She said you told her to come."

"I did nothing of the sort! It is much too far for her to travel for just a night. I never even told her of my travel plans. You must have said something."

Richard shook his head. "Not I. I have not written her in over a fortnight. Who else knew our plans? Mrs. Collins had never met her before today. Perhaps Anne wrote her. That must be it. But why would Georgiana not say so?"

"What did I not say?" Georgiana appeared beside the table, her brow furled.

Darcy embraced her. "I am delighted to see you, of course, but puzzled by your appearance here. Did Anne tell you our plans?"

She gave him an odd look. "Of course not."

"Then why are you here?" This was becoming worrisome. It was not like Georgiana to take initiative like this.

She dropped her eyes and wrung her hands. "You wanted me to come," she said in a bare whisper. "Crewe said so."

Darcy narrowed his eyes. "*Crewe* said so?"

"Was he not supposed to do so?" Georgiana peeked up at him through her lashes.

"No, he was not; or rather he was not under any instruction to tell you anything of the sort."

Georgiana bit her lip. "I am sorry. I will return to London first thing in the morning." She turned away, clearly ready to make an escape.

Darcy caught her hand before she could flee. "You are not in trouble, sweetheart. I am always glad to see you. I just did not expect you."

Richard's hand was over his mouth, but it did little to disguise his laughter. "Crewe! I should have known. But why in blazes did he want Georgiana here?"

Mrs. Collins said, "I fear I do not understand. Who is Crewe?"

"He is Darcy's valet, at least on the surface. Except when he thinks Darcy is making a mistake, in which case he fixes it without telling him. I wonder what he is up to now."

"As do I," Darcy said darkly. Crewe could not possibly disapprove of Elizabeth, could he? Darcy could not imagine it, and if it were true, Crewe would be looking for a new position. Even an old trusted family servant could not go that far.

Richard caught at the sleeve of a passing serving maid. "Would you be so kind as to go up to Mr. Darcy's room and tell his valet he is needed immediately?"

Darcy glanced at Elizabeth. "No, I will speak to him privately." If it was about her, he did not wish her to hear it.

"Whatever it may be, it is nothing negative about Miss Bennet. This whole jaunt was Crewe's idea." Once again, Richard seemed able to read his mind.

A weight lifted from Darcy's shoulders. He would hate to lose Crewe. "Very well then, bring him here. In the meantime, Georgiana, I have some exciting news. May I present your future sister, Miss Elizabeth Bennet?"

Georgiana's eyes grew wide and she clapped her hands together. "Truly? You are to be wed?"

"Quite truly." Darcy could still hardly believe it himself.

Elizabeth curtsied. "It is a pleasure to make your acquaintance, Miss Darcy. Your brother has told me so much about you, and I have longed to meet you." Trust Elizabeth to know Georgiana would need encouragement to overcome her shyness!

"He has told me all about *you* as well. I am so happy for both of you!"

He watched fondly as the two women he loved spoke, Elizabeth asking questions to draw Georgiana out. She would be good for his sister.

A shadow appeared beside him. "You wished to speak to me, sir?" said Crewe.

Darcy crossed his arms. "Yes, Crewe, I did. Perhaps you would be so kind as to inform me why you took it upon yourself to bring my sister here?"

"Of course. Is it your wish I tell you now or later?"

Richard guffawed. "Oh, no. No waiting until you are in private. I want to hear this!"

Darcy sent him a poisonous look. "You may tell me now."

Crewe, as always, looked completely unperturbed. "Very well, sir. May I first take the liberty of offering my best wishes to Miss Bennet?"

Of course, Crewe just assumed everything had gone according to his plans! "Later, Crewe. I am waiting."

Was that actually a slight look of satisfaction in Crewe's eyes? "Indeed. You will, of course, have already realized the great disadvantages to announcing your engagement, so I assumed you would be planning an immediate wedding. When I was in London to collect your special license, it occurred to me it would have much less of the appearance of an elopement if Miss Darcy was present on the occasion of your wedding."

Ignoring Richard's snickers, Darcy said dryly, "Pray remind me, Crewe, how it is I reached this realization?" If Crewe had a convincing reason why they should marry immediately, he wanted to know it. What he would not give for an excuse to marry Elizabeth right away!

"Lady Matlock has strong feelings about proper mourning etiquette." Crewe's eyes flickered to his absent black cravat. "She would be most distressed if you announced your engagement during the three months of mourning, and the wedding could not occur for a full six months. She would point out that starting your marriage with a scandal would create many difficulties for Miss Darcy in her come-out this Season, and that her marital prospects would be better if you did not announce your engagement at all until the season is over, a year from now. Naturally, you need not abide by her wishes, but she will share her opinion with you."

Devil take it. He had not thought about the mourning question and Georgiana's presentation in January. He would have to wait the three months, but that was all. "I have no intention of waiting that long. Lady Matlock does not make the rules."

Richard snorted at that. "Oh yes, she does."

"Of course, sir, you would make your own decision on it; but you will have taken into consideration that Lord Matlock will express his opinion on your engagement in the strongest terms and quite frequently. Those opinions would be likely to cause a rift between you and your uncle, but more importantly, it might be distressing to Miss Bennet to be the source of such conflict. By the time you marry, the damage might be irreparable. If, on the other hand, you present them with a fait accompli, they may be displeased, but they will make the best of it. There would be not be months of unpleasantness overshadowing your wedding."

"He has a point," said Richard. "My father will lecture you mercilessly on the disadvantages of the match – I beg your pardon, Miss Bennet; it is only because he has not had the opportunity to appreciate your sterling qualities – and it could be a nasty few months. Or year."

"While I respect my aunt and uncle, I will not marry precipitously to avoid their wrath."

"Of course not, sir. My apologies for my error." Crewe's lips curved up infinitesimally, and Darcy knew he was about to deliver the coup de grace. "No doubt Miss Bennet's family will quite understand the need to allow the scandal and gossip about her to continue for the three months until your engagement can be announced."

It took a moment for that to sink in. How had he missed that? He felt a smile growing on his face. A quick marriage was just the thing! He forced the smile back, and said sternly, "I suppose I have also considered how I could present the news of a secret wedding in such a way as not to cause even more scandal."

Crewe looked puzzled – and he never showed

an expression without a purpose. "How could it be a secret wedding if your sister, your cousin, and Miss Bennet's closest friend and cousin's wife are all present? It would be only appropriate to have a quiet, very private service in deference to Lady Catherine's recent demise."

Richard was shaking his head. "Crewe, Crewe, Crewe. You never cease to astonish me. Tell me, has Darcy already made arrangements for the wedding?"

Crewe bowed to Richard. "The curate of St. James's Church here in Folkestone will be available tomorrow morning at half ten."

But the silence from behind him was a reminder this was one decision he could not make himself. Elizabeth's expression was serene. That was likely a danger sign; he had seen her with many expressions, none of which could be described as serene.

His palms damp, Darcy slid his chair closer to Elizabeth. He reached under the table to cover her hand with his own. "What is your opinion? Crewe has some good points, but this is *your* wedding and it must be as *you* wish it to be. You have every right to be married in Longbourn church with your family around you. If you are dissatisfied in any way with these suggestions, pray tell me so at once, and I will put an end to them."

Her lips twitched. "Even though you would much prefer to marry right away, with or without your valet's carefully marshaled arguments?"

If only he could kiss that arch look away! "I would be hard put to deny a desire to make you mine as soon as possible, but my desire to make you happy is even greater than that."

"How lucky that you should have such a reasonable answer to give, and that I should be so reasonable as to admit it!"

Triumph surged within him. "Does that mean you agree?"

"There is one slight problem. I am not yet of age, so I would still need my father's permission."

Devil take it! If he had to ride to Longbourn and back, he would also need to announce the engagement...in three months' time. He spoke with great care. "If you did marry without his permission, would he be likely to attempt to have the marriage annulled, even after we have lived together as man and wife?"

A delightful flush rose in her cheeks. "No, I suppose not. That would be too much trouble, and he prefers the easiest path."

"I did call on him and told him of my intention to marry you, and while he did not give his permission, he also did not forbid it. I could argue that is the same as tacit permission. But more importantly, would it disturb you to marry without his formal consent? I would not wish to make you unhappy."

Her lips tightened. "My father, by withholding my letter to you and failing to tell you my whereabouts, was responsible for the most miserable time of my life. No doubt he meant well in his own way, but I would not allow his outright disapproval to stop me, so I will certainly not feel the lack of his formal consent."

At least he was not alone in his anger at Mr.

Bennet's interference! "So…"

She hesitated. "Is Crewe correct that an engagement announcement during the mourning period could be harmful to your sister's prospects?"

"He is correct, but it is not a serious issue. She is still the granddaughter of an earl with a large dowry. It would discourage only the highest sticklers that her brother has no sense of decorum."

Elizabeth laughed. "No sense of decorum indeed!"

He lowered his voice to a whisper. "I certainly had none when we were in the cove."

Color rose in her cheeks. "Perhaps, then, since your sense of decorum is so little to be trusted, we had best follow Crewe's plan. You did tell me once he was always right."

"And sometimes it is very annoying. Not this time, though."

Richard coughed loudly. "Well, Darcy?"

Electing to ignore him, Darcy said to Crewe, "I hope you brought me apparel suitable for a wedding."

"Naturally, sir. And for Miss Darcy as well."

Georgiana said, "But you said I was to bring my best clothes in case Darcy planned to introduce me to someone!"

Crewe inclined his head. "I find it is always best to be prepared."

Elizabeth laughed. "I see Charlotte and I will be the only ones ill-prepared!"

Richard muttered, "Not if I know Crewe."

"I took the liberty of obtaining Mrs. Collins'

best dress from the parsonage and certain items from Lady Anne's wardrobe which seemed likely to suit Miss Bennet. Naturally, I brought the Darcy sapphires from London."

"Naturally," Darcy said under his breath, then added more loudly, "Crewe, is there anything else I planned which I may have forgotten? I would hate to embarrass myself by being unaware of any particulars."

Crewe counted on his fingers. "License, church, curate, family, suitable apparel, jewelry; no, I believe you have taken care of everything, sir."

Richard said, "How remarkably poor your memory is these days, Darcy! Crewe, how did you manage to obtain a special license in Darcy's name?"

Crewe for once seemed at a loss and looked to Darcy.

Darcy cleared his throat. "Crewe was no doubt well aware I already had a special license in my desk drawer. I had obtained it prior to visiting Elizabeth's father, thinking he would wish a speedy wedding."

Mrs. Collins spoke up for the first time. "I find myself remarkably hard of hearing tonight. It would be improper for me to participate in plans which my husband might deem distasteful to her late ladyship. Tomorrow will no doubt come as quite a surprise to me."

Richard chuckled. "Had I only known Crewe had matters so well in hand, Mrs. Collins, I could have left you out of my little conspiracy, and your conscience would be quite clear."

"Oh, no," said Charlotte gravely. "I would not

have missed conspiring against Lizzy and Mr. Darcy for the world. In cases such as these, a clear conscience is highly overrated."

Under the table, Darcy took Elizabeth's hand and squeezed it.

After dinner, Darcy turned to his cousin and said abruptly, "I have not been thinking."

"To say the least!" Richard said.

"I am serious. Your father is absolutely set on marrying me off to Anne. He is not going to be pleased with you for interfering with his plans. There is little he can do to punish me, but you are a different story."

Richard's smile faded a bit. "I have considered that, but I am not going to hide my part in this, regardless of what he might do. It will be an ugly scene, at the very least."

To Darcy's surprise, Mrs. Collins spoke up. "What is the worst he can do to you?"

"Disown me," Richard said, his face a shade paler than it had been. "Cut off my funds. It would be difficult, but I could survive on my army pay."

Mrs. Collins leaned forward. "Did you not tell me you could not leave the army because of your duty to your father? What of that if he disowns you?"

A smile grew on Darcy's face. What a clever woman Mrs. Collins was! "If he disowns you, you can sell your commission and live at Pemberley."

Richard froze, his glass of port half way to his mouth.

"Oh, yes, Richard!" said Georgiana. "That

would be perfect!"

He set down the port carefully as if afraid the glass would break. "Do you...do you...I cannot accept your charity."

"It is not charity. You would do it for me – remember? Together, against all enemies?"

A bit of color returned to Richard's cheeks. "Together, against all odds. But perhaps you should consult your almost-wife before you invite me to live at Pemberley."

Darcy had not given that a thought. He would need to learn about being a husband. Husband. He liked that word. "Perhaps Elizabeth and I could discuss this privately."

"I cannot see why we need to discuss it," said Elizabeth warmly. "I would be very happy to see you sell your commission, Colonel."

Richard's shoulders lowered in relaxation. "Then you would have to call me Richard."

Elizabeth pursed her lips as if deep in thought, then said archly, "A difficult challenge, but I believe it would be within my capability."

With a laugh, Richard raised his glass. "To being disowned!"

"Hear, hear!" said Darcy.

Once they had all drunk a toast, Elizabeth said, "It has been a long day, and I believe I will retire early."

"An excellent plan," said the colonel. "One of you should be well rested, and Darcy never sleeps through the night."

Darcy ignored him, instead gazing at Elizabeth

with a slight smile playing around his lips. "Warm or cold?" he asked huskily.

Color rose in her cheeks, but she smiled. "Warm. Definitely warm."

Charlotte looked puzzled. "I am certain they will have lit a fire in your room. Mine was quite well heated."

"That is good news," said Elizabeth gravely. "I do so dislike being cold at night."

Chapter 20

WHAT HAD SHE agreed to? Not knowing when, or if, Darcy planned to appear, Elizabeth changed into her nightgown in record time. As she was brushing her hair, a knock at the door made her jump. Her pulses racing, she opened it.

Charlotte stepped inside. "I came to see if your room truly was warm enough. I can ask for more coal if you wish, and there is an extra blanket in the wardrobe should you require it."

If she felt any more overheated than she did at the moment, she might be in danger of going up in flames! Especially given that Mr. Darcy might appear at any moment for an even more embarrassing scene. "I thank you, Charlotte. As you can see the room is very comfortable. I was just about to go to bed." She hoped her friend would take the hint and depart.

"If you are certain the room is fine... I know you need your sleep. And Lizzy – should you have any *questions*, I would be happy to do my best to answer them. I know you were not expecting this situation." Charlotte's cheeks had turned as red as Elizabeth's felt.

This would be a *very* bad moment for Darcy to

walk in! "Dearest Charlotte, you are the very best of friends! I cannot think of any questions at the moment. As you know, my mother tended to be more free with information than I often wished – but should any questions arise, you will definitely hear from me." Impulsively she leaned forward and kissed Charlotte's cheek. "After all, if you had not brought us back together, I would not be marrying Mr. Darcy tomorrow!"

Charlotte's lips twitched. "Why, just this morning you were glaring daggers at me!"

"You deserved it – conspiring with Colonel Fitzwilliam, indeed! And you claim not to be romantic!"

"*Someone* had to try to bring the two of you to your senses. If this fortnight has been anything to judge by, your marriage will never be dull."

The memory of Darcy in his shirtsleeves before a flickering fire warmed her. "No, it has not been dull. In fact, a little less excitement might not be unwelcome," she said ruefully.

"I am only sorry your visit with me will be cut short! I am only teasing, of course. Sleep well, and I will see you in the morning."

"Goodnight, Charlotte." With a sigh of relief, Elizabeth shut the door behind Charlotte, then sagged back against it. Thank heaven she had gone! She hoped Darcy would take care in making his way to her, if in fact he did.

Perhaps it would be wiser to appear to the world as if she were asleep. She snuffed the two candles, leaving the darkened room lit only by the glow of the fire. After all, they had done well enough during the blizzard without candles.

She sat on the bed, wrapping her arms around her knees. She decided she would wait a little longer, and then go to sleep if he did not come.

The door latch lifted and a tall, familiar figure slipped inside. "Are you still awake?" he asked softly.

Elizabeth scrambled to her feet. "Yes. You just missed Charlotte."

He chuckled. "I know. I was starting down the passageway when I saw her knock on your door. I had to pretend I was going to Richard's room." He enveloped her in his arms.

How right it felt to be there! She rested her head against his shoulder. "I am glad we will not need to worry about secrecy in the future!"

"Tomorrow cannot come soon enough." He pressed his lips lightly on her forehead.

"I agree." She tilted her head back, thinking he would kiss her.

Instead, he stepped back and laid his forefinger against her lips. "I came here tonight hoping to sleep in your arms as I did at the cottage. After holding you on the beach, another night apart seemed intolerable. But if I start kissing you, I fear I will not stop at kisses. You tempt me more than you know."

Did he mean it? "I will take your word for it, but I will also be glad to sleep in *your* arms. How I missed that!"

His gaze grew more intense. "Did you?"

"Yes, I did." Unable to resist the opportunity to

tease, she added, "You made a lovely, warm pillow."

"A pillow, indeed. You were wearing more than this in the cottage, though."

She felt a tug on the belt of her dressing gown and looked down to see his hands sliding inside it. The warm weight of them on her hips through the fine linen of her nightgown sent shivers down her spine.

"We both slept in our clothes there. *This* is a nightgown."

"No, *that* is temptation incarnate! I think you had best sleep in your dressing gown as well, or all my good intentions may go for naught." With seeming reluctance, he removed his hands, pulled her robe together, and firmly tied the belt.

She crinkled her nose at him, unsure if she were relieved or disappointed. Her body, tingling from head to foot, voted on the side of disappointment. "Very well, if you insist. For tonight."

He groaned. "Do not say such things!"

"My, what a lot of rules you have tonight!"

"My, what an impertinent minx I have tonight!" He threw back the counterpane and gestured to the bed.

She hesitated. It should not be so hard to get into the bed. After all, she had lain with him on the pallet in the cabin, but somehow this seemed much more intimate. Gathering her courage, she lay back and held out her arms to him.

He slid in beside her, putting his arm under her head. "That is better."

She sighed with pleasure. "Much better. But

what if someone discovers us in the morning?"

"You need not worry. I always wake up before dawn, and will be gone before even the servants are about their business."

If only he would kiss her, it would be perfect! Snuggling close to him, she wondered how she could possibly fall asleep with him pressed against her. "Mm."

He kissed her forehead. "Sleep well, sweet Lizzy."

She opened one eye. "That is what you said at the cottage. I have treasured that memory."

"I have thought it every night since."

Blanketed in his care and concern, she fell under sleep's spell.

A persistent knocking roused Darcy from a most pleasurable dream of making love to Elizabeth in his bed at Pemberley. But this was not that magnificent oak four-poster, just a narrow inn bed, with sunlight pouring in the window and Elizabeth's head pillowed on his shoulder.

"Elizabeth?" It was Georgiana's voice.

And his sister was at the door.

What was wrong with him? He had not slept this late since… since sleeping in Elizabeth's arms at the cottage. What an idiot he was! He shook Elizabeth's shoulder. Scrambling out of bed with a finger to his lips, his eyes darted around the room. There must be somewhere he could hide. Devil take it, not enough space under the bed for him there!

"Elizabeth, are you awake?" That sounded like

Mrs. Collins.

Elizabeth hissed, "Behind the wardrobe!" Then she added more loudly, "Yes, just a moment. I shall be right there."

Darcy eyed the narrow space between the wardrobe and the wall. Could he possibly fit there? If it were anyone but Georgiana outside the door, he would simply brazen it out, but he could not do so in front of his little sister. With the force of panic, he managed to squeeze behind it.

Yes, it worked! At least as long as his head was turned to the side and he took only shallow breaths. What a ridiculous situation!

The latch clicked. "Good morning, ladies," said Elizabeth.

"I am so sorry to have woken you," said Georgiana, "but Mrs. Collins said we needed extra time to prepare you for the wedding, since we may need to adjust Cousin Anne's dress to fit you."

He prayed Elizabeth would manage to chase them away. He might strangle if he had to stay in the confined space much longer!

Mrs. Collins came to his rescue. "Lizzy, your room is very small. Perhaps it would be easier if we used Miss Darcy's room. There would be more space for all of us."

"An excellent idea," said Elizabeth. "Is there anyone in the passageway, or can I go in my dressing gown?"

"The coast is clear," said Mrs. Collins.

The sound of the latch falling into place was

one of the sweetest sounds Darcy had ever heard.

Elizabeth set a quick pace. The sooner they reached Miss Darcy's room, the better.

Charlotte caught her arm and whispered, "You wicked girl, Lizzy!"

"I beg your pardon?"

Her friend waited until Miss Darcy was opening her door to whisper, "Your wardrobe had *feet*."

"What do you mean?" Elizabeth had a sinking feeling she already knew.

"Four wooden legs and two human feet!" Charlotte was fighting not to laugh.

Elizabeth batted her lashes in mock innocence. "What is the point of being compromised if I cannot enjoy it?"

Miss Darcy looked back at them with a puzzled expression. "Is anything the matter? Did I do something I should not have?"

Elizabeth quickly hid her smile. "Nothing at all. Just giggling over the idea of being married so soon!"

When Darcy finally reached his room, he found his clothes laid out perfectly on the bed. Crewe sat in a straight backed wooden chair, his arms crossed over his chest.

"I was beginning to wonder if you planned to stop by," said Crewe pointedly.

Darcy scowled at him. "There is no need to look at me like that. Nothing happened. I overslept; that is all."

"You overslept." There was a world of disbelief in those two words.

"Yes, just as I did when I was stranded with her before!"

"At least she is an excellent sleeping potion, then."

"For God's sake, I will be married to her in a few hours, and I do not need to justify myself to my valet!" Especially after spending a quarter hour attempting to escape from that cursed wardrobe. Who would have thought getting out would be so much more difficult than getting in?

Crewe raised his eyebrows. "Of course you need not justify yourself to me. But if you wish to be at the church promptly, might I suggest, sir, that you wait to terminate my employment until after you are dressed."

"Do not be ridiculous."

"How very fortunate I arranged for you to marry her today. If you could not manage to wait one night, three months would have been a true disaster."

With his best Master of Pemberley glare, Darcy said ungraciously, "And I thank you for it."

Crewe almost smiled, then resumed his usual unreadable expression as he assisted Darcy with his dressing gown.

Chapter 21

DARCY STILL COULD not quite credit that they were married. Only the sight of the ring on Elizabeth's finger offered him proof it was real. But the ring could not sparkle nearly as much as Elizabeth's fine eyes in the bright sunshine as they walked the short distance from the church to the inn. So bedazzled was he by his new wife that he nearly collided with a plump woman standing in his path in front of the inn.

Darcy barely gave her a glance as he touched his hat. "Pardon me, madam."

"Mr. Darcy," she said crisply, "May I have a few moments of your time?"

Not someone begging a favor, not now! Brusquely he said, "This is a most inopportune moment."

"I am sorry for that, but I have come a long distance for the chance to speak to you. Do you not remember me?"

Annoyed, he turned his attention to her. At first she seemed a complete stranger, and then he saw through the years which had softened her face and added crow's feet by her eyes. He took an involuntary step backwards as he recognized the face that had haunted him for years.

"I see you do. I pray you, if you will only hear what I have to say, I will leave you in peace."

Everything in him wanted to refuse, but Georgiana, Richard and Mrs. Collins were only a short distance behind them, and above all he needed to prevent her presence from becoming known to Georgiana. "Very well, but only a few minutes. There is a private parlor in the inn."

"I thank you."

Darcy had forgotten Elizabeth's presence until her hand tightened on his arm. She gave him a questioning look.

He took a deep breath. "Elizabeth, may I present Mrs. Dawley. She is the last person before you to bear the title of Mrs. Darcy."

"Your wife? I had not heard you were married."

Elizabeth curtsied. "It was quite recent."

"Pray accept my felicitations, in that case."

Darcy glanced back over his shoulder. Georgiana and the others were already in sight. "Come, let us go in." He held the inn door open for them.

To his relief, Elizabeth took charge of arranging for immediate use of the private parlor and requesting tea, thus giving him a few much needed moments to remind himself he was the Master of Pemberley. Under her breath, Elizabeth asked, "Do you wish for me to accompany you?"

It had not occurred to him she might not. "Please."

Once they were settled and the door to the private parlor firmly closed, he said in his most authoritative manner, "So, you have gone to a great deal of trouble to find me."

Mrs. Dawley bit her lip. "Yes. When they told me you were not in London, I inquired as to your whereabouts. I thought it might be easier to reach you here. I wish to see Georgiana and to reassure myself of her well-being."

"Georgiana is perfectly well, and I wonder at this sudden interest of yours in a child you left behind long ago."

"If you think I have forgotten her simply because your father refused to allow me to take her, you do not understand how a mother's heart works. I have thought of her and missed her every day. When she reached the age I was when I met your father – and you – I began to think more about that terrible time, and to fear Georgiana might herself be placed in a similar situation. Finally I became so distraught over it that my friends suggested I try contacting you."

He would not allow her to manipulate him again. "I fail to see what was so terrible about it. Was it marrying a wealthy man or having to live at one of the most beautiful estates in Britain?"

Her brows tightened. "It was terrible for *me*," she said softly. "I married a man old enough to be my father, thinking he was enamored of me, and discovered he did not want a wife but an unpaid governess for his son. He sent me away from all my friends and family to a place where I knew no one except an eight year old boy. For years I had been waiting for my Season, looking forward to all the balls and soirees, laughing with all my friends – and instead I was whisked off to the middle of nowhere while my *husband* remained in London."

Darcy shook his head. "That is ridiculous. He had no need to marry to provide me with a governess."

"No, he could have hired someone, but you had taken a liking to *me* at a time when you were badly out of spirits. I was too well-born to be offered employment, so he married me instead to secure my services. You had been so withdrawn since your mother's death, and he had been at his wit's end to bring you out of it when he discovered you were happy in my company. My father was delighted at what he saw as a brilliant match. But no one asked *me* if I wished to be purchased as a playmate for a little boy."

His stomach clenched. "I had been under the foolish impression you liked me, but all you wanted was Pemberley."

"I *did* like you, but a young boy could not take the place of everyone else in my life. I missed my friends and my brothers. I hated Pemberley. It was my gaol, not my home. No one there wanted a seventeen year old mistress. They whispered behind their hands all the time." She shivered.

"If you hated Pemberley so, why did you attempt to kill me, if not so *your* child would inherit?"

She stiffened and drew back. "Attempt to *kill* you? That is utter nonsense!"

"True; you did not try to poison me, just to put

me in dangerous positions where I might be killed. Shall I list them all off for you? The unbroken horse, the cliffs, the trees?"

Turning white, she grabbed at the edge of the table. "*That* is what you thought I was doing? I thought if I showed everyone that you were not safe with me, your father would bring me back to London and my friends. Why else do you suppose I had you do all those things in front of the steward or your tutor? They were supposed to write to your father and tell him you should not be in my care! I never wanted to hurt you. Had I realized all it would do was make you be taken away and I would remain trapped at Pemberley, I should never have attempted it. You were the only pleasant thing about Pemberley for me."

His throat ached. Could it be true? He reviewed his memories. Had there always been someone watching his dangerous exploits? He could not remember one where he had been alone with her. But his tutor and his uncle had been so certain of her motives. "You left me alone without food or drink when I was ill."

She clenched her fists. "*That* was that horrible Reed woman, the housekeeper. I said the servants were not to *tend* you, not that they were not to *feed* you. If *I* had given such a ridiculous order, which I did *not*, the housekeeper should have ignored it. I told your uncle all this at the time. *And* I dismissed the housekeeper, something she thought I would never dare to do. And, as usual, your father paid no attention to anyone's reports."

"That seems a ridiculously farfetched explanation for your behavior. Surely there were more sensible methods to use to convince my father."

"It was foolish, I admit, but I was desperate — and practically still a child myself. I had pleaded again and again, both to your father and my own, to no avail. Your father cared a great deal for your happiness and very little for mine. He felt I was more than adequately recompensed as his wife. As if an estate alone could make me happy! That is all men care about, estates and money, but they meant nothing to me."

"Many women would tolerate much more than you did to be Mistress of Pemberley."

"Perhaps so, but I am not one of them. If I wanted Pemberley so badly, why did I ask to return to my home? Where, I might add, I was much happier, but I do not know why I am bothering to tell you this. It is clear you have made up your mind I am an evil, murderous villain." She pulled on her gloves with sharp, abrupt movements.

"Wait." Elizabeth placed her hand on Mrs. Dawley's arm. "You are asking him to change a belief he has held for years. I pray you, give him a little time."

Mrs. Dawley glared at her for a moment, then nodded slightly. "Very well. He looks a great deal like his father, and it brings back painful memories." Her voice quivered.

Conscious of Elizabeth's gaze on him, Darcy said carefully, "I was under the impression my father decided to send you away." But he could not recall his father saying anything about it. Had it just been his own assumptions?

"No, of course not! Why would he send me away? It was not as if he ever bothered to see me as it was, apart from those occasional visits to Pemberley he could not avoid. Once I realized he intended to keep me in the wilds of Derbyshire forever and would never permit me to live with him in London, I knew my only chance of happiness was to leave."

"I fail to see why he would not allow you to live in London."

She hesitated, then looked away. "You do not know?"

"Apparently not."

"He had ensconced his long-time mistress in Darcy House, and did not wish to move her out on my account. I can see you do not believe me. Ask any of the servants who were there at the time; they can tell you."

It felt as if she were taking his world apart, one piece at a time, and there was no solid ground on which to stand. Then he felt Elizabeth's hand grip his, and he looked into her eyes. *She* was his anchor.

He turned back to the other woman. "Mrs. Dawley, would you be so kind as to excuse me briefly? There is a matter I must attend to."

"Of course," she said, and Elizabeth gave him an encouraging nod. She must have guessed what he planned to do.

He had to stop half way up the staircase to regain his equanimity. Then he found Crewe in his room, laying out a fresh set of clothes.

"Crewe, I wish to ask you some questions about

my father." His voice felt rusty.

Crewe straightened. "Of course, sir."

"After my mother's death, did my father keep a mistress at Darcy House?"

Crewe did not meet his eyes. "Yes, sir."

"Even during his second marriage?"

"Yes, sir."

"Why did he send his second wife away from Pemberley?" He watched Crewe's expression closely.

Crewe hesitated. "I cannot say for certain, but I believe it was at her request. She came to London to speak to him. He was agreeable to it, but she became quite distraught, presumably when he told her he would not permit her to take Miss Georgiana with her. But this is solely my conjecture; he never said as much to me."

"Lord Matlock believed she was trying to harm me."

"Yes. Your father did not believe a word of it, but felt if you were happy at your uncle's house, there was no point in quarreling over it."

Darcy sank down in the chair by the fire and lowered his head into his hands.

"Sir?" asked Crewe tentatively.

"What?"

"Is all well with Mrs. Darcy?"

For a moment Darcy thought Crewe was referring to his stepmother, then remembered there was a new Mrs. Darcy. A smile grew across his face. "She is quite well, and I must return to her."

With a lighter step, he returned downstairs.

When he opened the door to the parlor, he heard Mrs. Dawley say, "I hope I have not given you a poor impression of your future home. Pemberley is very beautiful, a home anyone would be proud of. It was simply not a good place for a lonely girl who longed for the Devon coast."

Elizabeth smiled warmly. "I am very much looking forward to seeing Pemberley after all I have heard about it."

"Do you have no happy memories of Pemberley?" Darcy asked abruptly.

"Of course I have a few. Although one stately home is much like another to me, I loved the grounds at Pemberley." She paused, a misty smile lighting her face. "And our hiding place. I have very fond memories of that."

"What hiding place?" Darcy could not recall anything of the sort.

"Our cave, where we built the fire pit ring from river stones and lit fires to stay warm."

Darcy shook his head. "No, it was Richard who lit fires in a cave with me."

She looked taken aback. "I suppose you may have done it with him as well. But do you not remember? It was under Curbar Edge, not a true cave, just a hollowed out overhang. We even wove a little awning from willow branches to keep us dry in the rain. It was very ill-made, as I recall, but it served its purpose."

Weaving willow branches – yes, he could remember that. He stretched his fingers. It had been much harder than it looked, forcing the flexible branches into ever smaller openings, but he had done it until his fingers ached, and been ridiculously proud of himself for building something with his own hands. "I do recall," he said haltingly. "You made up stories for us to act out. Sometimes we were cavaliers hiding from the Roundheads, or wild Indians in America preparing to attack the British settlers."

"Or Robin Hood's men!" she chimed in. "That was your favorite."

"And I always said you should be Maid Marian, but you wanted to be Will Scarlett."

Her eyes crinkled as she smiled. "Will Scarlett sounded so much more interesting than Maid Marian, though I had complete sympathy with her desire to run away from home."

Yes, he had relished those games with her. Why had she troubled herself so much to entertain an eight year old boy? And at Curbar Edge of all places! His stomach lurched. There was no place near Pemberley where it would be easier to stage a fatal accident than Curbar Edge. Men had died there by stepping a little too close to the edge of the precipice. But she had taken him to the base of Curbar Edge, not the dangerous top. If she had been attempting to cause his death, she had thrown away an excellent opportunity on many occasions.

His uncle must have been mistaken about her motives. And that meant....

Abruptly, before he could convince himself otherwise, he said, "If you wish to meet with Georgiana,

I have no objection."

She clapped her hands together and pressed them to her chest. "I may? Truly?"

"I will call her now if you wish."

Her eyes were suspiciously shiny. "Nothing could make me happier."

Elizabeth rose. "I will invite her to join us."

Darcy gave her a grateful look. Elizabeth would know how to break the news to Georgiana.

Mrs. Dawley patted her hair, then wrung her hands together. "What does Georgiana know of me?"

"She believed you dead until last summer when she discovered the truth. I have said little but to confirm you are alive, and that it was our father's wish she have no contact with you."

She looked away, her lips tightening. "I will never forgive him for refusing to let me see her. No doubt he felt it would be in her best interest, but I cannot but feel it was cruel to both of us."

Georgiana had said something similar, had she not? "He never told me the reasoning for his decision."

"I know nothing about her. I hope she will not be disappointed in me. Will she think ill of me for not trying to make contact sooner? Forgive me; I am babbling. I do so hope this goes well!"

Before he could think of an appropriate rejoinder Elizabeth appeared in the doorway. Georgiana followed behind her, holding her hand, her face ashen.

He stood and bowed, then experienced a moment of panic. How did one introduce a woman to her grown daughter? Should he say it was her mother?

Elizabeth once again saved him. "Georgiana, dear, may I present Mrs. Dawley?"

Georgiana's curtsey was jerky. "I am pleased to make your acquaintance." Her voice was just over a whisper.

Mrs. Dawley hurried towards her and gripped Georgiana's hand in hers. "Oh, my dearest girl!"

Then, as Georgiana began to cry, her mother enveloped her into a warm embrace, tears streaming down her own cheeks.

Darcy swallowed hard. How much had his sister missed over the years from thinking her mother dead? He had never seen her sob like this, her shoulders heaving as she clung to Mrs. Dawley.

Elizabeth slipped her hand into his. "Perhaps we should give them a little privacy."

Leave Georgiana alone with his stepmother? It went against every instinct he possessed. But could his instincts be trusted? Looking down at Elizabeth's fine eyes, he realized it did not matter. *Elizabeth's* instincts could be trusted, and she thought they should leave.

And then he could finally be alone…with his wife. His *wife*! What an absolutely delightful concept! Tonight he would not have to restrain himself. His body suggested tonight could not possibly come soon enough.

"Come." He led her out of the private parlor into the main room, where Richard jumped to his feet from one of the benches by the fire.

Intercepting them, he tapped a rolled up paper against his hand. "Finally!"

Darcy held up his hand. "Richard I will tell you everything, but *later*." He put his arm around Elizabeth with a meaningful look at his cousin.

"Sorry; it will have to wait," said Richard. "We have a problem."

His heart sank. "What is it *this* time?"

"Our dear cousin Anne has taken it into her head to run off. No one knows where she has gone."

Darcy groaned. "How did you discover this?"

Richard flashed a grin. "An express for both of us. I opened it since the barman said you were not to be interrupted. Who were you speaking to?

"My stepmother," said Darcy absently. "But how could Anne run off?"

"*She* is here? Good God, Darcy, what is the world coming to?"

"Never mind that. All is well with her. Tell me about Anne."

Richard shook his head in disbelief. "If you say so. Apparently she had her trunk packed, ordered the carriage to take her to the coaching inn, and got on the London stage. When Higgins asked her where she was going, she told him it was not his place to question her."

Darcy whistled. "Just like her mother. What has your father done?"

"Nothing. He left Rosings shortly before she did. I suspect that is why she chose that time."

Damn Anne! It was his wedding day – soon to be his wedding *night* – and the last thing in the world he wanted to do was to chase after his foolhardy cousin.

"Well, she *is* of age."

"Yes, but you were appointed her guardian, and she has no knowledge of the world. Lord knows what manner of trouble she has got into!" Richard scowled.

"Devil take it! Richard, this is my wedding day!"

The lines of Richard's face softened slightly. "I know, and your family appears to be conspiring to ruin it for you. I wish this could be put off until tomorrow."

Elizabeth's hand slipped through Darcy's arm. "It is no matter," she said warmly. "We will have a great many other days when we will be together. We are married, and no one can take that away."

Except Mr. Bennet, if the marriage were not consummated. Darcy intended to make absolutely certain to remove that possibility as soon as he could, if his thrice-damned family would ever let him.

"Very well," said Darcy. "We will leave after our meal. Crewe has arranged a wedding breakfast for all of us, and we deserve at least that much of a wedding celebration."

After making arrangements for their departure, Darcy returned to the private parlor and found a tearstained but radiant Georgiana sitting close beside Mrs. Dawley, their hands entwined. At least that part of the day appeared to have been successful.

Mrs. Dawley looked up at him. "Thank you so much. I cannot tell you how much this means to me. My beautiful little girl, all grown up!" She touched Georgiana's cheek. "It is so odd to see myself reflected in you, my dear child, although I can see quite a bit of

Will in you as well!" She turned back to Darcy, her eyes frightened. "My apologies, Mr. Darcy, it just slipped out. I will not allow it to happen again."

To his astonishment, Darcy found himself saying, "I do not object if you wish to call me Will, although it is Fitzwilliam more often these days."

Tears filled her eyes. "You are very kind. Fitzwilliam was much too big of a name for a little boy, but it suits you now."

He swallowed hard. "Indeed it is. While I regret interrupting your reunion, the wedding breakfast is ready. Would you care to join us? It is a very small party, but enough food for a regiment." It was only for Georgiana's sake, of course.

Her brows came together in puzzlement. "Wedding breakfast? Why, who has been married?"

Georgiana giggled. "Fitzwilliam and Elizabeth. Just this morning."

Darcy said, "You caught us on our way back from the church."

Her eyes widened. "Your wedding day? Oh, I am so sorry! I would never have dreamed of interrupting such a special occasion had I known! What must you think of me? I had not heard anything about a wedding in the offing."

From behind him, Elizabeth said, "That is because we did not tell anyone. But I pray you, do join us."

"Oh, yes, if it please you," whispered Georgiana.

The older woman smiled tremulously. "If you

are willing to include me, I would be more than happy to join you."

It was an odd sort of wedding breakfast with only four people plus the bride and groom, but Crewe had outdone himself in making certain the finest foods were served. To Elizabeth's surprise, Darcy spoke openly about Anne's disappearance and the need to leave for Rosings after the meal despite Mrs. Dawley's presence. Georgiana's expression bespoke particular disappointment at the news.

"Georgiana, Crewe will escort you back to London with your maid," said Darcy.

Georgiana took a deep breath, then said, "May my mother come with me?"

Darcy glanced at Richard and chewed his lip for a moment. "If you and she both wish it, I have no objection if she joins you in the carriage."

"Oh, I do wish it! Thank you!" Georgiana rushed to hug her bemused-looking brother.

Mrs. Dawley spoke quietly to Elizabeth. "I cannot tell you how happy I am that Will is taking this so well. I was terribly afraid he would refuse even to speak to me. Until today, I never understood why he had taken such a sudden dislike to me as a child, but it was very painful. Even as a young child, he was very special. You are a fortunate woman."

Then Georgiana was back by her mother's side and the opportunity for private conversation ended.

Chapter 22

AFTER LETTING CHARLOTTE off at the parsonage, the carriage arrived at Rosings shortly before dark. A footman opened the door immediately, with Higgins just inside.

"Has Miss de Bourgh returned?" Darcy stripped off one glove, then the other.

"No, sir." Higgins cleared his throat.

"What has been done to discover her whereabouts?"

Higgins took a step back. "Sir, it is not my place to question the doings of my betters."

Richard snorted and strode past the butler. "Who saw her before she left?"

"Her maid, and the coachman who took her to the posting inn."

"What of her companion, Miss Holmes?"

"Miss Holmes went with Miss de Bourgh."

"Well, thank heavens for that!" said Richard. "Hopefully Miss Holmes has more sense than Anne does."

Darcy dropped his gloves on the tray. "Have her maid brought to the sitting room directly. I will be there as soon as I have shown Mrs. Darcy to our rooms. You must send someone to the parsonage for her belongings."

"Mrs. Darcy?" said Higgins skeptically, looking from Darcy to Elizabeth and back.

"Mrs. Darcy," he said firmly.

"Miss de Bourgh's maid, sir." A footman ushered in a woman of middle years.

"You wished to see me, sir?" Her hands clutched at her skirt even after she curtsied.

"Yes. I wish to know everything that happened yesterday leading up to Miss de Bourgh's departure."

"There was not much, sir. Everything seemed just as usual until breakfast arrived. She had it in her rooms, just like always, but this time she told me to have her trunk fetched from the attics. When the footmen brought it, she closed the door and told me to pack it."

"Did she give you any instructions on what to pack or how much?

"She pointed out which dresses should be packed, then told me to add everything else she would need."

Darcy willed himself to be patient. "How many dresses did she choose?"

"Ten, sir. Five day dresses and five evening gowns. And none of them were mourning dresses!" This seemed to shock the maid more than the fact of her mistress's disappearance.

So she intended to be away for an extended

period of time. "Did you notice anything unusual about her behavior?"

"She had been giggling with Miss Holmes all the day before, and Miss Holmes seemed very excited. But Miss de Bourgh usually sends me away when Miss Holmes is here except when it is time to dress or do her hair, same as she did when I finished packing."

Darcy found it difficult to imagine Anne giggling. "Have you heard her speak about wishing to travel anywhere?"

"No, sir, but she would not speak to me of such things."

"Does she correspond with other ladies?"

"Just Lady Matlock and Miss Darcy, and even those not very often."

"Does she have friends? People who visit her?"

The maid shook her head. "Not that I am aware of, sir. We do not receive many callers at Rosings."

That was hardly surprising. Lady Catherine had managed to annoy all the neighbors enough she was rarely invited anywhere, leaving her dependent on her parson for company. "Can you think of anything else?"

"No, sir, except that Mr. Collins has visited her every day since Lady Catherine's accident, but she never spoke to him for long."

Collins. Could he know something? Was he at the parsonage? Or might he be with Anne?

"Will there be anything else, sir?"

"No, you may go."

No sooner had the maid departed than Richard hurried in. "Any news?"

"Nothing."

Richard rubbed his chin. "I do not understand. Where would she go? And why would she leave no word?"

"I wish I knew. Did Mrs. Jenkinson tell you anything?" The chaperone had made her own way back to Rosings Park on the previous day after discovering Darcy's plans to marry Elizabeth.

"She claims to know nothing. My impression is Anne was not in the habit of confiding her."

From what little he had seen of Mrs. Jenkinson on their journey, Darcy was not surprised. "The question is what to do next. Do we simply wait for Anne to return, or try to determine where she may have gone?"

"Do we have a choice?"

Darcy passed his hand over his forehead. "Not really, no."

Perhaps Elizabeth would accompany him to question Mr. Collins. Not that he needed any assistance; he just wanted to be by her side.

They rejoined ranks just before dinner to pool their knowledge. Richard stretched his legs out in front of him in a manner he would never have used in front of Lady Catherine. "Miss Holmes's family knows nothing. She told them she would be staying with Anne for several days. No one gave it a second thought under the circumstances. She has said nothing about wishing to travel, nor anything in particular about Anne. Her mother reports that some months ago she said someday

Anne would surprise everyone, but she would not elaborate on it. Did you find anything?"

Darcy shook his head. "None of the grooms or stable boys knew anything of their destination. Two trunks were placed on the stage, a large one belonging to Anne and a smaller one for Miss Holmes. No one noticed any smaller bags suitable for an overnight stay in an inn, suggesting either they are within a day's travel or Anne did not know to pack a second bag."

"What of Collins? Did you find him?"

Elizabeth said with a smile, "Yes, and he took a very long time to tell us nothing at all. He had not even realized she had left. But, oh! The colors he turned when he discovered we were married! I do not believe I have ever seen those colors on a human before." She reached out to take Darcy's hand.

Richard frowned. "Anne seems to have gone to some trouble to hide her tracks. There must be someone else who knows her."

"There is her doctor, but he is in London. It would be a long shot, but worth pursuing since we have nothing else."

Richard nodded. "Assuming you are still going to London tomorrow, perhaps you could find him. I will remain here in case Anne returns."

Darcy said, "It is hardly fair to leave you cooling your heels here while we go to Town."

Richard chuckled. "True, but you are newlyweds, and you need to visit your lovely wife's family to share the happy news. I will be quite content exploring Lady Catherine's wine cellars. I have always suspected she had better vintages than she served to us. Besides, I enjoy Mrs. Collins's company. She is very restful."

As Elizabeth gave Richard a grateful look, Darcy said, "Very well. We will plan on that, then."

Richard yawned ostentatiously. "I think I shall retire now. It has been a long day."

Darcy glanced at the clock. It was barely eight o'clock, and Richard had always been a night owl. Then he saw his cousin wink at him.

"An excellent idea," said Elizabeth demurely.

Darcy flexed his arms after Crewe remove his fashionably tight topcoat. It was not what he would have chosen to travel in, but no matter.

He dropped into low chair and stuck out his foot. Crewe pulled at the boot expertly and it popped off immediately. Darcy remembered how he had struggled to remove them in the cottage, and smiled. At least in the cottage, no one had interrupted them, but now he would finally be alone with Elizabeth again, and this time he would not have to stop. "Crewe?"

"Yes, sir?" The valet tugged off the second boot and brushed off a bit of dirt.

"I do not wish to be disturbed by anyone tonight or tomorrow morning unless the house is afire."

Crewe's lips tightened as he tried to hide a smile. "I will make certain of it."

"On second thought, not unless this wing of the house is burning. The other wing can be reduced to cinders for all I care."

"And the stables? What if they were afire?"

It was unheard of for Crewe to tease him, but Darcy grinned. "Save Bucephalus, but do not disturb me. And Crewe?"

"Yes, sir?"

"Thank you for making all the arrangements for the wedding."

A broad smile crossed the valet's face. "It was entirely my pleasure, sir."

In the next room, Elizabeth sat very still at the vanity as Lady Catherine's French maid removed her hairpins. When she picked up the hairbrush, though, Elizabeth said, "I will brush it out myself, if you will be so kind as to assist me with this dress. I have never worn anything with quite so many buttons!"

Antoinette sniffed to show her displeasure at Elizabeth's lack of polish, or perhaps it was simply disapproval of her position. Several of the Rosings staff seemed to be under the impression that she had somehow stolen the position of Mrs. Darcy from its rightful owner. Elizabeth hid a smile, thinking what Darcy would say if he knew. She herself did not care; she would be leaving tomorrow and never see Antoinette again. But she would still have him. A shiver of anticipation raced through her.

Her wedding night. It still did not seem real, not without the weeks of preparation for a wedding she had always expected. In a few minutes, her husband would arrive to consummate the marriage. It was supposed to be the moment which would change her from a girl to a wife, but their courtship had been so unusual that this seemed more like just one step in the process. And if it was anything like what had happened in the cove, it would be very interesting indeed!

She stepped out of her dress and allowed Antoinette to unlace her stays, then dismissed her before she could assist with her nightdress. It was just her plain everyday nightdress, no frills or lace, not at all what the bride of Mr. Darcy would be expected to wear on her wedding night. Somehow she did not think it would matter to him, though.

A knock on the connecting door sent her pulses racing. Rising to her feet, she said, "Come in."

Darcy was dressed in his shirtsleeves and a pair of trousers, not the nightshirt she had expected. The draping linen revealed the strong lines of his shoulders, making Elizabeth catch her breath.

After halting just inside the door, he moved forward towards her slowly. He reached out a finger and entwined it in a loose curl. "You leave me without words," he said hoarsely.

Tilting her head to the side, she said archly, "Then we must find activities which do not involve speaking."

His eyes flared, growing darker than she had ever seen them. Then he pulled her into his arms and held her tight. Pressing his head against hers, he said, "I have been wanting to do this all day. I thought I might run mad during that interminable carriage ride, having you so close to me, yet unable to touch you."

She decided not to mention how frequently his

foot had touched hers. "And now?"

"I still think I might run mad. Elizabeth, I do not wish to frighten you, and I fear my passion for you may do so."

She tilted her head and brushed her lips against his. "My courage always rises with each attempt to intimidate me, and I am not afraid. Somehow it seems easier for having shared a bed with you before."

He nodded jerkily. "I feel the same. This afternoon I realized I have felt as if we were married ever since the blizzard and today only formalizes what already existed."

Warmth filled her. She placed her palms against his chest and stroked outwards towards his shoulders. "How I wished in the cottage to do this, and now I may!"

Darcy sucked in a deep breath. "Whereas I wanted you to unbutton my shirt and touch me. Though I suspect our story there would have ended differently if you had done so!"

With an arch look, she undid the button on his shirt, though her hands were not as steady as she wished. "Do you know, I almost regret that it did not. It would have saved us so much trouble."

He closed his eyes, but she could see his breathing had quickened. Slowly she let his neck of his shirt fall open, and with what was either courage or abandon, placed her hand over his heart. The roughness of his skin against hers shot a powerful thrill straight through her.

His hand closed over hers, then he raised it to

his lips and kissed the center of her palm. "Next time. I fear for my self-control if you continue now." His lips moved in a circle around her palm, then up her fingers where he scraped his teeth lightly along her sensitive fingertips.

Sensation flooded her, and without meaning to, she swayed forward. Then his hands were tangling in her hair, drawing her face closer until he captured her mouth with his in a kiss which seemed to break through every barrier between them.

As she pressed herself against him, everything was different. Before there had always been many layers of clothes separating them, and now there was only light muslin. She could feel his body, the heat of it and the hardness, and it made her legs tremble.

His lips moved down to her neck, exploring the lines of it until he reached the hollow at the base. How had she never known what pleasure could be had from that little spot? Then she felt his fingers trace along the neckline of her nightgown, dipping just inside it and sending a swell of passion deep to her center.

She trembled as he untied the laces of her nightgown. He froze and gazed deep into her eyes. "Elizabeth, are you well? Do you wish me to stop?"

She shook her head. "Pray do not stop."

"My dearest, loveliest Elizabeth," he breathed as his warm hands shifted the nightgown from her shoulders. It whispered against her heated skin as it fell to the floor.

Chapter 23

DARCY WAS NOT in a good humor as he approached Mr. Graves's house. He had managed to locate his direction with relative ease, but it had already been a long morning of traveling from Rosings. A smile spread across his face. Of course he might just be fatigued from a lack of sleep the previous night – in the best of all causes! Elizabeth had fulfilled his every passionate dream of her. And then, instead of a leisurely day in bed, he had been forced to leave Elizabeth at Darcy House with Georgiana and Mrs. Dawley so he could hunt his errant cousin. He scowled.

He found the modest house in the City and presented his card. After a few minutes, a maid showed him into a small sitting room.

Anne de Bourgh rose gracefully to her feet, her friend Miss Holmes by her side. "So you have found your way here. Mr. Graves is out on a consultation, but I presume you were looking for me in any case."

So taken aback he almost forgot to bow, Darcy said sternly, "I am glad to see you well, cousin. Richard and I have been very worried about you."

"Well, that must be a novel experience for you!

As you can see, I am safe and in good health."

"Could you not have left word where you were going?"

She tilted her head and appeared to consider this for a moment. "I could have, but I have spent enough of my life seeking permission for the slightest variance to my routine. I am seven-and-twenty years old, not a child, and I do not need your supervision."

Darcy took a deep breath to steady himself. It was hardly surprising Anne would not think of the common courtesy of giving notice of her plans; she had seen little enough common courtesy at Rosings. And he did not wish to quarrel with her over her manners. She would be distraught enough with what he had to tell her.

"Now I know you are safe, may I have a moment of your time? There is a matter I would like to discuss with you."

She motioned him to a chair. "Please."

He glanced at Miss Holmes. "May we speak privately?"

"You may say anything you wish in front of Carrie. She is my dear friend and now my companion."

Since there was nothing to be done for it, he settled himself gingerly. They were only a few feet apart in this small room, and he was accustomed to keeping his distance from Anne. "You know it was your mother's wish that you and I should marry."

"I should say *everyone* must know that. She said it so often."

"However, I cannot marry you." He waited for

the storm.

"So you have said almost as often." She seemed quite unconcerned by the news.

"Unfortunately, there are other ramifications for you. Your mother left you Rosings only on the condition that you are married to me."

"Again, I have known this for years. It does not matter."

Bewildered, Darcy asked, "You do not care about losing your home?"

Her lip curled. "Do you think I am such a fool as to allow that to happen?"

"A fool? How could I possibly say? I am rapidly discovering how very little I know of you."

"Very observant. But Rosings is mine."

"Thanks to your mother, it does not work that way. She chose to deprive you of it in hopes it would force my hand."

Anne tapped her lips. "As I understand it, her will says that if I am unmarried at the time of her death, I will only inherit Rosings if I marry you. However, I was married prior to her death, so that does not matter."

He must have misheard. "I beg your pardon?"

"You heard me. I married two years ago, soon after I learned the contents of her will. I was not willing to lose my inheritance simply because my mother always had to have her own way."

Darcy felt lost. Had Anne made this up out of whole cloth? There were no men in her life. Perhaps she was not in her right mind. He glanced at Miss Holmes, but she did not seem to find any of this odd. "Ah…why did you say nothing of it?"

"And give my mother another opportunity to write me out of her will? No, thank you."

"I meant to ask why you have kept your silence since her death." And put him through two bad days of needless worry when he should have been celebrating his wedding.

"I did not care to discuss it until my husband was available. I knew you would try to stop me."

"Might I ask the identity of your husband?" He could only hope it was not one of the footmen.

She shrugged lightly. "Mr. Graves, of course."

"Mr. Graves?" Of course – Graves, who was so dedicated he called on her every week, whether she was in ill health or not. Graves, who would recognize the fortune which he only had to be patient to claim. Graves, who was clever enough to arrange for a wedding in a different parish, and to claim he only wished to give Anne the experience of walking out with a gentleman.

"Why not Mr. Graves? He gave me my life back. More than that, he *talked* to me. He brought me novels and Ackermann's Repository to read. He asked my opinions and listened to what I said. He found me Carrie, who did not report my every move to my mother or force vile tonics down my throat. No one else ever cared as much for me. I was happy to marry him."

There was little to be said to that, since Darcy had made a point of not showing Anne any attention, never considering how it would affect her. Still, there was nothing to be done now. If Graves was a fortune hunter, it was too late. "I hope you will be very happy."

"I am already happier than I have been in years. I have my dear husband, and Carrie will live with us instead of on her brother's charity. So you need not worry; you are under no obligation to me, especially as a potential husband."

"That would have been impossible in any case. You are not the only one who thought to avoid your mother's demands via a secret marriage. When I said I could not marry you, it was the truth."

That caught her attention. "I cannot believe it! You are married?"

"Just yesterday. My bride is waiting for me at Darcy House."

"Who is she?"

"You have met her as Miss Elizabeth Bennet. She came to dine at Rosings with Mr. and Mrs. Collins."

"The one who alternately ignored you and stared daggers at you?"

Darcy smiled. Who knew Anne had observed so much? "The very one."

Footsteps sounded outside the room, and Mr. Graves entered. Spotting Darcy, he looked quizzically at Anne.

She held her hand out to him. "Darcy knows. I just told him everything."

Her husband – what a concept! – smiled warmly at her as he took her hand and placed his free hand on her shoulder as he stood beside her. "I hope it is not too much of a disappointment to you, Mr. Darcy."

"Not at all. You will need to visit the solicitor and prove the facts of your marriage. I assume you kept documentation? Then I can turn Rosings Park over to you, as I am technically Anne's guardian until that time." He would be glad to wash his hands of this nonsense.

"I am at your service, with both documentation and witnesses. We anticipated our marriage might be contested."

"Very wise. Well, I shall impose on you no longer. I wish you both very happy."

Darcy was already on his feet when Mr. Graves said calmly, "I imagine you must think me the worst sort of fortune hunter, but I am very fond of your cousin. I suggested to her repeatedly that she quit Rosings to live with me here, even if it meant being cut out of her mother's will. But keeping Rosings is important to Anne, and I respect that."

Anne's lips tightened. "After everything I suffered at my mother's hands, I *deserve* Rosings. I would *not* give it up, even if it meant living there with her. At least she could no longer make me ill."

Darcy shook his head. "She *made* you ill?"

Mr. Graves responded, "When I was first called to see Anne, she was not far from death. In fact, I am surprised she survived so long. Her previous doctor bled her every week and dosed her with purgatives. At his orders she was fed nothing but milk and bread, which he described as a suitable diet for a young lady. My treatment for her, if you can call it that, was to stop the bleedings and purgatives, to give her meat and fruit every day, to take her out in the sun, and to replace her mother's purging tonic with a benign one which looked and smelled the same. A few months later, she was as you see her now. Anne, my dear, would you be so kind as to remove your glove?"

Anne hesitated, then rolled down one of her ever-present elbow length gloves and displayed her forearm to Darcy. It was crisscrossed with scars, some thick and red, others fine and fading to white.

He recoiled, remembering Anne's sickly years when she was always white as a ghost and weak enough walking across a room tired her. "I am sorry. I had no idea."

"Of course you had no idea," said Mr. Graves crisply. "Lady Catherine hired what she thought to be the finest doctors in England to care for her daughter. It was Anne's ill luck their skill was not proportionate to their reputations or their prices. But you will understand why I was reluctant to leave her under Lady Catherine's care, especially once she was my wife."

"I am glad you told me. It explains a great deal." Darcy cleared his throat. "Mr. Graves, Anne is not the only one to have suffered under Lady Catherine's rule. The upkeep of the estate, and especially the tenant villages, has been much neglected, and the steward is both incompetent and dishonest. I highly recommend replacing him at your first opportunity. If it would be of any assistance, I would be happy to make a list of the improvements I suggested to Lady Catherine, including repairing the road on which she met her end."

Graves looked surprised. "I would greatly appreciate that. I have no experience with land management, and will have much to learn."

At least the man recognized the problem. That was something.

❧

Darcy's next stop was at Matlock House where he was immediately shown in to see his uncle. He took in the sweet, rich aroma of fine brandy his uncle poured for him and allowed the first sip to roll around his mouth. French, by the taste of it, and no doubt smuggled. He should enjoy it now before the discussion became heated.

"I thought you were still at Rosings," said the earl.

"I left yesterday after discovering Anne had taken it into her head to travel. There is no need to worry; I have found her, but it has raised an interesting question regarding Lady Catherine's will."

The earl cleared his throat. "Now, Darcy, I understand you do not care for the idea of marrying Anne, but we cannot let Rosings go."

At least now he could avoid telling his uncle he had planned to do that very thing. "As it happens, Anne was aware of that clause in the will and decided some time ago to take action on her own. She is married already, and has been for two years. The clause only applied if Anne should be unmarried at the time of her mother's death. Presumably Lady Catherine never conceived of the possibility of Anne marrying someone other than me."

"Married already? Why, that is ridiculous. The girl never left Rosings."

"Apparently she has more ingenuity than we gave her credit for. There is one man who spent time with her on a regular basis – her doctor, now her husband."

Lord Matlock slammed his hands down on his desk. "Good God! Tell me this is a jest!"

"Unfortunately, it is no jest."

"We must get it annulled immediately."

"There does not appear to be grounds for an annulment. She has been living with him for several days. The one advantage is it does keep Rosings in the family, whereas otherwise Anne would lose it."

"Not if she were married to you."

Darcy set down his brandy. Better not to be holding fragile objects when the storm broke. "That would not be possible in any case. Even before Lady Catherine's untimely end, I was already honor bound to another."

"Engagements can be broken."

"But lost honor cannot be mended. The point is moot in any case. She is now my wife." He braced himself for the explosion.

"First *Anne* makes a mésalliance, and now *you*, of all people?"

"The lady in question saved my life at the cost of her own reputation. I could hardly ignore that. Whether it is a mésalliance or not I will leave to you. Her father is a gentleman, at least."

The earl pressed his fingertips to the bridge of his nose. "But not a *good* alliance, I take it."

"Her father owns a small estate which is entailed away from the family. They have no significant connections of which I am aware."

"It could be worse, I suppose. Is she presentable?"

"Yes." The thought of Elizabeth made him smile.

"Very well, then. I hope you will bring her to meet us."

Darcy gave a slow, disbelieving shake of his head. "That is all? No storms? No threats of disowning me or annulment?"

The earl leaned back in his chair and folded his hands behind his head. "Darcy, I would have accepted almost any woman you wished to marry. I had given up hope you would ever find one you could trust enough to give your name. Mind you, I understand you have reasons for distrust, but it will not serve to put up a wall against all womankind simply because your father chose a bad one. So if you are married, I am pleased."

"But you wanted me to marry Anne!"

His uncle sighed. "I thought it was my best chance of getting you married, as you were more likely to accept arguments about saving Anne than about the need for an heir. Well, all is well that ends well. You do like your new wife well enough to produce an heir, I hope?"

Darcy smiled. "That will not be a problem. She is unlike any other woman I have ever met, but she is perfect for me."

"Well, then, shall we drink to the new Mrs. Darcy?"

They clinked glasses. But one thing remained unresolved. If his uncle was not angry about his marriage, he would not disown Richard, who would be trapped in the army by his duty. "There is one other matter."

The earl narrowed his eyes. "What now?"

"It is about Richard. The army is destroying him."

"So I have gathered. But why does he say nothing?"

Darcy gave him an incredulous look. "Because you wanted him to join the army, and he wants to do his duty towards you – even if it kills him."

Lord Matlock shook his head in disbelief. "Do children ever grow up? Tell him to speak to me about it."

He had never seen his uncle accept opposition so calmly. Perhaps Anne was not the only relative he did not truly know.

Darcy was so impatient to reach Elizabeth that he practically leapt from the carriage when it reached Darcy House. Who could have known that consummating their marriage would make it even more painful to be separated from her, even for part of a day? It was too bad he would have to share her with Georgiana for a few hours until bedtime, but at least he could be in her presence.

He strode inside and stripped off his gloves. Handing his hat to the butler, he said, "Where is Mrs. Darcy?" Why waste time hunting for her?

"In the drawing room, sir."

But even as he said it, Elizabeth emerged from the drawing room to meet him. It was not at *all* proper, and he could not be happier about it. Willing the servants to disappear, he caught her around the waist and twirled her in the air, then set her down and kissed her. Slowly. Passionately. And hoping Georgiana would not come into the entryway.

Breathless, Elizabeth broke away long enough to say, "The servants…"

"The servants had damned well better accustom themselves to it!" And he kissed her again. If only he could take her straight upstairs! But no, they would have to be proper, then sit through a long dinner with Georgiana and listen to her perform on the pianoforte before he could have Elizabeth to himself. These kisses would have to tide him over until then. God, but it was good to have her in his arms!

Reluctantly he released her, but could not resist caressing her cheek. "I am sorry to have left you here for so long. I hope there have been no difficulties."

Elizabeth's dimples made an appearance. "No difficulties at all, though it was a trifle odd to suddenly become mistress of a house I did not know! I had not been here an hour before the housekeeper came to consult with me about dinner. I was going to tell her to do whatever she would usually do, but Mrs. Dawley came to my rescue and asked me if I would like her to take care of it for me. I was quite happy to allow her to do so, though I did not predict what she would do."

Foreboding filled him. "What happened?"

"Nothing like that!" She took his hand and led him into the drawing room where Mrs. Dawley and Georgiana rose at his approach. "She told the housekeeper we had not had a proper wedding night yet, so they put their heads together and made a plan."

Mrs. Dawley chuckled. "The two of you will be dining alone in your rooms tonight. Georgiana will be accompanying me to dinner at my hotel so you will have some privacy. We were just about to leave, were we not, my dear?"

Georgiana nodded, blushing. "You do not mind, do you?"

Did he mind being alone with Elizabeth? "Not at all."

His sister wrung her hands together. "Mrs my mother would like me to pay her a visit in Devon so I can meet her sons." She took a deep breath. "My younger brothers."

An unexpected pang struck deep in Darcy's chest. For all these years, he had been Georgiana's only immediate family, and now he would have to share her with her mother and two new brothers. Would he lose her to them?

Georgiana must have seen something in his face, for she said hurriedly, "There is no need to decide now. Perhaps we can discuss it another time."

He felt Elizabeth's hand in his, reminding him he would not be alone without his sister. His family had expanded to include Elizabeth, and it did not mean he loved Georgiana any less. "If you would like to go to Devon, I cannot see why you should not. I was merely taken aback by the idea of you having other brothers!"

She giggled. "I cannot quite believe it either!"

To his surprise, Mrs. Dawley put her hand to his cheek for a moment. "I thank you from the depth of my heart, my dear boy. I cannot tell you what it would mean to me. Perhaps some day you would like to meet them also."

"Of course I would like to meet Georgiana's other brothers," he said, somewhat surprised to realize it was true.

A radiant smile lit up Mrs. Dawley's face. "Nothing could make me happier! But I imagine nothing could make *you* happier than to be alone with your lovely bride, so we will take our leave of you now."

Elizabeth curtsied. "I hope you have a pleasant evening, and I will look forward to seeing you again."

Darcy watched with amusement as Mrs. Dawley efficiently bundled Georgiana out of the house.

Elizabeth said archly, "I hope you do not disapprove of her plans for us."

A slow smile grew on his lips. "Disapprove of being alone with you? Far from it! In fact, I believe we should go to our rooms immediately lest we miss our dinner."

She laughed as he led her up the stairs to their rooms, then gasped when he opened the door to his private sitting room – now *their* private sitting room. There were flowers everywhere, spring flowers and exotic hot house specimens, and even several bunches of roses. Their fragrance was everywhere, like spring in a garden. In the room beyond, even the four-poster bed was sprinkled with rose petals.

Elizabeth touched one of the velvety roses. "How could she possibly have arranged for this so quickly? I thought the room was beautiful before, but now it is beyond even that!"

"At the moment, I could find it in my heart to forgive my stepmother a great deal." He put his arms around Elizabeth from behind and caressed the side of her neck with his lips. "You are beyond beautiful."

A maid appeared in the doorway. "Mrs. Darcy," she said respectfully, "Is there anything that you will be requiring?"

"Perhaps some tea would be welcome."

"No, Mrs. Darcy has no need of anything at the moment," said Darcy authoritatively, never removing his eyes from Elizabeth. She could almost see the banked embers of desire beginning to flare to life in him.

The maid glanced back and forth between the two, then said, "Yes, sir," and withdrew with a curtsey.

He closed the door behind her. In response to her raised eyebrow, he said, "I wanted to be alone with you."

Elizabeth coloured, her body involuntarily responding the look in his eyes. "What will she think?"

Putting his hand to her cheek, he kissed her lingeringly. "She will undoubtedly think I am behaving like a newlywed man with a beautiful wife." He traced his finger lightly along her collarbone, then moved behind her and began to remove her hairpins, alternating his efforts with light kisses to her neck which rapidly undermined her desire to maintain propriety.

"But it is still afternoon!" she exclaimed as her hair fell loose about her shoulders, his tantalizing kisses sending seductive currents of excitement through her.

He ran his hands down her sides possessively, making her ache for more of his touch. "Observant as always, my love," he murmured. "Now, if you would be so kind as to stand still for a moment...." He turned his attention to the closures of her gown, and, sliding his fingers inside, began to undo them one by one as his lips explored the exposed skin of her shoulders. When he reached the last one, he pushed the gown down her arms until it fell to the floor.

As his hands began to discover the curves of her waist through her chemise, Elizabeth gave up any remaining pretext of resistance. She leaned back against him with a moan, allowing him the freedom to caress her through the thin fabric. His satisfied smile as she shivered at the touch was just the beginning.

Chapter 24

THE MANSERVANT WHO opened the door at the Gardiners' house looked surprised to see Elizabeth, as well he might, since normally she would walk in without knocking. But it seemed unfair to spring Mr. Darcy upon them unawares.

"Miss Elizabeth, your sister is in the sitting room."

"Thank you." Elizabeth took a deep breath, then marched forward.

Jane's face drained of color when she saw Elizabeth. She hurried forward and took both of her sister's hands. "Oh, Lizzy, pray tell me it is not our father! Who is it?"

Elizabeth stared at her in confusion. Of course it was not their father with her!

Fortunately Darcy's wits were working more clearly than her own. "Miss Bennet, your family is in good health. Elizabeth is wearing mourning for my aunt, Lady Catherine de Bourgh." He touched his own black crepe armband.

Jane's head swiveled from one to the other.

"Mr. Darcy! Pray forgive me for failing to notice you. It was merely the shock."

"Perfectly understandable, Miss Bennet."

"But Lizzy, why are *you* in mourning for *Mr. Darcy's* aunt?" Then her eyes widened as she examined Elizabeth's left hand and touched the ring on her finger. "Are you...are you..?"

"Married?" Elizabeth wrapped her fingers around Jane's hand. "Two days ago, in a very quiet ceremony in Folkestone."

As Jane opened her mouth, Darcy forestalled the next rush of questions. "It happened quite precipitously owing to our circumstances. Might I inquire if Mr. and Mrs. Gardiner are available? It might be simpler to tell the tale once."

"It is quite a long and circuitous story," added Elizabeth.

Darcy took Elizabeth's free hand and raised it to his lips. "The outcome is most satisfactory."

As heat rose in Elizabeth's cheeks, Jane said hurriedly, "Allow me but a moment to find my aunt and uncle. I will return shortly." She practically fled from the room.

"I do believe you frightened her away," said Elizabeth with a laugh.

"Good. It has been hours since I have kissed you." He took immediate action to remedy that situation.

A cough from outside the door made them spring apart, but Darcy somehow managed to retain hold of Elizabeth's hand. She smiled at him, amused by his continuing need to remain in contact with her.

Mr. Gardiner was looking hard at Darcy. "Why, this is certainly a surprise. Mr. Darcy, may I present my wife? Jane tells me you have something to tell us."

Darcy bowed to Mrs. Gardiner. "I do indeed; or perhaps I should say *Mrs. Darcy* and I have an announcement to make."

"That is quite a saga," said Mr. Gardiner after hearing the entire story. "Mr. Darcy, I must once again apologize profusely for the part I played in keeping you apart."

"There is no need for an apology when you were acting in what you thought was Elizabeth's best interests. I am the guardian of a much younger sister, and I likely would have made a similar decision, knowing only what you did."

Elizabeth said, "I hope Mr. Hartshorne will not be too disappointed."

"He will recover; although he might have preferred a different outcome for himself, he always felt it was unfair to you. I know he will be pleased for your sake. And I did promote him to a position of more responsibility, so he has gained something."

"Pray tell him I will never forget his generosity in offering me a safe haven."

Darcy had heard quite enough about this saintly Mr. Hartshorne who had dared to look at *his* Elizabeth.

Mrs. Gardiner asked, "Lizzy, have your parents been told of your marriage?"

Elizabeth glanced at Darcy. "Not yet. We wish

to give them the news in person."

"In a few days," said Darcy firmly. "After all that has happened, I have an urge to stay in the same place for several days running."

Three days later, Darcy grasped Elizabeth's hand as the carriage turned into the lane to Longbourn House. "Courage, my love."

"I know it will not be so difficult, but part of me still dislikes disappointing my father. I hope we can persuade him to reconsider his opinion of you."

"He may not do so today, but perhaps as he sees us together over time, his views may shift.

"I hope so." She smoothed her skirt with her free hand. After Jane's reaction to her mourning garb, she had elected to wear her lavender dress to Longbourn. Of course, the full mourning had been necessary to impress the Earl of Matlock with her propriety and respect for his family, but no one at Longbourn was likely to care about Lady Catherine's death.

Darcy kissed her lightly as they drew to a halt at the front steps.

The maid seemed startled to see her. "Miss Lizzy, I had not heard you were returning!"

"It is a surprise. Is my father in the library?"

"Yes, miss."

Elizabeth squared her shoulders before knocking on the library door. Opening it in response to her father's call, she was enveloped by the familiar dry scent of old books. In the past, she had always associated it with safety.

Mr. Bennet was seated in his favorite large leather chair by the window. Setting his book aside, he removed his spectacles. "Lizzy, this is a surprise. Or perhaps I should say it is *two* surprises."

Darcy placed his hand on the back of Elizabeth's waist. "There is a third surprise as well. Your daughter and I are married."

The older man, halfway to a standing position, froze with his hands still on the armrests, then straightened slowly, like a man two decades older. "That was quick work."

"Circumstances necessitated haste, as you must be aware."

Mr. Bennet's lips tightened into a thin line as he turned to his daughter. "Nothing to say for yourself, Lizzy, or does he already speak for you?"

Having breathed a little easier after Darcy's announcement relieved her of the necessity of confronting her father with the news, Elizabeth's resentment now took hold of her. "I would like to know why you lied to me. You never saw him in London, you never gave him my letter, and you did not tell me when he came to see you."

Slowly he pulled out a handkerchief and began to polish the lenses of his spectacles. "I do not deny opposing the match, and doing what I could to prevent it. But what is done is done, and all I can do is to hope my concerns proved unfounded."

Elizabeth licked her dry lips. "Precisely what were those concerns?"

"What is the point? You are already aware of my sentiments on unequal marriages and the resentment of a man forced into a leg-shackle. I wanted you to have a husband who respected you, not one who was marrying you because he had no other choice. You will forever owe him a debt for rescuing your reputation, and he will never allow you to forget it."

Darcy stiffened. "Sir, you mistake the matter. If there is any sort of debt, it is mine. Elizabeth saved my life, and if our wedding restored her reputation, it also served my own purposes. If Elizabeth has difficulties owing to her change in station, it is *my* responsibility to ease them, to instruct her in anything she needs to know and to protect her from situations which could prove embarrassing until she has had the opportunity to learn what she needs. With her cleverness and wit, I have no doubt she will soon be as comfortable in those situations as anyone born to them."

Elizabeth stared at Darcy. His unusual fluency on the subject told her he had thought this through in advance, and his sharp tone showed his anger. Could he be correct, that her mother's embarrassing behavior might have been different, had her father spent more effort in helping her adapt to her new circumstances? But the answer to that was already before her; it would have taken effort on his part, and her father disliked putting forth any effort which could possibly be avoided. Instead, he had found amusement in watching his wife's struggles.

"That is very easy to say, young man. I hope you find it as easy to do it."

"I have no doubts about *your daughter's* abilities."

Sensing her husband's increasing agitation, Elizabeth broke in before he could say anything further. "Father, we came here to share our news with you. I hope over time you will be able to see Mr. Darcy for the man I know him to be. In the meantime, we must be back in London tonight, and it is up to you whether I should break the news to my mother or whether you would prefer to do so yourself." She almost hoped he would choose the latter, as it would protect Mr. Darcy from what might prove to be embarrassing raptures.

Mr. Bennet's lips twisted into something which might have been a smile. "I will never hear the end of it should your mother be deprived of the opportunity to learn all those details she will glory in relating to her friends. Only spare me from any discussion of lace and fripperies!"

It was as close to an apology as she could hope to get. "Very well, though I can assure you lace was the least of my concerns at our wedding. I wore a borrowed dress."

"In that case, I wish I might have been there! But you would be wise to imagine at least a small amount of lace, lest your mother insist you go through it all again in a proper manner."

"Heaven forfend!" said Darcy. "Once was quite enough."

Elizabeth placed her hand on Darcy's arm. "Is there time for a short visit to the barn?"

The barn? Darcy's mind immediately jumped to piles of hay, but that could not be what she had in mind, not with her parents standing right behind them. "Of course."

Mrs. Bennet said, "Oh, Lizzy, you cannot take Mr. Darcy to the barn!"

"I assure you, Mrs. Bennet, I have seen the inside of a barn before," Darcy said sternly.

The older woman waved her handkerchief. "Well, if you must…"

"I must," said Elizabeth firmly. She led him past the house, through the gardens, to a small outbuilding.

"What is inside?" he asked.

"It is a surprise." She opened the door and peered inside, then went in.

Darcy trailed behind her, his eyes slowly adjusting to the dim light. The grassy scent of hay was everywhere. He followed her into a back corner.

She looked from side to side. "Snowball? Are you here? I hope she is not out catching mice; I would be sorry to miss her."

Something tugged on Darcy's trouser leg. He looked down to see the familiar fluffy white cat. Crouching down beside her, he stroked her fur as she rubbed against him, purring loudly. "Hello, Snowball."

"See, Snowball, I brought you your favorite person in the entire world!" said Elizabeth.

Snowball deigned to allow Elizabeth to pet her, then returned to courting Darcy. He said, "She has filled out quite a bit."

Elizabeth laughed. "I used to bring her food,

and then I would sit with her and think of you. She heard quite a few of my thoughts for a time! I missed her when I went to London." Her voice was wistful.

He had forgotten how appealing the little creature was. "Would you like to bring her with us?"

"Oh, may I?"

"Of course you may. You are Mrs. Darcy now, and can do as you wish – as long as you continue to love me."

"Then I am in no danger!" Their lips met and clung.

At least they would be alone together after they left Longbourn! He was tired of sharing Elizabeth with other people.

A short time later, Snowball was ensconced in the carriage with them. Elizabeth had brought Snowball's favorite basket, but the cat seemed to prefer Darcy's lap, clearly unwilling to let go of him now she had found him again.

Elizabeth nested against Darcy's side in the carriage. "You were very brave in facing my mother's excesses."

"For you I would do far more."

"At least she is so in awe of you as to provide some restraint!"

"And your father appeared more cheerful by the end. I hope it was not too distressing for you."

"Not distressing enough to make me reconsider my decision! I know he was trying to protect me in his own way, but I wish he had allowed me to make my own choice, or at least told me the truth. But he is still my father, and I will try to forgive him. I hope someday you will be able to do so as well."

"I will forgive him for your sake, my love, but only because his schemes failed to prevent our marriage in the end."

"I refuse to even consider that possibility. Instead, I intend to think only of the past as it brings me pleasure."

He responded in the only possible way, but their kiss was interrupted when the carriage came to a halt.

"Why are we stopping?" she asked.

Darcy broke into a wide smile. "I wished to think of the past, or at least a part of it which definitely gives *me* pleasure." He set down the cat, opened the carriage door and jumped out, then handed her down.

They were stopped in front of a freshly white-washed wattle-and-daub cottage, roses blooming around the doorway and smoke rising merrily from the chimney. Elizabeth could not help laughing. "Is this what I think it is? It looks quite different without the sea of snow. But it must be it – I recall that paving stone. At least my toe recalls hitting it!"

"Let us see if the inside is as you recall it." Darcy stepped forward and lifted the latch.

"But the tenants…"

"The tenants are enjoying a stay in a much larger cottage not far away, and are perfectly happy to give us the freedom of this one."

"But…" Elizabeth shook her head in amusement. Clearly Darcy had gone to some trouble to arrange this visit, and in truth she was curious to see it again. She stepped inside as he held the door open.

It took a moment for her eyes to adjust to the dimness. The room was both familiar and different. She blinked twice. The walls were freshly painted here as well, and a simple carved bed stood against the wall by the hearth. A small table sat under the window, and marvel of marvels, the floor had been leveled and was swept clear. Yellow curtains fluttered at the window. But it was the same cottage, with the familiar shelves and wardrobe, and the hearth where they had passed so much time.

"Are you responsible for all this? Surely the silver you left them after our stay could not perform such a transformation!"

"It is all Crewe's doing. He apologizes profusely that he was unable to have the floor tiled before our arrival. Even he can perform only minor miracles on two days' notice." From behind her, he slipped his hands around her waist.

"But why? It is beyond generous, and for people we never even met."

"Their house and firewood saved our lives; but this is not for them as much as for us."

"For us?" She leaned her head back against his shoulder.

"Very well, for *me*." He nuzzled her neck, sending shivers down her spine. "There were so many times while we were here that I longed to kiss you, to touch you, to make you mine – and to see caring and concern in your eyes. So I arranged for a second chance.

We will stay here tonight, but this time Crewe will bring us dinner and breakfast, and we shall be much more comfortable. If you do not mind, that is; we can still return to London today if you prefer."

She turned in his arms and locked her hands behind his neck. "I can think of nowhere I would rather be -- as long as I am not required to produce onion soup."

He laughed and nibbled her earlobe. "I can think of better things to whet my appetite upon."

Once again Darcy awoke with Elizabeth's head on his shoulder and sunlight streaming in the window. With a contented smile, he pulled her even closer.

"Mm?" she said sleepily. "Where...oh, yes. Back to our cottage again."

"And very pleasurably so." He tangled his hands in her hair and kissed her thoroughly.

Sometime later, he curled a lock of her hair around his finger. "I am all astonishment that Snowball has not interrupted us yet. As I recall, she took her role as chaperone very seriously last time."

Elizabeth's dimples showed. "Perhaps she understands we are married now." She raised herself up on her elbows and looked around the small room. "She must still be in her basket." She pushed back the coverlet, allowing him to enjoy the view as she took the few steps necessary to reach the basket. As she looked inside, she burst out laughing.

"What is it?"

Still laughing, she said, "Snowball has been

busy."

Darcy padded over to stand behind her and put his arms around her waist. He could not resist the temptation to kiss the soft skin of her neck, which was much more interesting than whatever the cat was doing.

"Pray permit me to introduce to you Snowflake, Snowdrop, Snowdrift and...let me think... Blizzard."

Startled, he released her and peered into the basket. Four little creatures that looked more like mice than kittens were suckling on Snowball's exposed belly. He reached down and stroked one with a fingertip, its short fur downy soft. "They are so tiny."

"So it was not just better food that made her fill out, apparently. And I was worried enough about the reaction of the housekeeper at Darcy House to one small cat, and instead we will be bringing five!" Her expression of comic dismay made her look even more kissable than usual.

He decided to take advantage of his good fortune. "Since I doubt Snowball would be happy about traveling today, I suppose that means we must stay here another few days."

She smiled up at him with that delightful arch look. "I do wonder how we shall manage to pass the time."

He scooped her up in his arms and proceeded to demonstrate his solution.

Epilogue

MASTER RICHARD DARCY put his hands on his hips and addressed the white cat in his mother's lap. "*When* are you going to have those kittens? I have been waiting for months!"

"Days, perhaps," his father corrected him.

"But they were *long* days," the boy said gloomily.

His mother reached out and tousled his chestnut curls. "Remember, even once they are born, your kitten will have to stay with his mama until he is weaned."

Richard pouted. "Who chooses their kitten first, Jenny or me?"

His father smiled down at the infant in his arms. "I think Jenny is a bit young for a kitten. Perhaps you could choose one for her to have when she is a little older."

His mother smiled at him. "A good plan. Richard, I do believe you are more excited about the kittens than about your baby sister!"

He gave her an incredulous look. Who would

choose a squalling baby who could not even play games over a kitten?

Richard found a faded scrap of silk in Snowball's basket and carefully wiggled it in front of the sleepy white cat. She deigned to reach out a paw to bat at it. "She is not very interested," he informed his parents. "Perhaps she needs a new ribbon. This one is all tattered."

"Snowball is particularly fond of that ribbon," his father told him.

His mother laughed. "Snowball would be particularly fond of *any* ribbon."

His father's face lit with a slow, warm smile. "Very well; *I* am particularly fond of that ribbon."

She smiled back at him, and it was as if they had forgotten Richard even existed. "I am very fond of it myself."

Richard did not like being ignored. "What is so special about that old ribbon?"

"Your mother gave it to me," said his father.

Richard screwed up his face in puzzlement. "Why did she give you a ribbon? You do not wear ribbons, do you?"

His father coughed and covered his mouth. "No, I do not wear ribbons. It was a token of her affection."

"Shouldn't she have given you something you could use, like boots or a cravat?"

His parents seemed to find this eminently practical idea amusing, but fortunately Uncle Richard strolled in and crouched down beside the boy. "Allow me to tell you a secret, young man. Women are not always practical in matters of love – nor are men."

"Well, I hope no girls try to give *me* ribbons," Richard announced, then added generously, "But if they do, I will give them to Snowball."

ACKNOWLEDGMENTS

Dave McKee, Maria Grace and Elaine Sieff read early drafts of this story and offered helpful advice. Rita Watts, Catherine Grant, and Connie Hay helped with great feedback on the final version and are responsible for there being far fewer typos than there otherwise might have been! The readers and my fellow writers at Jane Austen Variations provided encouragement and occasional threats when I posted excerpts from the book as a work in progress.

My family, as always, deserves endless thanks for their patience and support. Samoa, Floof, Pip, Beatrice and Satsuki kept the house free of mice (no mean feat when you live in the middle of the woods), and Snowdrop the Miracle Kitten provided inspiration through her extraordinary will to live. You can read more about Snowdrop here:

www.austenvariations.com/writing-kittens-and-other-miracles/

ABOUT THE AUTHOR

Abigail Reynolds may be a nationally bestselling author and a physician, but she can't follow a straight line with a ruler. Originally from upstate New York, she studied Russian and theater at Bryn Mawr College and marine biology at the Marine Biological Laboratory in Woods Hole. After a stint in performing arts administration, she decided to attend medical school, and took up writing as a hobby during her years as a physician in private practice.

A life-long lover of Jane Austen's novels, Abigail began writing variations on *Pride & Prejudice* in 2001, then expanded her repertoire to include a series of novels set on her beloved Cape Cod. Her most recent releases are the national bestseller *Mr. Darcy's Noble Connections*, *The Darcys of Derbyshire*, and *Mr. Darcy's Refuge*. Her books have been translated into five languages. A lifetime member of JASNA, she lives on Cape Cod with her husband, her son and a menagerie of animals, including Snowdrop the miracle kitten. Her hobbies do not include sleeping or cleaning her house.

www.pemberleyvariations.com
www.austenvariations.com

Also by Abigail Reynolds

The Pemberley Variations

WHAT WOULD MR. DARCY DO?

TO CONQUER MR. DARCY

BY FORCE OF INSTINCT

MR. DARCY'S UNDOING

MR. FITZWILLIAM DARCY: THE LAST MAN IN THE WORLD

MR. DARCY'S OBSESSION

A PEMBERLEY MEDLEY

MR. DARCY'S LETTER

MR. DARCY'S REFUGE

MR. DARCY'S NOBLE CONNECTIONS

THE DARCYS OF DERBYSHIRE

The Woods Hole Quartet

THE MAN WHO LOVED PRIDE & PREJUDICE

MORNING LIGHT

Made in the USA
Lexington, KY
23 November 2015